ROAD RUNNERS

COMBAT JOURNALISTS IN CAMBODIA

HANEY HOWELL

D1560300

BERKLEY BOOKS, NEW YORK

ROADRUNNERS

A Berkley Book / published by arrangement with
the author

PRINTING HISTORY
Published in hardcover by Paladin Press, 1989
Berkley edition / May 1990

ISBN: 0-425-12141-0

A BERKLEY BOOK ® TM 757,375
Berkley Books are published by The Berkley Publishing Group,
200 Madison Avenue, New York, New York 10016.
The name "BERKLEY" and the "B" logo
are trademarks belonging to Berkley Publishing Corporation.

PRINTED IN THE UNITED STATES OF AMERICA

10 9 8 7 6 5 4 3 2 1

Preface

SAM SPENT A lot of time lying on the bottom of the pool. Spreadeagled in the very center of his universe, he viewed the war and Cambodia, for perspective, through eight feet of stagnant water. His days were insane, why should his nights be different?

At first, people would come to the water's edge and call down to Sam, checking to see if he was all right. Now they understood, and save for the occasional swimmer, Sam had the pool to himself. His trips to the bottom lasted longer and longer, as he learned to conserve energy, to overcome the natural urge to push up, to find air.

In Cambodia, the rules were different. Each person at the Hôtel Royale dealt with this reality in their own way. Sam knew that no one forced him into his air-conditioned Mercedes each morning, made him go down those highways, seeking out the war. Few of the people crowded around the tables by the pool chased combat, including the high-ranking Cambodian officers, who seemed to have a knack for avoiding it. The roadrunners were a strange elite, crazies, part of an endless stream of men and women who chose to live on the edge of war, hanging their asses out for a flat fee. Though America was bored with the politics of the Indochina war, a good combat story might get on the Evening News. TV dinners and the Indochina war. No wonder they tasted so funny.

But even here, in the pool, Sam couldn't escape. The water amplified sounds beyond the city, the clump of mortars, the solid thud of artillery, the shakes of the B-52 bombing runs, rumbles so low they were more felt than heard. Now, the attacks were getting closer and Sam imagined the bombs landing, digging twenty-foot craters in the earth, playing the spoiled child destroying what it couldn't keep.

He watched bubbles from his jeans and combat boots float slowly toward the surface, like movement in another dimension. Cambodia was like that, too. Quick moments frozen in time and space. In themselves, they were not significant or threatening, but they hung in the mind. Sam would take his solace to relive and replay these times, to try and sort out what they meant. There was nothing Sam could point to that would mark where things had shifted, but he had been drawn into something much bigger than himself. He tried to pinpoint his feelings, to work through them, face them head on. Was he really caught, or was his mind trying to find an out for the body, a reason to leave? After a trip to the surface for a deep breath, he drifted downward again, into the watery world he understood.

One thing was certain. Cambodia was coming apart, and so was Sam. Neither could control the things that were destroying them. What did the song say? "You can't run and you can't hide"?

I.

Mekong Convoy

SAND. IT STUCK in Sam's teeth, shirt and pants, trickled down his back, piled up where his flack jacket pressed hard into the sandbags. Every time he tried to move, his helmet dug deeper, cutting loose more sand. He cringed as another blast from an invisible machine gun sent colorful tracers curving inches above his head, the rounds drumming against the side of the old ship, rusting paint chips drifting down into the sandbag enclosure in front of the wheelhouse where he was hiding. Sam ground the sand around in his teeth, counting the seconds until he could get up and run. He plotted in his mind how best to extricate himself from the other five people huddled behind the bags.

He had to shit. In the worst way. His ass seemed to chew the hard steel deck, half from fear, half from need. He sucked in a lungful of air, trying to push back the pain from the cramps in his belly. Two days on the good ship *Manila Racer* had done little to improve his diet, and the constant series of ambushes along the river bank made every trip to the head an adventure. They were uncomfortable with no place to run, stuck here until the convoy reached Phnom Penh or stopped dead in the water. Like being stranded on a bad amusement park ride.

It was first light. They had just passed the river-crossing town of Neak Loung, the last major checkpoint before the final sprint up the Mekong to Phnom Penh. Before the war, all road traffic between Saigon and Phnom Penh stopped at Neak Loung for the ferry. No more. Like most of the other cities in Cambodia, it was controlled by the government, but isolated. Only the meagerly supplied shops, the hospital and nearby army post made Neak Loung any different from the rest of the countryside. Getting closer to Phnom Penh didn't mean much to the convoy. The channel of the wide river wound near the shore for many more miles, close to favorite spots for the hit and run ambushes. The last couple of convoys caught hell a few miles up the river.

"You squirm like a bitch in heat," muttered Steve Chan, who cradled a CP-16 television camera between his legs, his chin protecting the lens. "Your gut again?"

"Yeah," Sam groaned, hoping for a sympathetic audience. Few people who lived and worked in Cambodia had normal stomachs.

"Fetch that man a cork!" Marty Satterfield leaned against Sam's shoulder, a Clint Eastwood-style, rust-colored Stetson pulled down over his eyes.

"That's a myth. . . ."

"Asshole corks? Part of the kit, my man, part of the kit." Satterfield chuckled as he talked.

"Sammi. You must listen to me," Claudine Peirpoli said in her heavy Parisian accent. "You go straight to Bangkok, go to Bangkok Nursing Home, and have the test. You must have the test." She sat back on her heels, a Nikon with a telephoto lens jammed in a slot between the sandbags, ready to shoot if something interesting popped up. There were advantages to being crammed in so tight behind the bags; the feel of her breast on his arm helped Sam keep his mind off his stomach. He grinned at Chan behind her back, but got no reaction.

"Have a hit." Ty Stoneman handed Sam a Salem packed full of Thai Buddha weed. "Old natural remedy." Sam took a drag, then handed it back, his functioning-high threshold far lower than Stoneman's. Ty looked like a latter day hippie, long hair tied back in a pigtail, droopy moustache, and a constant haze of weed surrounding him. He didn't look like a man who'd spent ten years looking for war with his cameras. A lot of people wrote Ty off as a flake, but Sam knew better. Ty was a man he'd choose to be back to back with in a knife fight.

Sophan, the Cambodian soundman squeezed in next to Chan, had told them about Neak Loung, how he'd been garrisoned there with the French army in the early fifties. He didn't look that old to Sam, but then he had problems figuring Oriental ages. Women who looked seventy were thirty; grandfathers looked twenty. The tropics were not good to a woman's looks. Sophan filled the soundman slot, but his real job was keeping them alive. His survival instincts seemed flawless, powers he attributed to the small jade Buddha worn on a gold chain around his neck. Sometimes Sam tried to get inside Sophan's head, wondering what it was like to watch your country go slowly down the tubes.

By the summer of 1973, the war in Cambodia had come down to the slow choking of Phnom Penh, and now the Khmer Rouge insurgents were claiming control of the river routes into the capital. In three years of war, the country had shrunk from seventy thousand square miles to a few hundred near the major towns. Around the clock, American B-52 bombers and jet fighters held the insurgents back by dropping more bombs on Cambodia than the U.S. dumped on Japan in World War II. But the American public sickened of this war, and the U.S. Congress voted to cut off the bombing, the last gasp of the American presence in Indochina. When the warplanes left, Cambodia and Vietnam would have civil wars, and Sam and the other freelancers knew that while it lasted, any American angle helped sell the story. There would be few convoys once the bombing stopped. That's why they worked so hard to hitch a ride on this one.

"This little trip confirms my deepest thoughts," Satterfield said, his Oklahoma twang making his words more dramatic. "I don't want no part of no goddamn navy." Satterfield was an enigma to Sam. He'd wandered up to them in Vung Tau, the port in South Vietnam where they'd boarded the convoy, wondering if they minded if he joined their ragged band for the journey to Phnom Penh, as though the *Manila Racer* and the other ten ships in the convoy were a ferry service, not an ambush looking for a place to happen. Marty had told them a bit about his time in Vietnam, how he'd been a Green Beret and worked with the Montagnards, the highland villagers who fought so well for the French and Americans. One thing the past days had proven—very little upset Marty Satterfield.

"Have a shot . . ." Chan handed Sam a pint bottle of Mekong whiskey. "We ain't seen nothing yet."

"You're the fucking voice of hope . . ." Sam grimaced as the hot, raw liquid flowed down his throat. It did nothing to relieve the pain in his gut. From his pocket he dug out a small, white Lomotil tablet and washed it back with the whiskey.

"Lifeline to Phnom Penh . . . shit," Chan muttered as he took back the bottle. His flat Chinese features hid the Latin side of his nature, a product of his growing up as an American-born Chinese in south Los Angeles.

Sam chuckled, then nearly doubled over as another shot of pain ran through his stomach. "What do you think . . . can I make it to the head?" It had been awhile since the last ambush. Now there were only scattered rifle shots.

"They're on the starboard side. Go down the other . . ."

Chan gave Sam a hand as he got ready to roll over the sandbags.

"I must go, too," Claudine said, tapping her stomach and making a funny face.

"Take the head behind the wheelhouse. I'll find another one." Sam silently cursed his chivalry as another shot of pain ran through his gut. He pressed his shoulder against the side of the wheelhouse, duck-walking the twenty feet to the portal, one he'd never entered. The rusty handle stuck, but a burst of rifle fire gave Sam the energy to force its release.

Inside, red lights dimly lit the passageway. Sam had no idea where he was going. One promising door was tightly shut, the large handle refusing to budge. He found a ladder to the next level, feeling his way down step by step. The roar of the ship's engines could not blank out the metallic ringing of the bullets striking the sides.

Sam found a door that would open, and entered into a hold. He looked around frantically, hoping a seaman would tell him where to go, the countdown in his bowels about to end. Down another ladder to the bottom hold, a quick walk around the large containers, and the realization that he would again have to improvise. He found a pile of papers between two boxes, dropped his pants and let go. A wave of pain made his eyes tear. He only passed liquid, not enough in his mind to create all this discomfort.

When the cramps passed, he looked around, his eyes adjusting to the light. The container on his right had the name of a medical company stenciled across it, the one on the left with the familiar shaking hands symbol of the U.S. Agency for International Development. He was puzzled by the construct in the middle of the hold surrounded by sandbags. He buckled up, walked over and looked through a space between the bags. Wooden frames prevented the large green cylinders of ether, standing on skids of six rows of eight, from toppling over. Each of the long metal bottles had a red tag hanging from its neck cap, warning of fire and explosion in four languages. Sam shrugged. If the bottles blew, he'd never know it.

Two rockets hit the ship, the hold ringing like the inside of a bass drum, the noise seeming to search for the bottles. Sam scrambled back up the ladders, through the passageway to the door. He took a quick breath, then dashed down the walkway to the enclosure. As soon as he rolled over the sandbags, his stomach heaved again. No way, he thought.

Claudine had beaten him back, and was solicitous to Sam when he settled back against the bag. She poured water from a canteen into Sam's helmet liner, dipped in her cotton neckerchief, and wiped Sam's thin face. The water felt good, drops seeping into his red moustache. His body was folded double, long thin legs tucked under his chin, pressed hard against the flack jacket. The knees of his jeans were worn, the blue workshirt faded white from washing.

They were a superstitious lot. Claudine always wore white jeans and red tee shirt, Chan the same style bush shirt, Sophan his Buddha, and Stoneman his holy green fatigue shirt; none wanted to wear a military uniform, keeping themselves distinct from the soldiers, but Sam realized in fact that each had their own uniform.

"The little lady is right, Sam," Marty said, rolling the wad of tobacco in his mouth. "Once we get to Phnom Penh, you better knock off and get your gut fixed."

"Doesn't work that way, Marty. There are a lot of folks out there who'd like a shot at this job, and I can't afford to leave. Not now, anyhow." Sam listened to his own words and realized how strange they sounded. From a traveling salesman, they'd make sense; but for someone who hangs his ass out everyday, they sounded stupid. He knew his stomach problem was a slow bullet, that it could bring him down just like being shot. "You know the eternal New York question: 'What have you done for us today?' "

"That's the shits . . ."

"No, I have the shits . . ." Sam laughed.

"Then how do you top this story? Looks to me like you've got your dick in a ringer."

"Well put, Satterfield." Chan peeked over the bags, keeping an eye on the river. "Happens all the time. Once in Nam, we shipped a shitkick story to Saigon. Took us another two days to get out, and when we got home New York was screaming, why we'd been fucking off for two days." Chan didn't have good feelings toward New York. Someone, somewhere in the past decided that Chan didn't have what it took to be a staff photographer, and despite a decade of doing the job well, the rap hadn't changed. He trusted few people, and even Sam wasn't sure where he was on his list.

"Sounds like the Army." Marty shifted on the steel deck, trying to be more comfortable. "What do you call this job, anyhow?"

"Long time ago someone came up with 'roadrunning,' and it fits. Yeah, we're roadrunners."

"Like the bird in the cartoon . . ."

"I know that bird. . . ." Claudine kept her eyes shut, resting.

"Beep beep . . ." Marty tried it, and liked it. He kept going "beep beep. . . ."

"Yeah, well, if we could just do as well against the coyotes out here."

"Well, you guys are crazy. It's one thing to fight in a war, another to go looking for it."

"What are you doing then?" Sam felt a little anger rise in his voice.

"Looking for a war." Marty realized he needed to back off. "But once I find it, give it a good look, then I can leave. I don't have to keep going back. Not now, anyhow." The conversation dropped, each with their own thoughts. They all liked what they did, but to hear it spelled out made it sound crazy, almost evil.

"A couple weeks ago, this high-rolling book editor from New York came to town, looking for truth." Sam paused, remembering a conversation. "She said that journalists were shallow, thrill-seekers, who didn't care what happened here as long as we had a good time."

"I told ya not to take her to Chantao's," Ty said, referring to the opium den.

"Guess you're right. She must feel that way about the French ambassador, too, if she wants to put us in tidy little piles. I think he had a couple of pipes with us that night." Sam was bothered by such criticisms, and had given the subject a lot of thought. No doubt they all did seek thrills, but that passed quickly. He stayed because he liked the place, and yes, he liked the work. He'd accepted the fact that few people would accept that reasoning.

"Well, fuck her if she can't take a joke." Satterfield understood. "When you work on Madison Avenue, you're at the center of the world and can make such judgments."

"I met the lady. I thought she was nice," Claudine said, getting into the conversation.

"You would," Chan shot back. He wasn't happy that Claudine had come along, but then he hadn't been one of her great fans from the start. He could remember when Claudine had started hanging around the pool, asking photographers for tips on using cameras, bumming rides down the road. No one was sure how she got to Phnom Penh.

Sam let the comment pass. As far as he was concerned, she was just like him, learning her trade on the job. The nearest Sam and Chan had ever come to blows was Chan's contention that she only sold pictures to the papers and magazines by sleeping with the correspondents. He knew she wasn't selling anything sleeping with him, although the thought had crossed his mind that she did have a guaranteed ride in the car. No, he thought, leave good enough alone. Everyone here had their own ghost.

"Looks like we've got company. . . ." Ty watched as the low-flying Phantom jet fighters screamed by the ship, pulling up into the rising sun. Nearby, a Bronco spotter plane circled, keeping a watch over the convoy.

"Well, I guess if the Rouge didn't know we were coming, they know now." Marty was not impressed with heavy military hardware like airplanes. Too obvious, too noisy. He'd been a jungle fighter, like the guys loading B-40 rockets into the tubes a quarter mile up the river. In the morning light, the convoy would make a tempting target. So far nothing seemed badly damaged from skirmishes during the night.

"Here we go . . ." Chan started filming at the first "thunk . . . swoosh . . ." of the B-40 self-propelled rocket. It slammed into the side of the nearest oil barge, penetrating the metal, the escaping oil leaving a sheet of flame on the river.

"We're fuckin' sitting ducks," Marty mumbled, pulling his hat tighter over his eyes.

"Yeah, but it's good footage." Sam twisted around in the tight space, seeking shelter and a view. "How's the Buddha doing, Sophan?"

"Buddha OK. He say we get good story, get home OK." Sophan smiled, but Sam always had the eerie feeling that he was repeating something whispered to him. "You like Buddha? Sophan will get you Buddha."

"Sure, I'd like that. But it won't be as good as yours." Sam decided that all the hardware exploding on the river would make for a good radio actuality. He barely got the tape recorder turned on when another rocket hit the ship.

"Radio . . . radio . . . ," he said into the microphone. "We're rounding a bend on the Mekong River and we're now in range of B-40 rockets . . . (blam . . . clung . . .) from where we're taking cover on the bridge of a freighter, they all seem aimed at us . . . (clung . . . clung . . .). American F-4 Phantoms are covering us, firing at the riverbank, but right now they're circling for another pass . . . . leaving all the ships wide open for attack . . . there's a machine gun! . . ." Sam grabbed for his helmet as the bul-

lets pounded the side of the wheelhouse, the last of the
canteen water running down his face. Marty cursed as
sand sprayed into his eyes. Chan cooly continued to film
through his notch in the sandbags.

"An oil barge ahead of us is on fire," Sam continued
into the radio mike. "But the tug still pulls it . . . we're
now passing through the burning oil slick . . . we're not
about to stop. . . ." Sam's voice was tight, his throat dry.
The spotter plane pulled up just above their heads with a
roar, its white phosphorus rockets throwing up smoke from
the bank near the enemy launchers. Quickly, the Phantoms
moved in, battering the jungle on the riverbank with long
blasts from their cannons. The rockets and mortars
stopped, only the crack of automatic fire proving there was
still life in that jungle.

For the next hour, the ships caught rockets, more white
phosphorous markers puffed up from the shore, the jets
strafed and bombed. Then around the next bend . . .
bingo. So far the convoy had been doing pretty well. The
barge was still burning, the flaming fuel pouring harm-
lessly into the Mekong. There was smoke from one of the
freighters behind them, but it kept the pace. The Filipino
captain looked determined and cool behind the wheel.

"How much longer?" Sam yelled through the slit in the
wheelhouse bags.

"Two hours . . . maybe less." The captain grinned at
the group huddled behind the sandbags. They hit a long
patch of river where both sides opened to wide plains of
reeds. He assured them that nothing would happen here;
there was nowhere for the ambusher to hide. They gingerly
stood up, carefully stepping over bags and cameras,
stretching their cramped limbs. Sam saw little piles of sand
outside their hideaway, below the holes opened by the bullets. In the noise, he hadn't even noticed. He unsnapped
the flack vest, took off his shirt and shook out the sand.
Marty did a couple of quick push-ups on the deck, while
Chan changed the film magazines and cleaned off the cam-

era lens. Without shooting another foot of film, they had a hell of a story.

"Good place for a bridge. . . ." Sam felt adrenaline now, the pump keeping him alert. He wanted to do an on-camera voice bridge in case he needed it when he wrote the script.

"Looks fine, but better hustle. About five minutes to the next bend." Chan adjusted the viewfinder and wiped dust from the small glass opening. He made a dry run through his shot. Sam moved away from the sandbags and leaned against the front rail of the upper deck.

"How's this?" he asked as Sophan handed him the mike.

"Little more to the left . . . get the burning barge behind you." Chan held the camera slightly off his shoulder, to compensate for the difference in their heights.

Sam ran his fingers through his matted hair and put the helmet back on. Behind the camera, Claudine faked a pose, trying to distract him, her tall, slender body forced into curves, eyebrows raised haughtily over green eyes. Photographers took great satisfaction in making fun of television reporters going on camera. Stoneman rolled another joint, while Marty jogged in place, shaking his head at their kidding around. Sophan checked the plugs on the soundbox, put on the earphones and asked Sam for a mike check.

"One, two . . . hello . . . one, two . . . ," Sam said. Sophan nodded his OK, and Sam thought about what he wanted to say. Sam stared into the orange filter on the camera lens until Chan flicked his finger.

"Being aboard a Mekong convoy is like riding a target in a shooting gallery. The insurgents are determined to keep these supplies from reaching the capital. We are only a couple of hours out of Phnom Penh, but we'll be hit again. The convoy crew can only hope that the Air Force gets to the attackers first." Sam held his pose for a few seconds.

"Good one. Nice flare from the fire while you were talking." Chan lodged the camera back into the notch in the bags.

"Coffee?" A young Chinese boy shoved tin mugs of steaming brew into their hands. "Captain, he say you drink fast." The boy didn't hang around to collect the empty cups.

"That's encouraging," said Sam, smiling nervously. "Just like your last cigarette." They sipped the thick, strong coffee. Around the next bend, there was more company.

Three A-7 fighter-bombers screamed up the river, blasting the bank with cannon fire. Chan caught them as they cleared the ship, a long-sustaining shot that would edit nicely. The jets carried two pods each under the wings. The crippled barge took two more hits from rockets, and Sam thought he detected a list to starboard. Still, the tug pulled it up the slate gray river. Suddenly, all hell broke loose.

"Get down . . ." "I can't . . ." All six tried to kiss the deck as a machine gun drummed more shells across the bridge. Chan had the camera running by itself. A zipper of big dents ran down the roof of the ship's wheelhouse, a wisp of white smoke curled up from the aft deck. Downriver, Sam saw the jets turning for another run. "Heads up, Steve . . ." The jets passed between them and the bank, the pilot's head clearly visible. The canisters tumbled end over end. Huge sheets of flame exploded from the trees on shore, the machine gun stopped, melted by napalm. "He got 'em, he got 'em . . ." Even Marty was moved to cheer the Air Force now. The A-7s were smaller than the F-4s, and able to work closer to their target. The second jet followed the path of the first. The pods broke open above the ground, slinging grapefruit-sized guava bombs into the jungle. They went off like a string of firecrackers, each pod slinging steel needles in all directions.

"I don't want you to get the big head . . . ," Chan said,

looking through the viewfinder, "but this is the best damn bombing footage I've ever shot. We've got a winner here, Tiger."

The big show was over. The jets cartwheeled around and around, spraying the bank ahead with cannon fire, clearing a path for the convoy. Three ships were smoking, but there were no flames. The other barges seemed intact. Up ahead rose the smoke of cooking fires in Phnom Penh, the city waking up, oblivious to their adventure. Finally, they rounded the last big bend in the river, took the left fork into the Tonle Sap and headed for the piers. All the ships had been hit, but they had made it. Chan and Sophan wandered the decks of the ship, getting closeups of holes punched into the steel by B-40s, taking shots of the crew preparing to dock. Army trucks lined the pier, waiting to off-load the cargo.

"Answer me this, ace," Satterfield said, spitting a stream of tobacco over the side of the ship. "How *do* you top this? Seems to me that you guys can't win, with all the shit you say about them always wanting something better next week." Marty had been thinking about their discussion.

"Something better always seems to come along," Sam said. "The trick is being there when it arrives." This trip was a good example, he thought. Sophan had gone through a number about having to find the Chinaman to get them this ride. They were all willing to take these chances for a story, but the difficult part was getting there. Official channels didn't really exist in Cambodia. The mysterious "Chinaman" had more pull than the Army. What would they do to top this? Ty handed him another joint, which he hit and passed on to Marty. "But if you do miss it," Sam said, slowly exhaling the strong weed, "you can always stick your head in this stuff and forget."

Sam felt relief, and the sudden need to take another shit. This time it wouldn't have to wait.

II.

Pig Pilots

"I THOUGHT THAT thing was fixed." Kip Keaney stared at the fluctuating oil pressure gauge.

"Oh, man. It's flying, ain't it?" Tony DeRosa, his co-pilot, was turning more sour by the day, incessant gigs on the old DC-3 cutting into his sense of humor.

"Yeah, but it's nice not to have distractions."

"Distractions!" DeRosa was so cranked that he jerked the plane to the side. "What the fuck you call that?"

The vibration from the right engine wouldn't fade with a slight pitch change, so they left it alone. The passengers would be more comfortable flying than dying, and in this country, those were the choices. As it had done a thousand times before, the old Gooney Bird settled in once they got a bit of altitude and out of the humid heat. He let his fingers stroke the huge wooden yoke. No, he thought, I really don't want to fly anything else right now. Few things in life come along like the Gooney Bird. Studebaker trucks, maybe, or a Maytag washer. But this sucker was fun, like lap dancing with an old flame. What had Rey-

16

nolds said? Loving a Gooney Bird was like loving a whore. She'd be good to you all year but fuck you over in the end. Well, Kip was still waiting. Besides, he was president of the Phnom Penh Pig Pilots Association, and the DC-3 fit his image.

Kip let DeRosa do the flying on this leg, sliding down in the pilot's seat and lighting a cigar. A pig squealed and someone cursed in Chinese, a sound from Kip's past. He turned to see the three Chinese men crammed behind DeRosa's seat, sitting on their luggage. He needn't look further. The bags were Samsonite, straight from the Long Binh PX. He'd seen Uzi submachine guns broken down into those fiberglass cases, plus a hundred rounds. Neat packing but a bitch to carry casually.

"Check those dudes," DeRosa said as he twisted in the copilot's seat. "Do they look weird or what?"

"Sir, this is a class operation and I'm sure that Khmer International Airlines will have checked their bonafides closely before allowing them passage on this First Class flight." Kip straightened the glasses on his nose, then reached down to again check the engines. The right throttle wanted to stick.

"Shit, man. 'Bonafides.' Dude like you, college and all that big word shit, and here you are, flying dying tin in the asshole of the world." They couldn't be from more different worlds, Kip and DeRosa. Kip got here via Brown University, the United States Navy, and a parcel of jobs ranging from jets to spray planes. DeRosa had long since given up trying to find out what blot on Kip's copybook ended his Navy career. A man like Kip didn't casually walk away from F-4s.

"You speak poorly of my adopted land, DeRosa. Besides, I like flying for Mama-san. A truly unique test of interpersonal relationships."

"Bet you like hitting yourself in the head with a hammer." DeRosa was fiddling with the other throttle, which now wanted to slip from its setting.

They'd had it out with Mama-san that morning as she stood on the tarmac in Phnom Penh, counting her money like a Vegas bookie, cramming most into the opening of her baggy blouse. She was the Chinese woman who fronted the airline for the Chinaman, and Kip knew that when he and DeRosa asked for their pay, she would beg poverty, flapping only the roll of riels she'd kept in her hand. That's why Kip had switched to the Green Stamp system. A genuine U.S. hundred dollar bill per flight, people or guns, no questions asked. DeRosa still liked the feel of the huge wad of riels in his hand, even though each night at the bar he would curse her, having finally carefully counted the stack of bills, divided by eight hundred, and come up short. He'd learn, Kip thought, if he lives that long.

"You fly, you fly now," the round-faced Chinese lady had ordered, waving the money at the plane.

"We fly when it's ready to fly, Mama-san." Kip had eyed the puddle of oil under the radial engine. "You want to have an airplane, you let us fix it first."

"Nothing wrong. You fly." The pushing and shoving from the passengers already inside was rocking the bird, causing DeRosa, who was standing on a shaky ladder working on the engine, to curse. "You fly now . . ."

"Ah, put it where the sun don't shine, lady . . . ," DeRosa had shouted as they buttoned up the engine and flew, just like she knew they would. But DeRosa had some uses, thought Kip. A fast mouth and even faster hands. The grease on his long black hair was as thick as the oil on the ground. It was a long way from Elmwood Park, New Jersey to Phnom Penh, and sometimes the strain of distance showed. And Kip knew damn well that Elmwood Park was East Paterson. A tidbit he constantly held over DeRosa.

"You'd think that broad could afford a cylinder head kit for this piece of shit," DeRosa mumbled, bringing Kip's mind back to the moment. "My whole fuckin' GI Bill I blew on flying lessons, and I should'a gotten a mechanic's license.''

"Hey, the hours all count, my man.'' Below, the emerald rice paddies melded into the rise of the Carmadon Mountains. The colors were almost too vivid, like a cheap postcard with ink that bled. He followed the highway west, noting the smoke pouring from several huts in a village at a crossroads.

"I still think it's the gauge . . . ,'' DeRosa called out.

"What?''

"The gauge. Nothing wrong with the engine. It's the gauge.'' He tapped a black fingernail on the cracked window of the oil pressure gauge. As Kip watched, the needle swung through half the arc.

"Yeah, I hope so or we're in deep shit.'' He didn't believe his own comment, more saying it to keep the critters away. Oil pressure raised and stayed there, that's what he told himself. He played with the throttle, finding a point where the needle steadied.

"No fuckin' sense, man. It makes no sense.''

"Since when was it suppose to? You can always go back to the car wash in Ridgewood.'' Another tidbit of DeRosa's past that slipped out and Kip used as a bludgeon.

"You're a real shit, Keaney.'' DeRosa added more grease to his hair by combing it back with his dirty hand. Kip liked the instant confirmation.

"Let's climb . . .'' Kip pointed forward at the thunder bumpers building alongside the mountains. The airplane's sounds changed pitch, but she happily climbed as he turned northwest. Sucker's built to fly. Too bad it's such a dog on the ground. A pig got loose in back, and the scuffle to catch it caused the wings to dip. Weight and balance meant little around here, because they rarely carried maximum fuel. To Mama-san, it was a waste to put two thousand pounds of fuel in the tanks when that could translate into paying cargo. Besides, where would they go on a full tank of fuel?

The landing in Battambang was uneventful, the passengers pushing and shoving to get out long before DeRosa had a chance to swing the tail around and shut down the engines. Kip swung out of his seat, did a cursory check for loose items left behind in the rear, and jumped onto the tarmac, only to be met by the three Chinese passengers.

"We leave now." The man speaking showed no emotions, acting as though Kip had been awaiting his instructions.

"Not so quick, sir. I believe these folks hold prior reservations." Kip waved at the mob behind the rope, huge baskets of produce piled at their feet, waiting to be taken to market in Phnom Penh.

"They will be accommodated. Perhaps this will help you decide." The leader snapped off two one hundred dollar bills for Kip, two for DeRosa, then another five hundred for Mama-san.

"Good argument. Where to?" Kip waved DeRosa back into the aircraft, the crowd starting to surge behind the flimsy rope.

"We will show you." As they taxied out, the leader stood in the doorway, watching their every move. The plane leapt off the ground, happy with its loss of weight. They flew north, making minor adjustments to their course according to where the Chinese man pointed.

"Cambodia don't go on forever, you know," DeRosa said finally.

"Keep it to yourself." Kip shot him a hard look. "This is a profitable venture for both of us, so don't ask questions."

"Got it." DeRosa went back to flying. On instructions, they started a descent.

Below, there was a small clearing in the heavy jungle, a strip no more than three thousand feet long that seemed to curve, lined with tall trees.

"Well, it ain't Teterboro . . ."

"Ah, shit, man. We really going in there?"

"We shall try . . ."

"We shall try . . ." DeRosa mocked Kip's Ivy League accent.

"We the unwilling . . ." Kip started to quote his favorite ditty about leadership. He stopped, gave the controls a flick to let DeRosa know he was flying, and concentrated on the jungle. He would like to make a pass over the clearing, but didn't dare. They'd already announced their arrival, and the clock was ticking on how long they could remain.

"A windsock would be nice." DeRosa looked at trees, grass, anything, trying to find the wind direction.

"Makes no difference. We're coming in from here. We'll go out the same direction." Kip had seen that the trees were lower on one end. He wanted every foot on the climb out. Nodding at their guide, and getting confirmation, he banked the Gooney hard to his left, dropped in 30% of flaps and reset the power. They leveled out just above the last trees, nose high, and when Kip saw the first flash of grass, he chopped the throttles. The plane settled with a thump, rocking from side to side on the rough turf. The far treeline was coming up fast, but Kip knew he'd nailed this one. "Classic three pointer, my boy."

"I wonder if they're impressed?" DeRosa nodded off to the right, where two army trucks waited, surrounded by a motley band of armed men.

"Keep the customer satisfied, that's my motto." Kip locked the left brake, spinning the bird 180 degrees, ready for takeoff. He pulled the engines to idle, not shutting down. No place to do that.

"I'm coming, I'm coming," DeRosa yelled to the men outside who pounded on the cargo door. As soon as it opened, the three passengers started barking orders to the men outside, giving hand signals to the trucks as they backed up. The ground crew worked quickly and quietly, following DeRosa's instructions on where to stack the dark brown bags. They were sewn on each end, and Kip sus-

pected that this was only one leg on their journey. As the
first truck pulled away, a fourth man boarded the plane
and worked his way to the cockpit. He had light skin, a
flat face, and Kip figured he was Thai or Lao. He waited
for him to speak, but the man stared out the windshield,
scanning the treelines and the runway.

"Man, this shit is heavy!" DeRosa tried to shift one of
the bags to improve the center of gravity. The second truck
was stacked high with wooden crates, cylinders and cop-
per tubing. "We can't carry all of this."

Kip looked past the men, tried to guess the weight of
the bags. Maybe DeRosa was right, but they didn't have
much choice. Five more men surrounded the plane and
the trucks, M-16s unslung, watching. The two hundred
dollars tucked in his pocket suddenly didn't seem like
much. They knew something Kip didn't.

Suddenly the cockpit guard shouted, pointing down the
runway. Kip saw the whiff of smoke then heard the thud
as the M-79 grenade round landed fifty feet behind them.
The guards broke for the treeline, spraying short bursts
toward the smoke. For a moment Kip thought the guard
was going to fire through the windshield in his excitement,
but instead he scrambled off the plane. A neatly dressed
Chinese man ran wildly from the treeline toward them,
looking terribly out of place in this jungle, scrambling on
board and identifying himself to the leader. DeRosa yelled
at the truck driver to pull away so he could close the door.
It was partly unloaded. Kip stuck his head out the side
window and realized the driver had abandoned the truck.

"DeRosa, move it yourself," he yelled back, while giving the throttles a tap for good luck.

"Oh, mother . . ." Tony was in the truck when the
second round landed in front of the plane. He stalled the
engine twice, finally found low gear, and let it jerk forward enough to clear the tail. He caught himself reciting
the rosary as he ran back to the door, banging his head on

the overhead as he tried to pull it closed behind him. At that moment, Kip opened the throttles wide.

Ahead, two men emerged from the trees, firing rifles from their hips. Another M-79 round smoked off to the side. The gear dug into the soft earth, the tail seemingly stuck to the ground. Kip started counting, for no other reason than to put some order into the chaos. He didn't look as they roared past the men. Finally, the tail bounced off the ground, the main gear started to lighten and Kip figured they had a chance. DeRosa slammed down in the copilot's seat, looking for something to do. The tall trees loomed bigger, and as the bird broke ground, Kip turned slightly, aiming for a gap. The DC-3 shuddered as the right wing tip dragged through the top of a tree, but it stayed on course and started to climb. He instinctively reached for the landing gear lever when DeRosa grabbed his hand, pointing to the hydraulic pressure gauge. It was going down fast. The rate of climb indicator was inching up, and Kip decided to leave the gear down, one less problem to mess with on the other end. A minute passed before Kip or DeRosa spoke. They climbed blindly ahead, away from the ugliness behind them.

"Check your side," Kip said, looking out the window at the left engine. He saw no smoke.

"We caught a couple of rounds in the back."

"Just adds to the air conditioning."

"And something got the hydraulics."

"Brilliant deduction, Watson." Kip wisecracked instinctively, covering the clump of fear lodged in his stomach. "Did you get a good look at those guys?"

"Yeah. They weren't Cambodian."

"We're not that far from Laos." That made Kip check the fuel levels. They seemed to be holding at a half tank. No leaks there. He tried to compute the extra fuel burn with the gear down. Two hours. They should make it back to Phnom Penh. Could land in Kampong Chhnang, but if his hunch was right about this load, it was well worth the risk to push on. The customer would be displeased that some was left behind, but he had the bullet holes to prove the discretion of an early departure. He then realized they wouldn't have gotten off with the full load. For once he appreciated being shot at.

"Did you see the guys doing the shooting? They weren't in anyone's army I've seen around here." DeRosa repeatedly rerouted the grease in his hair, glancing nervously at the leader, who looked ahead with a stoic gaze.

"Local commerce, my boy." Kip thought they'd been in deep shit the day the thirty hogs got loose in back, but this trip set a new standard. What bothered him even more were the clients. He'd been around these folks in his Air America days, working in Laos. The big reshuffle was on in the world of dope, and Kip and DeRosa had unwittingly joined it. This sort of knowledge could be harmful to one's health.

"I must speak to Mama-san about the unsavory clientele of late," he said, spinning the trim wheel, realizing that he'd been holding the yoke back for climb with brute force.

"Mama-san don't care. She gets her cut." DeRosa was learning fast.

"Right. Now here's the drill when we land. We'll shut down and leave this conveyance on the ramp. I've already made the acquaintance of more of these gentlemen than I care to know. We'll let the nice lady figure out the holes."

"Copy." DeRosa stared ahead, stunned. He'd found the adventure he'd searched for, but now he was understanding the price. You couldn't just come and fly around, you got sucked into the game.

"Look at it this way, Tony. When your kids ask you what you did during the Indochina war, you can tell them you were a Phnom Penh Pig Pilot."

"Big fuckin' deal." DeRosa was still shaken.

"Well, you must admit this has turned into a profitable trip." Kip tapped the crisp bills in his flight shirt pocket.

He'd seen weirder things here, but something about these guys stuck in his mind. DeRosa grinned as he tapped his pocket. Not the time to talk, he decided as he realized the leader was giving their conversation his full attention. In the back, the other two men tried to calm down the one who had run from the woods. A city boy if Kip had ever seen one. The throttle slipped again. "Let's get that thing fixed."

"Yeah, well the only way you're going to fix this bastard is to jack it up and drive another DC-3 under it."

"Explain that to Mama-san." Kip stared out at the Tonle Sap River and marveled at the huge craters along the banks dug by B-52 bomb loads. Looked like the earth had caught on fire and God tried to put it out with an ice pick. It wasn't the flying that bothered him, it was what happened on the ground. Somehow he sensed that this trip would come back to haunt him.

III.

Hôtel Royale

"SIR, I SAY *sir*!" The muffled voice penetrated the water. Sam bubbled to the surface of the pool. Thick-heeled cork "catch-me, fuck-me" shoes clanked on the walk at eye level, so cumbersome the young Cambodian girl could barely walk, much less run. A pair of worn combat boots pointed at Sam's face.

"Excuse me, sir, I'm Lawrence Incoming, from fun-lovin' Phnom Penh Radio, doing our poolside culture hour from the Hôtel Royale . . ." Larry Moss leaned over the pool, unplugged microphone in hand. "I'm told by your colleagues at yonder table that you run like you have a cob up your ass. Would you care to comment on that unsavory remark, sir?" Moss was Sam's main competitor, but a most likable guy, especially when stoned.

"First, I must consult with my lawyers before making a comment." Sam liked this bit, their Richard Nixon routine, perfected over the months by the two of them. "But let me say this about that."

"That about what?"

"I'm not a thief . . ."

"We're talking about your running . . ."

"We'll bomb them back into the Stone Age. . . ." Both laughed now, their wired minds on the same frequency. The shortwave radio played the Watergate shuffle constantly around the pool. The big news peg was a President bobbing and weaving for his political life. Cambodia was a diversion for the networks, a lively change of pace from the dull talking heads and White House standups. Sam and Moss competed here, but they shared the same problems of getting on the air. In fact, theirs was a mutual relationship, the appearance of one on the air almost guaranteed the same for the other. But neither wanted to lose, and Moss would have to scramble to top the river convoy.

"Hey, country boy . . ." Sy Rosen leaned back in his white pool chair, calling over his shoulder, owl-like horn-rimmed glasses down on the end of his large nose. "You keep hanging it out like you did on the ship, and we'll ship you home in a body bag." Rosen did not hide his distaste for the way the television crews and the photographers hunted for combat, but he also respected the roadrunners. He'd covered his share of battles for his New York newspaper but the Cambodia story for him was buried under the rocks at the Palace and embassy.

"Is he part of the program?" Sam asked Moss, loud enough for Rosen to hear.

"I think he slipped in through the fire exit. I hear he likes to grope little boys." Moss made a big show of combing his sun-bleached hair with his fingers, straightening his Hollywood sunglasses, then heading toward Rosen with the mike.

"Sir, have you something to say to our wonderful audience, especially the junior class at the Phnom Penh Medical School that took to the jungle to join the insurgency?"

"I would like to dedicate this war to the bubblehead television types . . ." Rosen was drowned out by the boos from the other tables. "I shall rejoin my young friend here if you don't mind," Rosen said over the catcalls. "I've discovered that her skin gets smoother and her English better with each bottle of Bordeaux."

"Hey, Sy," Bill Byers called out, his corpulent body molded into a lounge chair, "ol' Mekong Annie ya got there don't need much urging, so you can save your wine."

Rosen put his arm around the young Cambodian girl, her tight tee shirt and jeans strange on a body used to a sarong. "My friend here has certain redeeming virtues known only to a select few. I do not care for your insinuations, sir!"

"Using them big words again, Sy." Byers' attention was drawn back to the lady, or in this case, girl, who sat beside his chair, her sarong fanned on the grass. She looked ten years old. Several years before in Saigon Byers had shown up for the Bastille Day reception at the French Embassy with a young blossom in tow, and was taken aside by his fellows. "My God, Byers, the child couldn't be a day over thirteen, and you bring her to the biggest reception of the year?" they asked.

"Not to worry, not to worry . . . she's got the body of a nine-year-old." He favored youth in both booze and women, his years overseas with the wire services providing a lot of both.

"Hey, Stoneman," Sam called, "how 'bout a joint?" Stoneman sat at one of the tables in cut-off jeans, picking shrapnel out of the festering wound in his calf. Sam had tried to get Ty to the hospital in Saigon for treatment, but he'd refused. Too many bad memories of the Third Field Hospital, he said, from the other six times he'd been treated there for battlefield injuries. He grunted, but found his film can of dope on the table and started rolling, the loading procedure made more mysterious by his wispy Fu Manchu mustache which obscured the corners of his mouth. His body was covered with scars, like a tomcat who defended his fence each night; lasting mementos of firefights and mortar attacks, helicopter crashes and bar-room remedial conduct sessions. All the years of looking at war showed on his face, but at least here he was himself, something he could not be sure of in the outside world.

Moss carried the finished joint back to Sam in the pool, lighting it as he walked. He sat on the edge and watched Sam try to smoke it, arching his head to keep it out of the water.

"All right, asshole, what did you do to me on the convoy?" Moss was serious.

"Stuck it right in your ear. Some of the best bombing and close air support stuff I've ever seen. Chan says the same thing. It was worth the ride, despite the serious shits. . . ." Sam didn't boast. Tomorrow was another day. In their running television battle, he and Moss were about even.

"I take it you shipped?"

"Not yet. What's the rush? I'm exclusive, remember?" Sam grinned as he rubbed it in a little bit. Moss wanted to know when to get ready for the rockets from New York. He could breathe easy for a day. The weed was strong, some of Ty's special Buddha dope. The variety here was mind-boggling and cheap. Sam remembered when he first arrived and asked Driver Joe to pick up some dope, giving him five dollars, and how Joe returned with two large bags jammed full of the stuff. A far cry from when he and his Air Force friend Richard would hide on the end of a jetty at an Air Force base in Mobile, carefully smoking the cherished weed lovingly grown in a patch between the runways. The Air Police thought they were a couple of fags.

Moss drifted off, continuing his radio rap. He was now interviewing Dr. Jake, an Australian surgeon who spent his vacation each year doing hundreds of meatball operations at the Russian Hospital. He told Larry about a nice little place he'd found, Madame Lon's house of Oral Hy-

giene, guaranteed to clean your pipes. The doctor rocked
a bit, his chin drooping on his chest. He got like this every
night, rarely making it to the whorehouse, but no one
cared. Up with the sun, Jake operated with little medicine
and shaky electricity. They took turns getting him to his
room. Sam jogged himself to ask Jake about the ether.
Might be good for a follow-up story, a way to milk the
convoy for all it was worth.

"You seen Claudine?" Satterfield squatted by the pool,
spinning his cowboy hat on his finger.

"Should be around somewhere. Why?" Sam felt his ass
tighten a tad, wondering if Marty wasn't joining the long
list of potential Claudine suitors.

"She said she knows some dude, named Maurice, who
can probably find my man Pha Doh. He's the Montagnard
I told you about, my counterpart in Nam." Marty's right
arm showed a bullet scar that ran from his fingers to his
elbow, a sharp contrast to his long hair and beard. The
Stetson held his collection of military medals pinned to
the band of the hat, a Silver Star up front. Had Sam not
seen him under fire, he'd think that Marty was another
Walter Mitty bumming around the edges of the war. His
jeans had butterfly-shaped patches, and he wore an old
French camo bush jacket over his cowboy shirt. Sam still
wondered about his claim that he was back to write something about the Montagnards for *Rolling Stone*.

"I hear she's your main squeeze." Marty took a long,
involved hit from the joint.

"God, I wish. I'm just a country boy from East Tennessee who got lucky."

"Well, she sure makes all the blood run down to my
head." Satterfield dragged a vacant chair from under one
of the thatched huts that rimmed the pool. Sam looked
around, trying to measure the reaction to Marty. Anywhere else, he would be a conversation piece. Here, he
was just another player.

Sam dunked his head in the tepid water, trying to cool

his brain. Claudine was an enigma to him, but most European women were. Here he was in the land of hot and cold running pussy, and he found himself chasing a woman who had half of the men in this country drooling down their chins. Yet there was a bond, perhaps from getting shot at together, and the fact that they both hustled for their work. The old buddy in the foxhole bit. But he didn't want to fuck his buddy. Oh shit, oh dear, he thought, can't take this one home to Mama. Larry Moss wandered by and stuck out a beer.

"No, thanks. I'm drinking from the pool." Sam noticed the half-smoked joint was soaked with water from his fingers. Marty's face lit up and Sam knew without looking around that he'd spotted Claudine. She wasn't stunning, but there was something about the way she carried herself, her seeming total self-confidence, that attracted the type of men who studied war. This evening, she stoked Sam's fire with a thin korta shirt and white jeans. She mussed Sam's wet hair then spoke to Marty. "What the girls say, is it true?" she asked Marty with a grin.

"That depends on what you hear. You been talking to that little Chinese gal?" Marty faked an accusing look. Sam was impressed by how quickly he'd availed himself of the local talent.

"Yes, the Chinese. Is it true?" Claudine ran her fingers through her short hair, laughing. Sam was completely in the dark.

"What the lady here is referring to is my shortage of balls." Marty carefully put the hat on his head, low over his eyes. "A VC round removed the left one without the benefit of anesthetic. I've found the best way to answer that question is with a practical demonstration." He winked at Claudine. "It's good for openers. You interested?"

"You will make Sam *beaucoup* jealous. You ask when he not around." She took the drenched joint from Sam's hand, holding it out like a dead fly. "It is bad you waste such good marijuana. You must think of all the little children in Africa. . . ."

Sam laughed. He'd told her of his mother's favorite line to get him to eat as a child, and it took about ten minutes explaining to her, the language barrier obscuring the meaning. That happened a lot with them, Sam completely at the mercy of her English, his whorehouse French good enough to get him fed and laid. The locals loved to hear him struggle with the language, Cambodian French with an American southern accent.

"Marty, please, you come with me." Claudine grabbed him by the arm and started leading him toward the corner of the pool garden. Sam pulled himself up a little to the rim of the pool, and spotted Maurice greeting them at one of the small tables.

Fuckin' Maurice. That was the guy Sam couldn't figure. Claudine seemed to lose all of her cool around him, serious looks sweeping her face when he talked. More than one night at Chantao's opium den had been spoiled for Sam by Maurice's arrival. He was very pleasant, but Sam always felt he was condescending. A long-time French resident of Phnom Penh, Maurice seemed to always be living in two worlds, the French and Cambodian. Why would he know where Pha Doh was stationed? He watched as Maurice stood to meet Marty, his freshly pressed bush shirt and slacks setting off his dark tan. Sam could compete with men after Claudine's body. He couldn't handle the one who had her mind. Sam sensed that there was more to the thing with Maurice, something that went deeper than just friendship. He stuck his head under water to try and change the subject in his mind.

"Ribbitt . . . ribbitt . . . ribbitt . . ." Someone hiding in the bushes behind the cluster of French locals was making like a frog. The French didn't like to be called Frogs.

"*Monsieur, s'il vous plaît!*" The old schoolteacher, in

her long white pressed silk evening dress, tried to hush the intruder.

"Ribbitt . . . ribbitt . . . ribbitt . . ." The call was picked up by the others, a chorus of frogs calling in the night. The local French had to suffer it, though. Many had chosen Phnom Penh as their home after Hitler didn't quite work out. The farther from Paris, the fewer questions asked. For them, as for the journalists, the Hôtel Royale was the last thread to western civilization. But for the old teacher, the worst thing about the war was the siege on her beloved hotel by these barbarians.

The Royale reflected the old Cambodia. The peeling yellow walls, dark red tile roof, high ceilings and wide elegant staircases typical of late colonial architecture. It was diagonal to the Cathedral, where the Virgin perched between the spires, staring benignly down upon the Wat Phnom, the holiest of Cambodian Buddhist shrines, which sat on a knoll at the end of the long, wide boulevard. The five floors of the main hotel spread in a horseshoe, with wings and rooms tucked under the eaves, and cottages around the back pool area sealing it off from prying eyes. The hotel seemed to expand each time a new influx of foreigners arrived. Residents had hot water maybe twice a week, but Sam could walk out of his roadrunning clothes at night and find them neatly pressed in the morning.

Sam lived well here. If you're going to study war, might as well study it in style. Even cold-hearted corporations had a hard time playing cheap with people who got shot at every day. They did what the executives wouldn't do, and the company paid for that guilt through the nose. The Japanese fed the Kamikazes well before they shoved them on the plane, too. The big difference was that Sam and the others could duck out before the big fight. At least most of the time.

In the early days, when the roadrunners traveled far into the countryside, there would be a vigil under the huge banyan tree in the parking lot of the hotel. Kate Webb, who survived forty days of captivity, called it the "weeping tree." It was here they cried for those who didn't return by nightfall. More journalists died here than in Vietnam because they were on their own, without the backup of the American army. The heavyweights abandoned Cambodia, leaving it to the Sams and the Stonemans, only returning when the story was hot. Dying wasn't part of the ritual of getting your card punched and going on to a cushy assignment Stateside or in Europe. Sam figured that was what bothered the New York book editor, the lack of handsome thumbsuckers who mulled the political and moral implications of the war. Sam would have been more than willing to go after that angle, but it didn't sell back home. Nope, they were creations of the television beast, rejected by the same souls who decided what went on the air.

"Considering all the lovely talent around this pool, I don't understand why Rosen always goes for that particular lady." Larry returned to poolside with a fresh joint.

"Has to do with her eagerness to play 'swallow the swan.' " Sam took a deep hit and looked at the chubby girl, deep in conversation with one of her friends.

"The swan?" Larry missed his analogy.

"She gives great head. . . ."

"Lot of them do that. . . ."

"Well, she has moved it up to a new art form. . . ." They watched the crowd of girls around the pool. Sam didn't really consider them whores. Like everything else around here, the whores really never had time to get their act together. They were more like local talent willing to barter favors for an entrée to the pool. From the corner table, Sam could hear Claudine laughing with Marty and Maurice.

"Hey, Michaels," Byers bellowed, "that convoy shit had better be as good as you say." Sam had pitched Byers on Ty's pictures, giving him the details of the trip for the endless mill of the wire service news cycles. It didn't hurt to have the producers back home reading about their adventures while deciding whether to satellite for the pictures. Byers detested Stoneman's lifestyle, so it took a little prodding for them to do business. Byers claimed Ty had gone native, the way he spoke whorehouse Cambodian and all.

"Trust me, Byers. They're great pictures." At the moment, Sam was very high. What he did was go from one high to the next. A ditty ran through his mind, like the old song, *Sugartime*. "Adrenaline in the morning, opium in the evening, weed at supper time; everybody keeps doing it, trying to get high." Here that wasn't difficult.

"Goddamn, boy," Byers muttered in his Alabama twang. "I don't know where you've been, but you look like you been rode hard and put up wet." His big belly shook through the little half moons down the front of his too small bush shirt, his chubby face and bald head burned pink by the sun.

"Those fuckin' rednecks always look bad," Rosen said, diverting his attention from Mekong Annie, who was trying to fog his belt buckle.

"We got you outnumbered, slick." Byers nodded at Sam. He was one of those Southerners who figured a couple of rednecks equaled a mob. Sam had fought his way out of more than one bar with Southern friends who shared that philosophy.

"Hey, Sam, what did they bring in on that convoy? Last one was loaded with frozen fish and ladies' hats." No matter how sloshed, Rosen thought news. Even with Mekong Annie.

"Ship we were on had a bunch of food, medical supplies and the like. Most of the barges had fuel. Would you believe a shipload of rice?" Before the war, Cambodia had been a major exporter.

"Well, the Chinaman has strange taste. The embassy tells me it's about a week's supply."

"Well, I'd do a little hoarding, because there ain't no

way they'll get up the river once the jets are gone.'' Sam
was glad to feed information to him. Rosen was the doyen
of the press corps, the class act on a talented stage. When
Rosen wrote it, television crews went out to find it. The
honchos at the network read his New York paper like the
Bible as they munched their Post Toasties each morning.
They smiled if Rosen's story had been on their Evening
News; they frowned if it hadn't.

"I'll get that in my morning file; good setup for the
next one. Nothing I can do now but let this lass have her
evil way." Rosen turned back to Annie, and Sam slapped
the water with his hand, a private celebration. If Rosen
mentioned the convoy in his paper, it would play high in
the Evening News, and the producers would think it was
their idea.

The war ended for the journalists at five. Communica-
tions to the outside world shut down, the airport closed.
They covered stories at night in the city, but those were
rare. No one would beat you by filing at night. Thus the
lifestyle.

Moss was now leading one table in the Horst Wessel
song, the volume increasing as the French protested. Sam
could see that Claudine was through with Marty and Maurice. It was time for him to leave the pool and take off his
roadrunning clothes, get ready for dinner and a trip to
Chantao's opium den.

"I send the telex to *Paris Match*. I think they will like
my pictures. Perhaps we should celebrate." Claudine had
returned and was standing over him, the bottom of her
firm breast visible to Sam from under the shirt.

"Good show. Let's do it." Damn right, he thought.

"I would like to dedicate the glee club's next number
to Sam Michaels," Moss yelled from his new perch on
top of a table, "who's been hiding a hard-on in the pool
for the last two hours." Sam grabbed a handful of water
and tried to spray the singers.

"For staying in the line of fire far beyond the call of

duty,'' Moss droned, like a military posthumous awards ceremony, ''for his total disregard for his own safety, for his dedication to the company, for his shitting on vital government documents, we would like to sing the following ditty.'' The singers started three songs at once, quickly breaking into laughter and shouts.

Sam felt warm in the pool, the day's victory acknowledged by the man who'd get the shitty cables. Today he'd won the gold star. Claudine pushed his head underwater, and when he emerged, pursed her mouth in a kiss. Maybe the God of the Groin would prevail, and she would help him make it through this night. The sun would shine on his name at the company for the convoy story. But in the back of his mind, he remembered what his Pappy had always told him.

''Son, the sun don't shine on the same dog's ass all the time.''

IV.

Renegades

ENG HAULED THE wooden box down the slope, putting it upside down next to the gate to the docks. He arranged the bottles of soda on the flat bottom, creating an instant roadside stand. He hunched down on his heels, assuming the stoic posture of the vendor awaiting business. He tugged at the edges of his white shirt, making certain it hung free.

From where he crouched, he could see ships unloading, the large cranes slowly lowering cargo to the docks, where it was loaded onto a catch-all collection of army and civilian trucks. He tilted the edge of the box until he saw the antenna of the small walkie-talkie. Everything was now in place. All he had to do was wait.

A year ago, Eng and his comrades in the Ninth Brigade had been gung ho troops, proud of their reputation as one of the best units in the Cambodian army. They'd fought all around the country, moved from crisis to crisis, the one outfit that could open a road or push the insurgents out of captured towns. General Chandaran, their commander, trained them well and kept them alive. The General was a shrewd trader, swapping unsuited equipment for the things they needed; armored personnel carriers for jeeps with machine guns, a couple of tanks for a division's share of rockets and mortars. Other generals thought the big guns and tanks would keep the enemy away. Chandaran said the only way to fight this war was to be light and fast, surprise and overwhelm.

The Ninth was proud, and the men wore their blue beret that way. Sure, Eng thought, they tore up a few bars and demonstrated their skills on the heads of other units, but nothing out of the ordinary. No, their downfall was politics. When the Ninth became good, the generals who were politicians panicked, fearful of Chandaran. They called the Ninth a "private army." The elite forces of the Ninth were assigned to the mountain, the useless mountain.

For nearly a year, they'd been stuck out there, in the middle of the Carmadon Mountains, waiting for relief, for resupply. It never came. The insurgents picked away at them, lobbing shells daily into their fixed positions, hitting the edges of the perimeter with raids. Without resupply, the unit could not replace weapons or men. The insurgents were doing what the politicians couldn't do—bleeding Chandaran's forces until there was nothing left.

Finally, they'd had enough. They gathered their families and arms in the dark of the night, fought their way off the mountain, through the insurgent lines, to the highway, and returned to Kampong Sneu, Chandaran's home and power base, to regroup. His orders were strict. The men were not to advertise their return, the government was to think they were still slowly dying on the mountain. They continued to check in each day by radio, begging for relief. No, the men of the Ninth were going to get their payback their own way. The fifty men with the blue berets would have one more mission, then leave. It was clear that the war couldn't be won, not with the best forces wasted. Now they must look to the future.

Eng watched as large skids loaded with green bottles were lowered to the docks. He shifted slightly, keeping the truck being loaded with the first of the bottles clearly in sight. Over the next hour, Eng observed, selling a few green sodas to thirsty workers. He gave one to the guard on the gate, who then forgot he was there. He wanted to brace the man, chew him out for his sloppy uniform, his dirty rifle. But Eng had to remember he was a soda salesman, not a captain. Those powers were left behind with the uniform.

He ran the plans through his mind. When the loaded trucks with the bottles left the gate, Eng would give the signal. Men waiting in the market would slowly move into position. They knew what to do when the convoy arrived. He glanced back up the slope, checking for the tenth time that the Peugeot taxi they'd stolen was still in position, ready to pick him up.

He felt excited, yet disappointed. The General was right. They must do things now for themselves. This was the end of Cambodia for them; they would have to find new homes. What they were doing now was very dangerous, taking on the Chinaman, but they were men with few choices. Eng had seen enough of the enemy on the mountain to know he wouldn't live very many days if the insurgents won. They had killed too many of the enemy for that. He was a marked man, the General told him, and he needed to take care of himself.

The unloading was going smoother than he'd expected. As each truck filled, it pulled up behind the one ahead, waiting until all the trucks were loaded. They'd gambled the convoy would move out as one unit, and now the pieces fell into place. Finally, the last truck was loaded. A bored sergeant blew a whistle, waving at the drivers to follow him in the first truck. As they rumbled toward the gate, Eng lifted the box, slipped the radio under his shirt, and climbed up toward the taxi. Out of sight of the guard, he keyed the radio and said, "Unit Seven, going on break." He listened long enough to hear a "roger," and his message repeated back, then jumped into the taxi and urged the driver toward the paved road near the docks, the one the trucks would use.

There was no traffic; the road had once been the entrance to the long, graceful Japanese Friendship Bridge which crossed the Tonle Sap River. It now lay in three pieces in the water, the pylons blown two years before by rebel sappers. If the government was stupid enough to let them infiltrate the city and blow the bridge, Eng thought, this plan could work.

He counted again as seven trucks passed, the coded message alerting his fellows to the size of the convoy. The taxi slipped in behind, Eng breathing fumes from the smoking truck ahead. God, he thought, I bet they've never heard of oil seals and rings. It wouldn't matter; the trucks weren't going far.

They turned on Monivong, past the Calumet French Hospital, the Hôtel Royal and the Cathedral, then headed into the center of the city. At the abandoned train station the convoy halted, the sergeant jumping down from the truck, chatting with a civilian in a jeeplike Mini Moke. Eng pulled the radio from under his shirt, waiting for their next move.

After a short conversation, the sergeant walked back to the truck, shouting directions. The trucks pulled away, turning right. Eng took a deep breath of relief. They were right on the second count. The Chinaman wasn't showing any pretense of taking the ether to the hospital then stealing it from there. It was headed straight for the lab. He ducked his head slightly in case someone was watching from the last truck, and keyed the radio, listening for the repeater to clunk, making sure he could be heard. "Unit Seven, back on duty. Checking western quadrant." He heard the reassuring clunk, then the voice on the other end acknowledge and repeat.

They picked up speed, flying through Ponchetrong Market, horns blaring as they passed the airport on Highway 4. No one challenged them; no one cared. They were just another convoy. The taxi hung back, keeping the trucks in sight, trying to be part of the scenery. He tried to look ahead of the trucks, making certain no armored jeeps joined the convoy. As they approached the town of Ang Snoul, they slowed, the market overflowing into the road, cutting it to one narrow lane.

Abruptly, up ahead, there was an explosion. Eng reached under the seat for his M-16. He leaped out, ran toward the door of the last truck and yelled at the driver. "Take cover, take cover . . ." Now was the time to sound like a captain. He fired a few rounds into the air, adding to the noise, running up the row of trucks, shouting warnings to each driver. He pointed toward a wall across the street where they hid, happy to be away from whatever was going on.

Ahead, a cyclo smoldered in the middle of the road, blown to bits by the explosion. Chunks of fresh meat and clothing were scattered on the road. All the blood and gore left the drivers stunned. Eng grinned to himself. A pig wrapped in explosives and some torn rags did make a mess.

He saw two of his men leading the sergeant down an alley, pushing him ahead with their rifles, their insignia that of the local unit here. Satisfied the chaos level was at a peak, Eng gave a signal with his hands, and seven men appeared from the crowd, jumping into the cabs of the trucks. Eng ran back down the line, just as one of the drivers jumped the wall, running for his truck. Eng pulled the trigger on the rifle, stitching red holes across the boy's stomach. For a frozen moment the stunned boy stared at Eng as he toppled backward, blood spurting from his mouth. Eng sprayed the rest of the clip at the wall that hid the others, jumped into the Peugeot, and ordered his driver to pass the trucks.

They threaded their way past the soldier's body and cyclo wreckage, continuing west for a few kilometers. Then they turned left, bumped down a dirt road into a village. Each truck picked out one of the houses on stilts, easing under them, tarps ready on the sides to hide them. The men gathered at one of the trucks that had some boxes besides the bottles. They tore into the cartons, laughing with glee at their find. General Chandaran walked toward Eng, smiling, the first part of the plan complete. Now they must wait for the Chinaman to react, before they would make their next move. At the far end of the village, Eng could see men loading another truck with artillery shells. Under the house, he could see the barrel of a One-Oh-Five ready to be towed. Since they'd left everything behind on the mountain, they'd had to steal this one, a part of the Ninth's plan, like hijacking the trucks. They could use the gun to crank up the pressure. Soon it would leave, moving to a spot near the city. Eng turned back to watch the antics around the truck.

The men ignored the officers, occupied with the task of splitting up the booty. Some waved the bras and women's panties over their heads. Others tried to wrap them around their uniforms, humming dirty ditties and grabbing at one another. Let them play, Eng thought, for soon it would be time for work. Events would happen fast. The General smiled too, but in his face Eng could see the worries of his mind. He thought of the many nights he had drunk strong coffee and talked with the General, listening to his descriptions of an American general called Stonewall Jackson, who held back a great army in the great Shenandoah Valley with few men, constantly moving his armies around, tactics that Chandaran said they were using. It was nearly a year before Eng discovered that Stonewall Jackson had died over a hundred years before. To him, the battles were fought yesterday.

One of the younger soldiers was now completely dressed in women's underwear, bras to the front and the back. A bottle of Mai Tai was passed around, long swigs a toast to the booty of the day. The men would be popular at the Chinese whorehouse tonight.

V.

Evening Song

"FUCK YOU, BYERS." Stoneman grabbed back the five rolls of film, stuck them in his jeans pocket and headed for the door of the bureau office on the ground floor of the hotel.

"Hey, asshole, I said I'd buy them. What the hell else you want?" Byers' pudgy face reddened as the argument grew. "I told ya I'm sorry about you getting chopped up, but you're a stringer. I can't pay your medical bills. But I can buy your pictures." He felt like a stuck record, repeating the same lines three times in five minutes.

"I don't want your God damn sympathy, motherfucker. You can find sympathy in the dictionary, right between two other things I don't need, shit and syphilis."

"Give me the goddamn film." Byers held out his hand, knowing that eventually Stoneman would turn the rolls over; economic facts would force him to. He did feel bad about the medical bills, and in a way it was his fault. When Ty got shrapnel in his legs the month before, Byers sent off a panic telex to Hong Kong, receiving the standard bureaucratic reaction of no responsibility. He'd envisioned weeks in a hospital and surgery, not to mention the couple of weeks R&R on the company that staffers considered part of the bargain. Instead, Stoneman only wanted $450 for the initial treatment at the French Hospital and some money to cover the week he couldn't work. That was all. But now that Hong Kong knew, there was no way to hide the bills on the bureau books. He'd fucked up, but didn't need to be reminded of it.

"One of these days," Ty said, slowly handing back the rolls, "you're going to get somebody killed, then deny that you hired them." There was an unwritten agreement with the stringers that they had some off-the-book medical coverage. Shit, the television network stringers were treated just like staffers when they got hurt. They even managed some off-the-books R&R. Sam's network had paid out full death benefits to the Indian sound stringer's family when he was killed on Highway 3 the year before.

"You make it sound worse than it is. I'm buying your stuff every day. . . ."

"Nah, nah I don't. You're going to buy up a bunch of pictures from me to cover my losses. Then you'll dry up." He pulled out a Salem packed with weed and lit up, a move he knew would distress Byers. It did.

"Goddamn it, Stoneman, this is a fuckin' office, not a hippie dive. . . ."

"That's more like it, fuckhead," Ty said, pleased that he'd irritated Byers. "I need the money quick, man. Choe is saving it up."

"You mean that hand-me-down blossom you live with."

"Watch it, Byers." Ty felt his temper rise.

"Who you hang out with is your business, but when it comes to money, a chick will suck you dry." Byers showed his redneck grin.

"Meaning what?"

"Meaning, I don't know why women complain. They've

got half the money and all the pussy. . . ." Byers was laughing at his own joke before he hit the punch line.

"Some day, Byers, some day," Ty said, heading out the door. He mulled over the conversation, one part of him realizing that he antagonized people, the other part defensive of his style.

It was uniquely his. Anybody can be like me, he thought, chuckling to himself. Just run away from home and join the Navy when you're fifteen, get caught and booted just in time to turn around and join the Army at eighteen, then head straight for Vietnam. Stir in six months of paddy dike-running and combat patrols to learn the fine art of staying alive, add a late-blooming interest in cameras and a willingness to re-up, and you're a lifer combat photographer.

Byers wasn't the first person he'd pissed off in his long career. The sergeants and officers quickly learned to stay off his back, give him plenty of film, and in return he'd come back with good pictures. It was a deal they could both live with, until the American involvement in the Vietnam war ended. He was an E-6 by then, an NCO rank which carried with it certain responsibilities in the peacetime army. After a six-month tryout in Colorado, he and the Army reached an agreement. He'd leave the service if they'd discharge him in Vietnam. After a good look at their creation, the Army was more than willing to grant his wish. Twenty-four hours a civilian, he'd found a new home in Cambodia.

Ty had been injured worse in the past, but for the first time he was thinking of someone else. There was a lady in his life, and fuck those who didn't understand. He loved her. That was the catch. He'd been around war long enough to know when one was winding down, and the end was in sight. He didn't want to leave her behind.

The street was noisy with the afternoon trade, sidewalk merchants leaving only a narrow path for him to pass. Some smiled at the familiar foreigner, holding up produce

and goods, hoping for an overpriced sale. He paused to
watch the dentist, crouched on the curb, his tools neatly
laid out on a cloth, the patient gripping his ankles to kill
the pain of an extraction with what looked to Ty to be a
pair of rusty vice grips. He took a few pictures and moved
on. The oversweet smell of ripened mangos filled his nose
as he headed for the doorway of the whorehouse. Over the
downstairs shop was a sign for a tourist agency. The Chinaman should do something about that, Ty thought; the
cover was pretty transparent. But who really cared?

Choe was waiting for him in the little room they shared.
She was half Thai, of slight build, and to Ty's eyes, beautiful. He could hear the other girls giggling and gossiping
down the hall, it being too early for many customers to
call. Ambulance drivers were drifting back in, engaged in
a heated card game in the big room. Stoneman traveled
with them to the heaviest action, and a few hundred well-
placed riels assured him of a seat out to the field, the first
photographer there. They also knew all the good rumors
of heavy action, the down and dirty stuff that kept Ty
ahead of the other stringers.

Choe had spoken to Mama-san about Ty. Mama-san was
pissed that she'd let him live there for a year, and now the
ungrateful bastard was trying to take one of her best and
most attractive workers. But the pain in her arm where
she'd had diamonds buried to stake her on the new life
bound to come reminded her of the truth. Going with Ty
would be Choe's ticket out. She promised to ask the Chinaman to let Choe go with Ty. He'd spent a fortune buying
her out of the whorehouse, night after night, so she could
be with him and the others around the pool. He wondered
what Byers would say if he knew how he spent his money.

Choe rolled a killer joint, and choked as she tried to
light it. Mama-san stocked the finest dope, an incentive to
customers and a crutch for the girls. He laughed and
reached out and took her in his arms. Someday he wouldn't
share her with anyone, not for love, or money.

⊕   ⊕   ⊕

Claudine knew someone had been in her room before she opened the door. She'd learned over the years to trust her instincts, and they now told her to check each corner of the room, every object. She felt the anger rising inside her. Why couldn't they leave her alone?

A year had passed since she moved to the Royal and started on her new life. She loved photography, always had, even when she modeled briefly in Paris. On the art table in the window alcove were letters from *Paris Match* and *Photo*, both encouraging her to keep submitting material. She dropped to her knees and pulled out the long boxes of contact sheets, prints and negatives. She couldn't tell if they'd been disturbed, but none were missing. She grinned ironically when she found the little box at the bottom of the pile. She didn't have to open it. Someday, when I'm old and wrinkled, she thought, I'll be glad that I have pictures of my body, but boy, would I love to have the negatives. She'd discovered quickly that the line was thin between modeling with and without clothes.

The room boy had tidied up, the bed was made, and her clothes neatly folded in the armoire. She relaxed, sat down on the bed, then saw the little box, sitting square in the middle of her desk. The knot in her stomach tightened and her mouth dried.

Slowly, she unwrapped the paper. Inside were two metal film cans, tightly shut, along with a two-inch square envelope filled with powder. There was no note, no need for one. She paced the room, walked to the window and felt like screaming. She could see no way out. When she started stringing, she was certain that the past would melt away, releasing her to a new life. But they saw her job as good cover, and while she fought every intrusion, she knew she was compromising her new friends.

Hanging on her bedpost was a red kerchief, one of Sam Michaels'. It was there as a joke, Sam trying to stake out her bed as his own. Now it made her want to cry. Whatever the reasons for her taking up with Sam, she found that she liked him now. Others saw him as only another channel to the outside. She'd held her ground last month when they wanted to increase the volume. No, no, she'd said. Only the samples. And when things settle down, no more.

A shiver of revulsion ran from head to toe. Even when she brought forth her greatest resolve, the tingling worsened, and the conversation with herself always ended the same way. One more day, just one more day, the voice in her head would say. Tomorrow, you can walk away. After all you've been through in your life, treat yourself. Only the best, it would say, you're on the top now, you deserve the best. She grabbed the packet and headed for the bathroom.

Just one more day.

VI.

Studio 5

SAM CURSED THE cold water hitting his back. In the months he'd lived in Studio 5, he'd had hot water for two weeks. A candle flickered outside the bathroom door, gaining strength on the dying twilight. If Sam had a choice in the evenings, he'd take the hot water over electricity. Tonight he had neither.

He stared down at his body and noticed that his ribs were showing. Cambodia and dysentery had to rank as the world's most efficient diet, he thought. Maybe he could package it for Bloomingdales, shipping out vials of the local water in fancy bottles. "La Potion du Cambodge," he'd call it. The product would be a nice sideline for the old room boy who spent his days boiling drinking water, then pouring it into jugs freshly rinsed in polluted tap water. Sam guessed his weight around 140, twenty-five pounds below his average. He was slightly over six feet tall, but the thinness added to his height.

The electric razor ran slowly, in bad need of a recharge. How many days had it been since the power had been on

for more than a couple of hours at a time? Once, he'd
cranked up the portable Honda generator that was stashed
on the studio balcony to get a charge.

He found himself laughing at the image of the modern
man removed from the convenience of electrical sockets.
Over the whir of the blades, he could hear Sophan laughing, keeping time with the music from the battery-powered
stereo. He'd dropped by the studio with his girlfriend Ming
to listen to music.

Sam remembered the time, shortly after he'd arrived,
when Sophan offered him Ming for the night. He didn't
know how to handle it, not wanting to insult the man, but
unable to explain his reservations, his own cultural hang-
ups. It only complicated matters when he realized that
Ming was a full partner in the proposition. She didn't feel
used. Instead, she felt honored to be the symbol of Sophan's growing attachment to Sam. It was then Sam realized how deeply their feelings ran, how much Sophan
really cared. Chan had bailed him out, carefully explaining to Sophan and Ming that while Sam was honored, he'd
rather Sophan keep the lady that particular night, that he
had other plans.

He smiled into the mirror, checking his tobacco-stained
teeth. "Sam Michaels, Phnom Penh," he said out loud,
still getting accustomed to being a television reporter, a
real change after years in radio. He rarely saw his stuff,
and this was a way for him to get reinforcement and the
ego rush. He was in over his head, and he knew it. But
what the hell, he thought, life is shot full of bullshitters,
and he had the knack.

Ten years before, his goal had been to work at a radio
station in Atlanta, the ultimate fantasy. He pursued the
dream by wandering the South, working as a disc jockey
and newsman at various stations, living on minimum wage
and all the freebie McDonald's coupons he could rip off
from the station prize room. In between he crammed in
college, and finally the Air Force called, breaking his pro-

vincial pattern and showing him the world. When he discharged, he took the little money he'd saved and headed for Europe and bought a battered Volkswagen van. He hit the hippie highway, heading down whatever road met his fancy, but always east. Six months in Afghanistan had taught him to live on the edge, and a couple years in India was a graduate course in getting by in the Third World. He often wondered what would have happened if India and Pakistan hadn't gone to war, if he hadn't met Tom Rider in the hotel, hadn't gone to work for the network. Probably would still be on some mountaintop in India, looking for truth. War wasn't conducive to that sort of quest, but it certainly was more interesting.

Sam wrapped himself in a towel and wandered through the loft, searching for his favorite cut-off jeans. He'd left them in a pile the night before. Sophan watched him for a few moments, dug under one of the pillows and tossed him the ragged Levi's. Ming smiled at some comment in Cambodian, her fragile features highlighted by her smooth, dark hair.

"Did you hide them?" Sam kidded, as he slipped into the jeans inside the bathroom door.

"No. You lose them doing boom boom," Sophan said, using the GI slang for sex. They continued to kid around about women as Sam trotted down the spiral staircase to the office, to look for more tape recorder batteries in the cabinet. He found four in a forgotten box, and underneath he found a stack of glossy 8 $\times$ 10 photos, stuff left behind in the old bureau. Many of them included Sophan. He took them back up to the loft.

"Check these out," Sam said, tossing the dozen pictures on the mats. "Keep them. They're all of you." He fiddled with the Sony stereo, changing the batteries, while Sophan showed the pictures to Ming.

"Here Tom Rider," Sophan said, holding one of the pictures toward Sam. Rider, Sam's rabbi at the network, was sitting in a cyclo, rum crook cigar stuck in his mouth,

like a sultan taking in his domain. Sophan stood grinning
to the side, a coolie hat cocked on his head.

"That's your problem, Sophan. Always letting people
push you around." Sam laughed and gave the photo back.
He put on "Tea for the Tillerman," by Cat Stevens, dug
under the large brown armoire for the lacquer box filled
with clean weed. As he finished rolling the joint, he realized that Sophan was quiet. Looking around, he saw
tears welling in Sophan's eyes.

"What did you find, man?" Sam crawled over the cushions to Sophan's side, looked at the picture in his hand.
Two Americans and an Indian stood with Sophan, their
arms wrapped over each other's shoulders. Sam recognized Karana, the Indian, and the other two looked vaguely
familiar, like long lost relatives in the family album.

"This John Morton . . . this Peter Strauss . . . ," Sophan said, pointing to the two white men. *"Morte . . .
fini . . ."* This was the crew killed on Highway 3, the men
who did not listen to Sophan's Buddha. It seemed long
ago, but they'd died only the year before.

"You still blame yourself for that, don't you?" Sam
could tell that there was no use in trying to change Sophan's mood.

"Yes . . . no . . ." He slowly shook his head and stared
at the photograph. "I tell them not to go, but they not
listen. I can do nothing . . . nothing. But maybe Sophan
save them if Sophan go. . . ."

". . . or get killed with them. Sophan, you can't look
back."

"Then, before this," he said, nodding at the picture,
"it was good. We go many miles, take good pictures,
everybody happy. War good then too. Everybody want join
army, everybody want to kill VC. Sophan make beaucoup
money, buy nice car, marry second wife. Much fun."

"We still do all right, Sophan. You still have the car,
the wives, not to mention Ming." The lady smiled when
she heard her name.

"Yes, we do OK. I like working with Sam, Chan. But it different. Sophan do good in war, but now he see too much, lose too many friends." He took a final look at the picture and put it on the bottom of the stack.

"Try some of this, maybe it will cheer you up." Sam dug under his clothes in the armoire, locating the full bottle of Jack Daniels. It was worth its weight in gold. "Where I come from, Sophan, we call this 'mother's milk.' "

Sophan took a long hit from the bottle, then giggled. *"Lait de la mère?"*

"Yeah, as good as the stuff from old Mom." Sam felt strange trying to cheer the Cambodian. To Sam, Sophan had seen it all in this part of the world. He'd been captured with the French army at Dien Bien Phu as a young man, traveled all over Indochina as a soldier, had hustled hard in the guided tour business at Angkor Wat. Ming choked on the whiskey, paused, then took another swig. Yeah, thought Sam, at this moment Sophan was on top of his world. He was able to provide for two wives, assorted children and Ming, but the picture had touched more than the sadness of seeing dead friends. It had reminded him of how things once were here, and how they'd changed. How much longer could it last? A year? Two years?

"Sam, you hide good whiskey from Sophan!" He gave Sam a gentle hit on the arm.

"Goddamn right, I do. That and the peanut butter." Sam laughed as Sophan made a face. He'd given him peanut butter once and Sophan had nearly choked trying to swallow it whole. Sam knew that this man filled a role in his life that no other man had. Sophan was Sam's Zorba the Greek, the man who was teaching him how to sing and dance. For that he loved him. He never failed to make Sam laugh, and when Sophan was sad, the whole world seemed sadder.

They alternated hits from the bottle and the joint, giddy

in the candlelight. Sam heard the door open downstairs,
someone bump into the desk.

"Hello. We're up here." He picked up the candle in
the dish and walked over to the head of the stairs. Claudine was working her way up the steps. She was dressed
in white cotton, baggy Indian cloth that flowed from her
body. Only the red scarf tied around her head broke the
whiteness.

"Sammi . . . I need favor. I have some film, things I
want to keep for myself, and I want to get it developed.
Can you ship it for me?" She pulled out an envelope with
a half-dozen film cans.

"No problem," he said, tossing the envelope into a
yellow mesh shipping bag by the rail. "Michael's Fast
Photos to the rescue."

"You are having a party without me, Sammi!" She
made an aside to Sophan in French. He laughed. Now that
she knew it was Sophan and Ming in the loft, she relaxed,
helped herself to the whiskey. Sam felt good now, surrounded by his friends. He protested when Sophan got up
to leave.

"I must go see number one wife. She cook tonight."
He helped Ming get up from the mats.

"She doesn't have to go unless she wants to," Sam
said, wondering what he did with Ming when he went
home. Sophan talked a moment in Cambodian. "No, she
must go home. She say maybe next time." They eased
themselves down the dark steps and quietly out the door.
The tape had ended. The tall windows rumbled for a full
thirty seconds, echoing a B-52 strike miles away.

"Do you have some of the little cans? I do not feel like
going out for the food."

"Sure." Sam went downstairs and prowled through the
small room that was once the kitchen. A dozen green boxes
were stacked in the corner, full of C rations. He found
cans of fruit cocktail, salisbury steak and ham and limas,
a concoction generations of GIs swore were the work of a

culinary sadist. He hated ham and limas, but Claudine loved them.

From his desk he took out his Swiss army knife, found a plate behind the chair. Feast time at the Royal. Upstairs, Claudine played a tape, one he'd misplaced. He opened the cans, listening to his own voice from above. He'd made it for his family, shipped the original home for safekeeping. One side described his life here, how living in Phnom Penh was different from New Delhi, what it was like being a roadrunner, going down the highways each day to find the war. He described the studio in detail, how the high windows rattled with the bombs, the view of the overgrown tropical garden through the dirty glass.

The other side, playing now, contained splices of action from the road; mortars crunching, machine guns firing, bombs detonating, pilots' voices squawking through the static on Sam's portable radio. He liked the part where his crew was pinned down by crossfire. They'd followed the army in, and before they realized it, the government troops retreated, leaving them in the middle. His voice was so tight he couldn't even complete a sentence. He'd saved that part to remind himself of pure fear.

"Sammi, what is this tape?" She watched him from the shadows as he tried to carry the whole meal up the stairs at once along with the candle.

"I made it for my family." He placed the dish and cans on the floor.

"You are cruel. They should not listen to such things." She spoke softly, but firmly.

"They wanted to know what I did here, so I told them." Sam didn't sense the flippancy of his comment, but he was taken aback by her reaction to the tape. "Don't you send pictures to your friends?"

"I send them pictures, but not like the tape." She listened to his frightened voice under the gunfire. Sam reached down and turned it off. "You are a very strange man, Sammi. . . ."

"Some folks think that, yeah. . . ." He sipped the juice from the green can of fruit cocktail. "Do you say that just because I make weird tapes?"

"No." Claudine stirred the ham and limas around in the can with her finger. "How many times I have come to your room at Chantao's, here to the studio, and you just talk. Other men, they always just try to make love to Claudine. But you like to talk."

"Shit. I wish I'd known."

"No, no, it is better this way. I like being here, just the talking. It is very nice. But it is difficult for me to understand. I never know when you want to talk, when you want to make love. . . ."

"Try me. . . ."

"Sammi, do not make the jokes." She gave him a serious look, and Sam decided to let her have her say.

"I do not always want the sex, either. Many times when we are together, well, I do not know what it is I want. To be near is important. Some men, they want Claudine around, they say they want to take me here, take me there, to show me off. I watch you with other women, and you are kind to them, like you are with me. In France, men would not treat me that way. You make me feel important, like friend. Oh, Sammi, you know what I mean. . . ."

"I think so." Sam shook some of the fruit cocktail around in the can. He felt like she wanted to say more, but had cut herself short. "My daddy always said treat women you're with the way you would want your sister to be treated. Well, I worship my sister, we were very close. She was my closest childhood buddy, so I knew what he was saying. That's simplistic, I know, but it's not a bad place to start. I get along with women better than men. They're my best friends."

"Didn't you have good men friends when you were the boy?"

"Sure, a few. But I didn't do the things other boys did. I played some sports, that sort of thing. But when the other

kids played ball, I was at the radio station. I couldn't wait
to work, but now that I'm older, I find myself trying to
get back some of that freedom I missed. You might say
that I was a 'serious child,' with a terminal case of the
fuckoffs.'' Sam propped a cushion under his back.

"Well, Sammi, whatever the reason you do things, I
like them. I find it difficult to understand your wants, your
desires. You are crazy in the pool. Up here, another person. Which Sammi should I like?'' She flipped a lima out
of the can toward Sam.

"Damn,'' he said, laughing, turning the slimy bean in
his hand. "I don't see how you eat these things." Sam
consumed the fruit cocktail, mulling over her question.
"I'm shy, Claudine, really I am. It's not that I didn't want
you, it's just that if I have to make a choice between having
a good friend, or risking the friendship trying to be lovers,
I'll go with the friend.''

"I thought all men wanted the lover.''

"That's too easy. I can get laid at the snap of my fingers
around here. So can you. I feel like I know you well, then
you drop another bomb. . . .''

"Drop the bomb?''

"You know, like your husband in Africa, things from
your past. I think sometimes that we were both a little
lonely when we were young. That's why we hold back.''
Sam was trolling now, hoping for more detail of her life.

"You, you are right. That is why I love the man in the
desert. He treats me in the same way you do. He is very
gentle, he listens to me.''

"So you are really married to him.''

"Yes . . . and no. I am married to him when I go there.
When I come here, that is something different.''

"Tell me about it. . . .''

"I go there many years ago, to get away from France.
I met him in Paris, at the University. He invite me to come
to desert. I traveled with the tribe, riding the Sahara and
living in tents. One night, he comes to my tent, ask me

to be wife while I'm with tribe.'' She lay down next to Sam, pulling a pillow under her head. "I ask him what other wives think . . . he has three . . . and he tells me to ask them.''

"What did they say?''

"Yes, they say yes. Then they make me a dress, like they wear, you know, the robe. I become his wife.'' She smiled, her mind drifting thousands of miles away, into the desert. "The first night, I stay with him in his tent. In desert, there are no roofs. The stars, they light up our bed. He was very gentle, very nice. You see, Sammi, that time of my life was not good. I did not think that I would love again.''

"Why's that?'' He spoke softly, not wanting to break her train of thought.

"Before, I live in Paris. In the 14th Arrondissement, just off rue du Chateau. There, I met a nice man. He was a singer, how do you say, folksinger? We start living together. After one year, we find out that we are brother and sister.''

Sam tried not to look shocked. He stayed quiet, stroking her arm, hoping that she would continue talking.

"During the war, we are separated. I was born in Germany.''

"But I thought you were French. . . .''

"My mother, she French. My father, German. Just before the war, my brother went to France, to live with aunt. My father, he die in war. I do not like to think about those times, Sammi.''

"Well, don't then.'' He'd sensed some of those deep scars in her soul. Now they made sense. He decided to get off of the war. "What happened to your brother?''

"He try to suicide himself. Put his head in the stove at our little flat. I found him, saved him, then he ran far away. That is why I do not like going to Paris now.'' She rolled over, held Sam tightly, like a child looking for comfort. He knew she'd revealed some inner parts of her life to him that weren't common knowledge, but he knew she held back even more. Sam was at a loss for words.

"Sammi," she whispered, "when I first start taking pictures, I stand up in combat all the time. Stand there and take my picture. People they call to me, 'get down, Claudine, get down.' But I do not care. Maybe sometimes I want to die, but I am like my brother. I cannot do it myself."

"You don't feel that way now, do you?" Sam remembered her on the ship.

"Most times, no. Not when I'm with you, or my friends. Oh, Sammi, why do we talk about such things." She reached for the bottle of whiskey, took a long hit and passed it to Sam. As he drank, she stood up, pulled off her blouse, slowly pulled on the cord that held up the baggy pants. "You say you are shy. Well, Claudine is not shy. Right now, we make love." She stepped from the pants, kneeled between Sam's legs and started unfastening his jeans. "What would you like, Sammi?"

He watched her fumble with the brass buttons, raised his hips as she pulled down the cut-offs.

"Lady's choice."

VII.

The Sniper

SOPHAN CAUGHT THE little Buddha falling from his mouth with his hand. His blue shower shoes flew in the air behind him as he ran. A sniper had the short Cambodian in his sights from several hundred yards down the street, and Sophan still had twenty yards to go.

"Come on, Sophan . . . run you bastard, run!" Sam winced, making himself small behind the low concrete wall as he watched him sprint across the rutted road. How many dead Cambodians had he seen with Buddhas still stuck in their frozen mouths? His sweat-soaked jeans stuck to the mire beneath him, his red hair and mustache dripping from the tropical humidity.

He was pissed. It was his idea to push farther into Ang Snoul and now this. They'd found some scattered fighting, but a sniper here didn't make sense. The convoy story aired yesterday, and they wanted to follow up fast with another good one. Now they'd gone too far, trapping themselves on the wrong end of this battered town, a few miles west of Phnom Penh, a world away from the Hôtel

Royal and a breakfast of French coffee and fresh croissants under poolside thatched huts.

"Fuck the soundbox, Sophan . . . ," Chan yelled from behind the black camera. "Move . . . move . . ." Two more sniper rounds slapped into the wall near them as Sophan grabbed at the shoulder strap to the soundbox. Chan's camera was rolling, even without the soundbox. Eight had crossed the street; Sophan made nine.

Crouched on one knee, her camera pointed straight at them from across the street, Claudine propped the barrel of her Nikon telephoto lens on a chunk of rubble from the shell of the building that protected her. She was recording each dash from behind, the expressions of the watchers the pictures she wanted. Who knows, if she got lucky they might be on the cover of some slick European magazine.

Sophan giggled as he dived into the crowd of photographers vying to be in front for the best shots. Larry Moss lay flat in the filthy alley, his cameraman on top of him, the bulky camera braced on his shoulder.

"Son-of-a-bitch, I think he broke the eyepiece." Chan was trying to pull himself free of the pile with his camera, staying within that invisible line just outside the bullets' range.

"I'll buy you a new one." Sam was relieved now that Sophan had made it, but he tightened back up as he watched Claudine tuck her arms around the three cameras that hung from her neck, to protect them for the run. Sam stared at the black muck on her white jeans. She looked like a tourist in her damned red tee shirt, and the color made her a good target.

Sam's body ached from the massive rush of adrenaline. He'd long since learned to control the fear, to use the rush that consumed it and drove him on. It was addictive, like opium smoking. Nothing like being in sniper range, one on one, to crank the high up a couple of notches.

"Here at the Ang Snoul Olympics, the numbers are in on Put Sophan's run . . . five-five, five-three, five-four.

Good speed, but a little shaky on the style.'' Moss shook with a nervous laugh. It relieved the tension. With nine runners for practice, he had to get his range, although Sam suspected the sniper was just playing with them. Still, Claudine had nowhere to go but across that road.

Sam felt the twist in his stomach, the rumble in his bowels. He didn't like what he felt right now, the sort of feelings that could get them hurt. One of the first rules of war, as his daddy had told him about life, was not to get your bread and meat from the same place. Chan had pissed and moaned when Claudine started roadrunning with them, worried that Sam would make mistakes with her around. He was right, but it was too late to change.

Sam realized that he had the radio microphone in his hand, set to do a radio spot. He couldn't speak. None of the reasons that pushed them this far an hour ago seemed to matter now.

"Here she comes. . . ." Chan turned on his camera with the others, the whir-click of the motorized Nikons a soft counterpoint to the cracking of the rifle.

Claudine's long legs pushed her jungle boots into the dirt, her mouth shut in a tight line, eyes fixed on the small opening where the others hid. The sniper held his fire for a moment, surprised by a woman appearing in his sights.

"Ah, motherfuck . . . ,'' Sam groaned as she tumbled face first into the street, a burst from the gun kicking up dirt where she lay ten feet in front of them. He felt a wave of nausea start low in his bowels.

"Claudine! Claudine! *Lève-toi*!'' Sophan jumped up, pushing past the others to reach her. Sam grabbed the back of his shirt.

"Hang on, don't go out there. . . .''

Suddenly, Claudine moved, took three digging steps then dived over the top of the cameras, a fullback goal line move. They all cheered.

"Alllllright . . .'' Ty Stoneman broke her fall. Sam laughed, watching Ty cop a feel, the reason for his outburst. Claudine smiled and took a playful swipe at Stoneman, but her fingers shook as she wiped the Nikon lenses with her tee shirt. Sam resisted the temptation to crawl to her side.

"Let's *didi mau*," ordered Chan, using the Vietnamese for "move fast." "This ville is going down the tubes." He unhooked the umbilical cord that ran from his camera to Sophan's soundbox and unraveled his legs from the pile. As Sam shoved the mike into his hip pocket, a jet screamed overhead, cutting across town on a bomb run.

"About fuckin' time the cavalry rode in," Sam said, trying to see between the houses to where the Phantom was bombing.

"Before we move on to the napalm-slinging event, let's meet the winners of the Main Street Sniper Dash," Moss said as they worked their way down the alley. "The bronze to Ty Stoneman, who despite years of training on a rigid dope diet could still run in a straight line. . . ." The group jogged now, cameras and ditty bags slapping their hips and backs. The cars were a quarter of a mile away, parked on the edge of the village.

"Second goes to Steve Chan, proof that the master race may well be Chinese children raised on Mexican cooking." Chan shot him the bird over his shoulder. "And the gold medal to Put Sophan, who proved that God didn't mean for man to wear shoes."

He was screaming over the screech of a second F-4, invisible behind the trees. They could hear the distant crunch of a napalm canister as it hit the ground, the whoosh as the jellied gasoline sprayed out, sticking to and burning whatever it could find, buildings, trees or human skin.

Sam was puzzled. Ang Snoul was only halfway to the front. The Khmer Rouge couldn't hold this town, not with the big government base a couple of miles away. Snipers usually covered troop movements, held a position for a short time, then disappeared. What could they be covering in this town? There was action across the paddies, but what was happening here?

"Hey, Michaels," Moss said, falling in beside him, "you really let me down just now. I was going to make sure they spelled your name right and everything."

"Same to you, fellow." Sam got off on Moss' odd humor.

"All the same, that could have been great shit back there," voicing what they'd all been thinking. You couldn't take pictures of flying bullets, only the people dodging them, and somebody getting blown away on camera is rare. Definitely an Evening News lead, even if it's one of your colleagues. How morbid can I get, Sam wondered. As it stood, neither of them had shit. A fuck-up didn't qualify as a television story.

"You can't go anywhere out here without getting shot at," Moss continued. "Wanna bet on who controls this town right now?" Moss looked around as he ran, his California good looks out of place somehow in a war. Too many wrinkles had forced him out of the anchorman business. He was now biding his time until graying temples made him an older, distinguished anchor at one of the major TV markets Stateside. He contented himself with chasing battles and getting on the air a lot.

"I don't know," Sam said, looking at the shuttered windows and abandoned bicycles on the street. "I think he just got lonesome."

"Ah, yes. The old Lonesome Sniper scam."

The two Mercedes were where they'd left them, under the trees, out of the midday heat. The group split up as they approached the cars. Ty Stoneman hung back. He'd ridden out with the ambulance drivers early that morning. Driver Joe was waiting, the trunk open, iced towels and cold beers in the cooler. Sam dug out two beers and tossed one to Moss.

"A lot of pissing in the wind, I might say." Sam wiped

his face with a cold towel. How the quality of life could improve in ten minutes around here.

"Indeed. And I think I'll call it a day. Last night was enough to kill two men." They'd done some heavy singing and dancing around the pool, warming up on a case of Dr. Jake's Foster's beer. Moss was a staff correspondent, and his paycheck didn't depend on filing everyday. He worked hard, but he didn't have to constantly hump like Sam and the others.

"Think we'll look around for another element. Hate to let this whole day go to waste."

"Ah, yes, the fine television art of making chicken salad out of chicken shit." Moss downed the beer and headed for his car. His driver wasted no time turning around and speeding toward the city. The Cambodian stringers had bummed a ride with him, leaving Sam with his normal contingent.

Sam started to open the car door, then heard the jets turn in for another run. He looked at Chan, getting a thumbs up. "Five minutes . . . that's all . . ."

Sam called to Claudine, who was reloading her cameras on the hood of the car. "You going with us?" A roadrunning team was a democracy, with a majority of one. No one was required to go anywhere, all in agreement before they set out

"Certainement . . ." She shook her head at the question, her pursed lips showing her disgust in the Parisian manner.

This was how the freelancers, or stringers, made their money. For them, five more minutes could mean getting the element that would sell a story. If no one used the story or picture, a whole day of ass-hanging went to waste. Ty sold to the wire services, sometimes to the newspapers. Claudine sold mostly to European magazines and papers, so they didn't compete.

"It's nape, man, it's nape . . . ," Stoneman called back. He had taken the lead down the highway, his ponytail flop-

ping against the ragged fatigue shirt, the Nikons swinging
to the side. They could see the fire now, black smoke
pouring from a treeline across the paddies.

The jets were spots now, circling wide and finding their
range. Overhead, a Bronco buzzed around like a worried
hen, checking the target, keeping score of the hits.

"We got it all right here, Tiger." Chan dropped to one
knee, getting the wide shot of the edge of the paddy,
zooming in on the spotter plane. "Won't be anything like
the river stuff, but it's something. I'll get them on the next
run. . . ." Chan sat on the ground, practicing the arc he'd
have to make with the camera to keep the jets in the lens.
The gunfire was heavy, but none seemed directed at them.
Chan wiped the sweat from his eyes on the sleeve of his
bush shirt.

Sam got behind Chan, to stay clear of his shot. He could
see himself in the reflection of Sophan's wrap-around sunglasses. The Cambodian twisted the knobs of the foot-long
soundbox, enjoying the off and on sounds in his headset.
As a soundman, he left a lot to be desired.

"Hey," Sam said, nudging Sophan, "check the Buddha."

"Buddha say OK . . . we OK today." Eight of the
twenty foreign journalists who'd died in this war did it
twenty miles farther down this very road. Sophan had refused to go. The reporter from Sam's network hired another driver. The crew from Moss' company followed,
afraid of being scooped. The lead jeep was hit by a B-40
anti-tank round. The five who survived the ambush got to
dig their own graves the next morning. You bet Sam listened to Sophan's Buddha.

"Ah, you're just in a rush to service your number two
wife. Can't you keep that thing in your pants for just one
day?" Sam slapped Sophan on the back and laughed. He
kidded him constantly about his two wives and beautiful
girlfriend, but he envied his stamina and his ability to lead
many lives. The buzz among the drivers was that none of

Sophan's women complained from a lack of physical attention.

"I got 'em, I got 'em. . . ." Chan panned with the jets as they came in from Sam's right. Stoneman and Claudine followed with the Nikons, both praying for that one picture that showed the bombs dropping. Sam pulled the microphone from his hip pocket, checked the small Sony tape recorder that hung from a canteen case on his belt, then moved away from the crew, describing the scene for radio.

"I can see the bombs dropping now . . . ," he said, talking close into the mike, the tone of his voice saying more than the words. ". . . they are tumbling end over end, going into the trees . . . there's the flash! It's napalm!" He held the mike toward the trees, hoping that the whoosh of the fire would be captured on the tape. He'd long since disabled the automatic gain control on the tape recorder which made the loudest explosions sound like firecrackers.

"These bombings have intensified, as the government wants to hit every target before the bombers leave. But the insurgents know full well that it is only a matter of time, and my sources say they are laying low, awaiting the day they can move freely, without being spotted from the air. Sam Michaels, Ang Snoul, Cambodia."

Sam almost doubled over from the shot of pain in his gut. He muttered something incoherent to Sophan and duck-walked toward a clump of bushes, trying to pocket the microphone at the same time he unbuckled his belt, an awkward task. He didn't have time to choose a place, he just squatted as soon as he was out of sight of the others. His eyes squeezed shut and he saw colors in his head as his bowels once again tried to turn themselves inside out. One of these days, Sam thought, I'm going to have to get my ass out of this place and have this taken care of. But not now, not yet, not until we see what happens when the bombing ends.

As his stomach settled, Sam tackled the next problem—
retrieving the wad of toilet paper from the left hip pocket
of his jeans. As he finished he realized someone was
watching him. A young Cambodian government soldier,
wearing a blue beret, stood fifty yards away, M-16 slung
to the side, just watching.

Sam stood, then started toward him. In one smooth
move, the soldier raised and cocked the rifle, a signal for
Sam to stop. Sam raised both hands in a signal of recog-
nition, trying to think about his next move. They stared at
one another for a full minute, until the man finally smiled,
lowered the gun and walked away. Sam watched and wondered why, then turned to see Claudine standing behind
him. The soldier had acted like he knew her, but that was
impossible, Sam thought. No, he just wasn't in the mood
to put holes in pretty girls. Claudine said nothing as they
rejoined the group.

"I don't know what's going on here, but I just saw a
government troop in the bushes, and he didn't act so
friendly." Sam shut up as Chan gave him a sharp look
from behind the camera. He was still shooting. The jets
made a final pass at their target, both doing a slow roll as
they climbed and headed back toward their base in Thailand.

"I don't know about you, man. . . ." Chan was pissed.

"Sorry." Sam felt a blush.

"Just watch it." Chan shouldered the camera and
started walking down the highway. "Did you see his outfit
patch?"

"No, but he had a blue beret, like the Ninth Brigade's."

"Wrong, Tiger. They're based at Kampong Sneu, but
the last I heard, they were stuck on a mountain." Chan
was saying what Sam was thinking. That was at least
twenty miles down the road.

"Well, the way they juggle troops, maybe they moved
up here."

"For what? Prek's not about to post them down here."

"I don't know, but they've been around the whorehouse for the past week," Stoneman said. "They're off the mountain, you can bet on that. Did you hear about the paymaster?"

"What are you talking about?"

"The Ninth, man, the Ninth. They were bullshitting with the ambulance drivers. Seems they hadn't been paid or fed out on that mountain for months. Government sent out a paymaster to settle them down."

"And . . ." Sam nudged Ty into the story. This could be good.

"Well, I think the Ninth ceased to be an effective fighting force the day they ate the paymaster."

"No shit!"

Ty looked hurt. "You think I'm lying?"

"No, no. That's incredible. So what are they doing now?"

"Getting laid."

"Other than that . . ."

"They're out of the war, that's for certain." Ty had shared enough to whet their appetites.

"Well," Chan said, swinging the conversation back to the story, "you can't use any of that. We don't have pictures of your soldier."

"Hey, I'm just commenting on what I saw, that's all." Sam felt Chan was punishing him for getting them pinned down.

"Sure, sure. I believe you." Chan didn't sound convinced.

"Sammi, Ty . . . come, look," Claudine called from a patch of bushes nearby. "What is happening here," she said, kneeling next to the body of a small child. Her face was intense, and Sam noticed the same expression he'd seen as she crossed the road.

"Ain't this a pretty sight." Sam looked around the area, a series of dugouts covered with green military tarps, surrounding an empty artillery mortar position. Spent shell casings were scattered about, cooking pots lay on their sides. Fresh tire tracks through the bags showed that the gun had been quickly dragged from its position. Three women's bodies hung from the foxholes. The hand of one reached over the dirt edge, toward the child next to Claudine, her fingers six inches from the little body.

"Oh, fuck this war," she said as she patted the dead child, moved back and cocked her camera. Sam was in her first picture.

"Why do they stay on the front lines?" Sam asked, knowing well the answer. The Cambodian army had no lines of supply, no way of feeding their troops. The soldiers took their families along, exposing them to battle. More civilians died than soldiers in mortar attacks on the army camps. Claudine focused on the child, crouching low to get his face. The little boy seemed asleep, his tiny arm under his head, his legs spread comfortably.

"Hey, Sam . . . let's move . . . ," Chan was calling as he broke through the bushes, but cut it short when he saw Claudine.

"Right, but we've gotta get this." Sam moved back to let Chan and Sophan work. Chan had made his point.

"Wonder where the gun went?" Stoneman said, picking up one of the brass casings. "Hasn't been long since they fired from here. Still smell the cordite."

"Well, somebody wanted it pretty bad to do this," Sam said as he looked at the bodies.

"If you're going to do a close, do it here." Chan didn't look up from the camera. With this element, they had enough to stitch together a story. Sam walked over to get the mike from Sophan, who stood shaking his head. "Very bad . . . this very bad," he said, the emotion hidden behind his mirrored sunglasses.

"Yeah, yeah, it is," Sam said, Sophan's grief shifting him rapidly from seeing the bodies as part of a story to the human side. Sam had seen a lot of bodies in his years of chasing wrecks and wars, but for Sophan it was different. These were his own people dying. The Cambodians never wanted this war. In fact, they tried for years to avoid being sucked into the abyss that consumed their neighbors, Vietnam and Laos.

"Come on, Tiger . . . let's wrap it up." Sam took the mike from Sophan and moved in front of the camera, dropping to one knee. He checked himself in the orange eye of the camera filter, could see the sides of his hair sticking out like wings, black gunk on his shirt. He ran his hand through his hair once, cleared his voice and nodded at Chan.

"Rolling . . ." Chan's finger flicked toward Sam.

"Close . . . close . . . Ang Snoul . . . take one. . . ." Sam paused to give the editor time to establish him in the camera. "This is thought to be a secure area, under the control of the government. But even here, small actions take place, and they take their toll. But for this woman and her child," he said, indicating the bodies near him, "the military implications don't matter. For them, the war ended sometime early this morning. Sam Michaels, Wat Kambaul . . ."

"That's a keeper . . . let's go. . . ." Chan reached back to unhook the sound cord. Claudine walked up to the child and covered his body with one of the green tarps.

"Adieu, mon petit soldat," she whispered, pausing beside the child a moment before joining the others.

They double-timed back to the car. The houses of the town were shuttered and empty, bicycles and carts abandoned in the roads and gutters. Driver Joe had the engine running, the doors and trunk open. The dignified, white-haired driver spoke five languages and provided full service with his car. Sophan grabbed an armful of local beers and white towels from the cooler in the trunk. Chan jumped in the back seat, pulling the film magazine from the top of the camera, quickly replacing it with a fresh one in a black sack to keep out the light. To Sam, it always looked like he was playing with himself, fiddling around in the bag on his lap.

"I don't think I'd buy a house down here. . . ." Chan was only serious until the story was done.

". . . or loan anyone money." Sam took a beer from Sophan and leaned against the car, watching as Ty and Claudine stopped for a couple more shots of the smoking town. "Let's take this straight to the airport . . ."

Sam was interrupted by a commotion in the distance, beeping horns and roaring motors. A jeep, driven by a small, dark, wiry soldier wearing an American Green Beret, led the way. Riding shotgun was Marty Satterfield, one hand holding down his brown Stetson. Behind them stretched a ragged convoy of jeeps, Peugeot taxis, army trucks and cyclos, each piled full of people, arms and supplies.

"Afternoon, chappies. I got here just in time to join the retreat." Satterfield leaned over the side of the jeep, cutting loose a brown stream of tobacco. "Like you to meet my partner, Pha Doh."

Sam looked past the vehicles, at the smoke rising from the other side of the river. "I take it we're now part of the rear guard?"

"At least on that side of the river. No need to waste these fine Montagnards on a bridge no one's going to use again. We just blew the fucker." Pha Doh barked at his little army in *Rhade*, taking advantage of the stop to reorganize a bit.

"*Fini bibi,* to quote the Vietnamese."

"Yeah. Too bad." Satterfield eyed the pouch of Levi Garrett tobacco stuck in Sam's shirt pocket. "Looks like our noble allies dropped and ran." He picked up the microphone to a field radio lying behind the seat. "Just like old times, calling in the airstrikes. Nothing like a little nape to open the ferry crossing one last time."

"Yeah, we saw that." Down the road, the crack of automatic rifle fire increased.

"Got something for you, man. Tall thin army dude asked Pha Doh to get this to you." Marty dug out a small movie film can from his bush shirt pocket.

"Great. Sir Charles strikes again." Charles was a Cambodian army photographer who moonlighted with the networks. He could get places they'd never see. Now they might have a story.

"Tell you what's weird, man. There's been pushing and bumping going on in this sector for the past two days, but there have been no reports of enemy movements. Pha Doh got smart and decided he had no support. Nobody would tell him what to do. So he decided to boogie."

"Yeah, well we got pinned by a sniper in the village, and God only knows where he came from." Sam looked at the piece of paper taped to the film can, the shot list neatly written in Cambodian.

"Well, I had fun." Marty smiled, then pulled the tobacco pouch from Sam's shirt. "Hey, Claudine, Maurice was right. Pha Doh was right where he said."

Claudine wandered around the convoy, taking rapid fire pictures with the Nikon. She smiled knowingly at Marty.

"Hey, Tiger, let's go." Chan stood next to the Mercedes, door open, ready to leave.

"Buy you a beer at the hotel." Sam wanted to talk more with Satterfield. He had a suspicion that Marty was up to his neck in this war, and now he had some proof.

"Deal. But I can't drink without my personal escort," he said, nodding at Pha Doh.

"Sure. Just look for me in the pool."

The moment they all crammed into the car, Driver Joe made a fast U turn and headed north. Sam rolled down his window. The noise of the rifles was closer as they skirted the main street. Should they suck in a bullet, he didn't want to eat window glass.

"Tiger, you looked a little puckered back there in the alley." Chan was unwinding now.

"Ol' buddy, you couldn't have shoved a pin up my ass

with a sledgehammer.'' Sam lapsed into his East Tennessee drawl now, feeling that they'd made up for his mistake.

"Sammi, sometimes the things you say, they do not make sense.'' Claudine shared the front, her body tight against his in the leather bucket seat. Smudges of dirt streaked her face; her wide mouth and white teeth set off her big green eyes. She rested her head on his shoulder and took a deep breath.

"Sophan, translate this, will ya?'' Sam handed him the dope sheet, then dug his reporter's notebook from the glove box of the car.

"He say he have stolen convoy. Have pictures of trucks, picture of One-Oh-Five, picture of soldiers.''

"Big fuckin' deal. The Cambos are notorious for hijacking their own convoys. No fighting?''

"No. Just pictures of trucks, guns, soldiers.''

"Looks like Sir Charles let us down.'' Sam had given the cameraman that nickname because of his regal air.

"You can still use it. Just cover it with a couple of lines about resupply problems or something.'' Chan wanted Charles to keep sending them film first, so he pushed Sam to use his footage. More than once he'd gotten great stuff.

"Yeah, OK. Why this convoy?'' Sam couldn't figure why Charles would take those particular pictures. Maybe he was just hungry and needed money.

"He say it the 'Renegade Brigade.' ''

"The what?''

"You know, the Renegade.''

"Maybe that's the name they've given themselves.'' Chan was impatient. "Just write it into the script. We've got the story.''

"As you say, Master.'' Sam adjusted himself in the seat, Claudine moving so he could type. A soft breast pushed in on his arm. Sam glanced over the seat, saw Chan arching his eyebrows, slowly shaking his head from side to side. As he wrote, they sped through a few hundred yards of deep jungle, then curved left, now running high up over the paddies that stretched out on both sides of the road, a silhouette target. Chan always said riding in the car was the part he hated most. Things were totally out of his control. The spotter plane buzzed over the car, checking them out.

"I hope he knows the good guys ride in white Mercedes," Chan quipped, sticking his head out the window to keep his eye on the plane. It flew on. Sam was thinking about the village, about how to work the trucks and gun into one story. If the gun were captured, Sam wouldn't want to be in those woods when the B-52s announced their arrival with a string of five-hundred-pound bombs. If true, the wine glasses would surely dance tonight on the tables in Phnom Penh.

VIII.

The Lab

PAO WAS SCARED shitless. Events had left him in a daze, barely able to think or function. Sleep was impossible. The only way to keep his sanity was to work, and that would soon be done. Then what?

He'd felt the bad karma when he arrived up north, just in time to watch them tear down the lab. Then the flight to Phnom Penh, Pao almost getting shot in the jungle clearing. But by whom? And the lab. Some critical parts were left behind, and by only the most diligent scrounging around the military thieves' market was he able to rebuild the lab at all.

Pao nodded to his assistant. At least the process was going well. The solution on the makeshift lab table was cooking smoothly, granules of substance gathering on the bottom of the flask. He walked down a darkened corridor, ducked through a blackout curtain and entered the front room. Sitting patiently were the two men who'd never left his side. Pao tried to imagine the layout of the village. He guessed it to be twenty miles out of the capital, judging from the car rides. They only let him out after dark, and after the firefight and bombers, he wasn't anxious to wander far.

He poured a cup of tea, walked between the men and stood at the front door. The porch of the house was five feet above the ground, supported on poles. Woven thatch loosely formed the walls; mats covered the floor. The only change in the ancient design was the tin roof, patched together from U.S. Government shipping cases. The village streets were deserted, but music from radios and a low murmur of whispering voices attested to life somewhere out there. It was an hour after curfew. His eyes followed a slow-moving Mercedes as it eased down the dirt street, dome light on, the driver's white face his passport in the night.

Pao wasn't happy with the arrangement, not one bit. When they'd approached him in Hong Kong two weeks ago, the deal seemed simple enough. Break down and re-establish the Cambodian laboratory. Done properly, it should have taken two weeks and he'd have been back on Nathan Road, playing mah-jong with his friends. Yes, the money was there in his account. That wasn't the problem. Someone had gambled bringing him here. These weren't his people, but the money talked. They needed a pro, and they needed him now. Pao didn't want to know who the Chinaman was. To him, it could be fatal information. He watched as the car pulled behind another house, fifty meters away. A moment later, he heard loud voices arguing in French and Cambodian.

He finished the tea, put the cup on the floor and sat with his feet hanging over the edge of the small porch. He thought about his immediate problem. He didn't have time up north to sort out all of the equipment. When he arrived, he discovered that the lab pieces had been scattered into six separate boxes, neatly packed for the move, but in no order. That, in addition to the boxes abandoned at the airstrip. The men wouldn't listen to reason. They wanted it finished now, back in production. He was worried about several of the fittings. The proper ones just couldn't be found, and he had to improvise. They worked, but somehow didn't seem to be quite the right combination. He was a master chemist, not a mechanic. Years ago, when he was learning the trade, he'd built and maintained labs. But you forget, and others do things differently.

And it was big. What he had going right now was only the start. Three more areas would be built, and that would mean forty kilos a day. He'd never seen this big an operation in one place. That bothered him too. Would they let someone who knew about this lab go home, back to Bangkok, free to talk? Deep in his gut, Pao had the sinking feeling that he knew the answer.

The shouting from the house grew louder. One of his guards grunted, signaling to Pao to go back into the lab. He wanted a cigarette, but he did not dare smoke in the lab. He stood back from the bench, following the intricate tubing with his eyes, trying to find a mistake. Tomorrow would be the final test.

The large ether bottles clanged together as he brushed by, sending a chill up his spine. Soon enough he'd be hooking them up, ready for the final step. He took the next few minutes to carefully watch the process, going through it step by step in his mind. He'd heated the morphine and an equal amount of acetic anhydride in a large glass flask. For six hours it had cooked at 185 degrees, until the morphine and acid became bonded chemically. It was impure, but it was diacetylmorphine. Heroin, to the users.

He then worked through the next three steps, the water and chloroform treatment, adding the sodium carbonate, to make the heroin solidify, then filtering off the heroin with a suction pump, reaching this point. Pure lumps of heroin clung to the bottom of the flask. He removed them, adding them to the small sample tin.

But that was as far as he could go. Only four bottles of

ether were on hand, and no hydrochloric acid. He'd been promised that they'd be waiting for him here. When these two elements are added to the solution of heroin and alcohol, white crystals start to form, the flake white powder so prized by American addicts. He guessed that this particular batch would be about 90% pure, certainly in the Number 4 category. He tasted a cooling sample and quickly felt the rush. Tonight, he could use some himself, but he held back the urge. Tasting in this kitchen could kill the cook.

He understood why they wanted to move here. The war was creeping up on the border lab, no doubt about that, and he guessed that the Chinaman was afraid it would be cut off, along with the product. Yet the move was too hasty, and no one had told him why the other master chemist had left, or even where he'd gone. He felt the dread return. Why hadn't he asked these questions in Bangkok? Get the process running and get out of here. That's all Pao wanted now. Even the money was worthless as long as he was stuck here. And when he left depended on the Chinaman's orders to the men out front.

For the first time he thought of escape. He'd risk being tracked down later. This operation couldn't last very long, not with the war, and he'd rather be holed up in Kowloon than dying here. He drew on his memory for Chinese connections. All overseas Chinese had relatives scattered throughout Asia. He'd heard about an aunt in Cambodia, several times removed, but she would have to do. He knew she wouldn't be hard to locate, not with her notoriety.

Pao's thinking was interrupted by loud yelling, and a commotion in front. "The Chinaman, he will not like this news." The one speaking followed the other four into the lab, then stood next to Pao, slowly moved his eyes from man to man, scanning the small circle gathered in the room. "You want me to tell him this thing?"

There were no answers. Two of the men wore uniforms; they watched the speaker like poker players. Pao noticed that the other two wore rubber thongs, signaling the limits of their westernness.

They spoke French, and Pao feigned ignorance, fiddling with the tubes, shaking the bottles, anything to stay out of this fight.

"It is too late to turn back, if that is what you are suggesting." The Cambodian army captain smiled softly, his sunglasses blocking the top of his face in the dark room. "You must give this situation a positive face. Let us think of it as a hitch in the pipeline, as our American allies like to say."

"Ahhh . . . ," the Frenchman hissed, slamming his fist down on the bench. "The stealing of the ether is not a hitch!"

"You are right, of course," said the major, waving his hand toward the speaker. "But it is not for us to argue such things. What is done is done."

"What do you want?"

"Half of it."

"Half of what?" The westerner stiffened even more.

"Half the heroin." The captain looked over the top of his sunglasses.

"I must tell you again. You do not have heroin. You have ether and hydrochloric acid bottles. It is only worth something here. But you must have a lab to make the heroin. That is why you are making a mistake."

"Yes, but you fail to understand. There is a positive side. You, you have the laboratory. I, well, we," he said, waving vaguely at his comrades, "have the ether to make the heroin."

"You have the Chinaman's ether," the Frenchman said, as though the use of his name would get a reaction from these common soldiers.

"Ah, yes, the Chinaman. We have his chemicals, but he has much more. That is what I would like to discuss with the Chinaman."

"You tell me . . ."

"Enough. I have told you enough. You tell him that we will talk only with him." The captain turned, quickly followed by his juniors. "And tell him that he will find it most difficult to transport his morphine base without the proper protection. That is what we want to discuss. Protection."

"Are you saying that you will do it again, try and hijack the base . . ."

"And again . . ." The captain flipped his beret at an angle on his head, chilling the Frenchman with his professional air. "You must hurry and tell him. We will have more news soon. We also have a gun. A One-Oh-Five. It is terrible what a One-Oh-Five artillery piece can do to a city. Terrible. Even the President would be upset with the Chinaman. Of course, the President would know that the Chinaman could prevent it."

"You will regret this. You will not live to see the money or the heroin," he shouted as the men left the lab.

Pao was in deep now, and he knew it. Something drastic had gone wrong, and he had no chance now, not after hearing this. The Frenchman grabbed the sample bottle and stormed out. Soon Pao heard the car start and roar off.

He heard his guards discussing the showdown, he heard the President's name, the American name Reilly, like in the "Life of Reilly," the TV show he'd watched growing up in Hong Kong with Cantonese voices. How could he forget that name.

Pao returned to the tubing, when one of the guards came in the lab. The guard said nothing. He just pointed his finger toward Pao like a pistol, and pulled the imaginary trigger.

Pao knew he'd seen the Chinaman.

IX.

Rang's Message

THE HOUSEBOY PADDED across the polished concrete deck toward Reilly. The gin and tonic was topped with one of those unknown sprigs which the houseboy insisted helped the drink. Shit, thought the Colonel, I'd just as soon skip the glass, ice, tonic, and that piece of weed sticking out of the top. But Reilly stuck with the ritual, forced himself to hold tight for this moment, when he lit his own drinking light.

He cursed silently as the boy messed with the folding table by the chair, the tall glass tilting at a threatening angle. What a dumb little fuck. I use this table every night at the same time, but it never occurs to these folks just to leave the goddamn thing up. His skin itched now, the inside of his mouth consumed by the chemical backtaste of gin from nights past. Reilly was counting bottles again, and that made it even more antsy with the boy. Under the bed, in the dresser, a pint for the briefcase.

He grabbed the glass from the tray and took a long drink. Within a minute, the taste and the itching passed.

There was a time that he liked that feeling, getting past the nasties. But now it was only a fleeting moment on the trip toward oblivion. Those goddamn hidden bottles. Shit, there were five cases of hard liquor in the storage room. But he didn't touch those. Only for parties. Those were the counted ones, the known ones.

Hobart Reilly didn't have to look very far for reasons to drink. He'd finally gotten a slot that could lead somewhere, but events and history were against him. What happened on paper and what really went on around here were two different things, and the constant juggling of balls would drive any man toward drink. Those who'd filled this position as the primary contact between the United States military and the Cambodian government in the past had been rewarded with stars, but the string was running out, and Reilly knew it. This was a sloppy war, as the world's worst army slugged it out with the world's second worst army. It certainly looked now like the government army was attaining the distinction.

Reilly was a lifer, a career soldier who'd started out as an enlisted man in the Big War and was now one step away from a general's star. If he could hang in six more months, six months without major battles, big losses, or heaven forbid, an enemy victory, he'd make the General list. Nothing could stop him now. Nothing but the people who really held the power here; people who had interests other than turning back an insurgency.

A large bird cawed from the banyan tree in the garden by the patio. It cocked its head at the man seated, watching. Reilly heard the bird, a creeping feeling moving down his spine that the bird was waiting him out, letting him destroy himself, looking for easy pickings. A vespa horn bleated repeatedly as it whined unseen down the alley behind the wall. He wondered if the rider was making room or waking up the guard detachment that reportedly secured the back of the villa.

He wished that Colonel Rang would show up soon so

they could have their little chat and he could get on with
the night. Things were starting to get out of hand. How
much could he ignore? Sure, everybody had their scams,
the place ran on *baksheesh*, but a sixth sense told him that
the Cambodians no longer feared him, that they'd happily
watch him go down the toilet. Sweet Jesus, he thought,
I'm tight-jawed about gooks. There had to be a reason.
Rang had insisted on a meeting tonight, something about
losing a gun. Why get turned inside out over one gun in
a country with thousands floating around?

Reilly shut his eyes and tried to focus on good thoughts.
Too many things were pressing in. Here I am, living in a
villa with more servants than I can shake a stick at, one
of the top ass kickers in this little drama, and it's all slipping away. He was losing his grip. Right now, the only
thing he worked toward was this moment, what he was
holding in his hand.

He was fucking up with the Cambodians, and he knew
it. He'd been hit with a ration of shit at a bad moment,
and now that the bombing would end, he'd lost his ace
card. They'd proven time and again that no amount of
hardware issued to their army would turn events around,
only the relentless bombing. He certainly wasn't working
in a vacuum. There seemed to be one journalist for every
soldier, and just let those weak-minded fuckers find something to take pictures of, and it suddenly became the biggest thing around. Half the time they didn't know what
they'd seen. He grinned ironically, and dug under the chair,
opened his briefcase and extracted the silver pint hip flask.
He took a long hit, then refilled the glass with straight gin.
Now that was what he'd been looking for.

He didn't want to lose it, he really didn't. Phnom Penh
suited his needs right now. Entertainment was not a high
priority, and he had his time for thinking. Shit, he'd earned
it. He deserved it. Once I get out of here, get that star,
everything will square up. I'll be back in the real world,
will move my act back to the Officer's Club, have a few

toddies with the boys and leave it at that. But not now, not with all this pressure. He smelled the gin, swished it around in the glass, spoke to it. I'll drink you if you promise me that nothing will happen tonight. That you'll have the strength to deal with this fucker. He threw the drink back in one long hit. How could his best friend let him down?

⊕　　⊕　　⊕

Colonel Sek Rang was tired. Last night, after a big party, he was about to go to bed when a call came from the palace. President Prek was slowly falling apart, seeing ghosts in the middle of the night. That's when he called Rang. All night long Rang watched the President pace up and down the war room, talking to somebody who wasn't there. Today, Rang could barely stay awake.

The President was a military man, not a politician. Rang thought about the changes in Prek since the heady days following the coup that overthrew Prince Sihanouk, how the General had been transformed from the flashy field leader of a phantom army to the head of a nation in distress. Before the coup, Prek cut a sharp figure around the capital, quoting André Maurois and giving Sihanouk's government the semblance of military presence. His downfall came with the Americans, who convinced themselves that Prek could replace the dynamic but unbridled Prince. They were so unsure of the move that they waited for Sihanouk to return, only taking over power after a week of uncertainty. Rang, for one, was convinced that the communists took advantage of the situation by keeping the Prince hopscotching from one bloc nation to the next. He just couldn't picture Snooky, as the Americans called him, happy in North Korea or Peking. He was certain that the Americans only wanted to frighten Sihanouk and bring him in line with their thinking. Those times of 1970 seemed decades ago.

It didn't take a genius to read the tea leaves now. Men like Rang who'd enlisted in the effort were looking to the future, making arrangements for life beyond Cambodia. He would like to consider himself above such, but this call on Reilly was proof enough that Rang was a messenger for the only real power that was left. What had begun as a little nest feathering had now turned into his primary job.

It was late when Rang swung into the front seat of his jeep on his way to Reilly's villa. His driver turned the vehicle onto the deserted boulevard. A sleepy sentry mustered the energy to salute, barely rising from his stool. During the day it was a different scene. They would fight into the flow of traffic; bicycles, cyclos, Peugeot taxis crammed with people and produce. Smoking army trucks roared above the noisy confusion, relics from the American surplus truck lot. Women in sarongs crowded the curb with twin baskets dangling from the ends of bamboo poles balanced on their shoulders, bare-assed children in tow, heading for whatever they called home. Soldiers in ill-fitting fatigue shirts, sarongs, and rubber shower shoes mixed with the crowd.

Rang could half close his eyes and picture himself on a wide street in Paris; Phnom Penh was a tropical copy of the French capital. But here concertina wire rusted on the tops of villa walls, colorful blossoms springing from the razor-sharp coils. Rang remembered the day a young boy had lost control of his bicycle in front of the Information Ministry. Before they could untangle the child's body, all his blood drained out from a thousand fine cuts. When the war began, men gleefully piled on Pepsi Cola trucks, riding to the front to face the enemy. The novelty was gone now. In the city, people had been out of range of the shooting war. But each day, it moved closer. Every day, another chunk of land or another village was gobbled up, the perimeters of the war becoming smaller and smaller.

Rang was a movie maker, a man of the arts, not a career officer. He'd spent his life before the war trying to capture the variety and spirit of his country on film, the energy that flowed through the fabric of their lives like the Mekong. Those were the good days, when Sihanouk shared his passion for movie making, and gave him whatever he needed—the best equipment, plenty of film.

Being Chief of Information was the price Rang paid to keep making a few movies a year. His only source of film now was from the television people, and he was not averse to bartering information for a few hundred feet of fresh color stock. All the movies were one hour long and were shot on an hour's worth of film. Same actors, same scenery, same antique camera, same theme. But now he was recapturing a time he feared would never return.

Since the 1970 coup, Rang had watched his country fall apart. First to go were the eastern provinces along the border where the communists set up their bases for attacks into Vietnam. Sihanouk had turned a blind eye, hoping the communists would be satisfied, trying to keep his country from being sucked into the surrounding war. Then came the B-52s, clandestine missions with mealtime names that spread the war even farther. Finally, the invasion, which pumped life and bodies into the insurgents' camp.

Rang now thought of the map of his country like a movie frame stuck in a projector, the film melting on the screen before his very eyes.

The American Embassy loomed from the dark like a bunker on the corner of the wide street. The building was surrounded by a ten-foot-high concrete wall, coiled concertina wire on top and firing platforms with machine guns every fifty yards. Sandbags filled the corners and were stacked around the gate.

He hated coming here, this evening more than usual. When he'd reached Reilly on the phone, he'd hoped for an early meeting, so he could duck out of his office to get a few hours of rest. But Reilly was afraid to talk at the embassy, and he could not very well refuse the man who controlled the supply linc to the Cambodian army. Rang didn't like the idea of being dependent on Reilly, but his instructions were clear. To Rang, Reilly symbolized all the things that had gone wrong in his country, how outsiders had tampered with the precarious balance and had thrown his countrymen into the war. But his job was to get along with the Americans, and his position was perfect as a go-between, since he dealt daily with the key people.

They went past the embassy proper, turned down a parallel street to the entrance of Reilly's villa. The Marine guard looked at him a long time before saluting and letting the jeep through the gate. Standing in the entrance, he waited for another Marine on the other side to check him out on the television monitor by his desk. The door buzzed, and he entered the lovely gardens where he'd spent several unpleasant times waiting for the American. They were even more paranoid than Prek, and that was saying a lot.

"Yes, sir, can I help you?"

"Colonel Rang to see Colonel Reilly." The Marine behind the long clean desk looked young to Rang, very young. As the boy turned to pick up the phone, Rang pressed his eyes shut. If he could get this over with quickly, he'd be able to get some sleep.

"Major Bishop will be down to get you in a moment. Would you please sign here." He pushed a clipboard toward the Cambodian. Rang signed his name. Let the enlisted man fill in the boxes.

"Sorry about the hour, Colonel Rang, but Colonel Reilly has been tied up all day. Nice to see you." Maj. Larry Bishop stood holding open the thick, leaded glass door that led through the villa onto the patio. He was a rod-straight West Pointer, Reilly's aide and buffer. As they walked, Bishop jingled his keys. "I ordered you a martini. That is what you like?"

"Yes, that is fine." He'd never developed a taste for American drinks, barbarian compared to the French taste.

"Let me see if Colonel Reilly is busy." Bishop pushed the button on the intercom even though Reilly sat in full view outside on the patio. Rang was always taken with the American fascination for gadgets, things that talked, lights that flashed. "He's ready to see you now. Would you follow me?" The men walked the ten yards to the Colonel's patio.

"Colonel Rang, sir." Reilly was standing at parade rest, staring at the map, his back to the men.

"I appreciate your taking time to see me." Rang resisted the temptation to sit, despite his fatigue.

Reilly walked behind the chair, waiting for the Cambodian to take a seat. After an awkward pause, both still standing, he started talking. "What is bothering you, Colonel?" Reilly had a hard time calling Rang "colonel," as though the insignia on his uniform came from a cereal box.

"A problem has come up that we think you should handle." Rang ignored Reilly's tone, attributing it to the drink in his hand.

"That's what I'm here for, Rang. To help you boys with your problems." He didn't like the way this conversation had begun.

"Let me first say that I'm here representing mutual friends, not the President."

"Understood." Reilly's mouth was drying up again. Where were those martinis?

"It seems this friend had a sizable consignment of goods aboard the latest convoy. We know the cargo was on board when the ship arrived, but it seems now to have disappeared."

"Colonel Rang," Reilly answered, irony in his voice, "if I went chasing everything that disappeared in this country, I would never sleep." Even the most optimistic figures showed that more than half of the supplies never reached their destination.

"Quite so." Rang paused, having learned that Reilly detested silence. "This delivery is different. It consists of medical supplies for the hospital. If we don't recover this shipment, many people will suffer." Rang knew that Reilly didn't believe a word of it, but certain games had to be played.

"Just what sort of medical supplies?"

"Morphine, ether, bandages. Among other things."

"What other things."

"We haven't confirmed it, but it appears that at least one One-Oh-Five artillery piece and ammunition has been taken by the same group." Reilly was standing tougher than Rang had expected.

"And what do you expect me to do? Find one gun? The medical supplies are probably on the street, or on the other side."

"We have reason to believe that is not so."

"What's this 'reason to believe' bullshit, Colonel? You either know, or you don't." Reilly waited for the kicker.

"Could we take a walk, Colonel?" Rang knew better than to talk where there might be a microphone. Reilly would take some convincing this time.

"Certainly. Let me help this drink." Reilly topped off his earlier drink from the flask, then showing the way with his hand, directed Rang toward the gate to the alley.

"I have been instructed to tell you about certain photographs that are in the possession of our friend." Rang noticed that the Cambodian guard didn't stir as they walked down the alley. Garbage rotted against the high concrete walls, services in the city long since suspended.

"Pictures of what?" Reilly had an edge in his voice.

"Of you, Colonel Reilly." Rang paused again. "Pictures from Bangkok, I believe, taken with a certain young gentleman."

"Are you trying to blackmail me?" Reilly felt he'd been kicked in the balls.

"We do not like that word, Colonel. On the other hand, our friend is more than willing to see that your superiors hear of the good work you've done here, the kinds of words that would serve well for future promotions." Rang knew Reilly's dream.

"And the pictures?"

"Should this matter be satisfactorily resolved, the pictures and the negatives will be returned to you, for your personal files. There could also be some financial reward as well." Rang couldn't resist the dig. Three years in the States had schooled him in verbal dueling.

"I still don't know what you want me to do. Where are these 'medical supplies'?"

"They were loaded into army trucks. Those trucks were hijacked outside the docks. Our information is that they're somewhere west of the city."

"Look, if you can give me some idea where they might be, I'm sure we can arrange an airstrike in the morning and take them out. That way we know they haven't gone to the Khmer Rouge."

"I appreciate that, Colonel, but it is most important that we recover these supplies intact. It is very difficult to replace them."

"Well, I can do it. I'll go over to Saigon and push them through, fly them in."

"Colonel, let us not delude ourselves. Too many questions would be asked, and our friend doesn't like that. And we both know that the river convoys are no longer dependable. It is most important that these particular supplies be recovered and the gun neutralized, quickly. Our intelligence indicates they are in the same place, near Ang Snoul." Rang knew he held the trump.

"I will need some cooperation from your people. I can't go wandering the countryside looking for trucks and a gun." Reilly had a frantic edge to his voice.

"True. You locate the supplies and provide the cover, and we will secure them. How you handle the One-Oh-Five is up to you, perhaps this will give you a chance to use your bombers. That shouldn't be asking too much." They'd circled the villa, and were near the rear gate.

"I suppose these instructions come from your 'Chinaman'?"

"Some call him that. It would be to both our advantage if we settle this matter quickly. Our friend wants it done quietly, without attention." Rang led the way back to the patio, turned, and smiled at Reilly. "Look at this as an opportunity to enhance your future."

"You tell the Chinaman that I don't like to be threatened." Reilly tried to bluff once more.

"Then we must consider what to do with these photographs."

"When this is over, you can shove them up your ass." Reilly lost his cool. Who'd set him up in Bangkok? Too late to wonder about that. He had to get the pictures back, and what they were asking didn't seem to be too much. "OK, first thing in the morning."

"I was certain you'd understand. Our friend will be pleased to hear of your willingness to cooperate."

The men shook hands, holding the grip, neither wanting to be the first to give in. Reilly finally slapped Rang on the shoulder like he was one of the boys, purely to end the handshake.

Reilly watched as Rang walked across the dark patio, noting how poorly his uniform fit. Typical of the Cambodian army, he thought. Hell, they may not even learn to salute before they lose the war. But he knew he was dealing with more than just the army, that his career was on the line.

Rang felt better once he was moving in the jeep. He smiled, pleased that he'd gotten out of the villa before the martini arrived.

X.

Chantao's

THE ONLY LIGHT in the cramped room was the blue haze of the bizarre lamp. God knows how the Howdy Cola bottle had gotten there. I'll never forget the Howdy lamp, Sam thought. It's what I'll always remember about Chantao's. Mother Chantao, Poppy Mother. Howdy, pipe. Howdy, high. Howdy, Chantao. Crazy howdys rang through his brain.

Chantao prepared another pipe for Sam, while Claudine stretched out on the mats, her eyes closed. The heavy Chinese woman rolled the raw opium on the tip of a long steel needle, slowly heating the paste over the flame of the lamp, the sawed-off Howdy bottle forming the chimney. While it cooked, she wound the opium around a second needle, then shaped the plug on the smooth surface of Sam's pipe. At the perfect moment, she deftly implanted the plug of opium in the small hole and turned the round, hollow bowl upside down to place the opium over the flame. Sam moved the small, hard pillow beneath his head to find the right distance from the end of the two foot long stem of the pipe

to the lamp. He recognized Claudine's taste on the moist
bamboo. Pulling and pulling the smoke into his lungs in
one long draw, he could hold no more just as the plug of
opium disappeared.

Sam wondered how many pipes the Poppy Mother had
made in her lifetime. Legend was that she learned the art
as a child, when she and her sister sat on either side of
their grandma and fed her two hundred pipes a day. Twenty
is considered addiction. Later, Chantao worked for Madame
Tang, perhaps the most renowned opium madame in Asia,
whose funeral in 1960 was covered by the French media.
Chantao opened her own smoking den on a dark side street
near the American Embassy, hidden behind her house. It
was one of the most exclusive clubs in the Orient, catering
mainly to foreigners.

"More pipe?" she asked, the word "pipe" sounding
like "peep." A wave of nausea pierced his stomach but
quickly passed. Tingles spread through his body as the last
pipe took hold, jacking his mind up still another notch.

"Non, merci . . ." Claudine didn't open her eyes. Sam
wondered how many years she had been coming here.
He'd worked hard for his entrée to the den, stayed on his
best behavior to curry the favor of Chantao. You didn't
come here without being introduced to the Chinese woman
by a regular customer. If she liked you, you could stay.
Otherwise, you could never return.

Chantao gathered up her sarong and stood, gently moving the pipe to one side with her bare foot. He loved that
pipe, given to Claudine by Chantao. He thought about
having one for himself, but owning a pipe worried him.
Was that a step beyond casual smoking into the gray area
of addiction? Last week, he'd caught himself looking at
his watch at ten in the morning, counting the hours until
he could return to Chantao's, to the ornately carved gold
inlay pipe which never left these rooms. He'd decided he
wouldn't go to dens in Bangkok or Hong Kong again. No,
he'd save opium smoking for here, at Chantao's.

At first, he'd been bothered by the way opium seemed to suppress his sex drive, how things shifted away from his body to his mind. Now he thrived on the sensation, craved it, would seek it out. With opium he'd discovered new levels. When Rabbit, Chantao's helper and masseuse, gave him a rub, he would concentrate his whole awareness on the inside of his thigh muscles or wherever her fingers might be working on a tight spot.

Once, he'd started to make love to Claudine, but found himself so totally involved with her left breast, with how the blood throbbed against the whiteness of her soft skin, that he'd never gotten any further. He was amazed at the physical gratification, without the effort of intercourse.

Sam was rarely surprised anymore; not by Asia, at least. Yet he was more intrigued than ever, lured by its mystique. He would never share all of its secrets, but opium helped him stop trying. It provided sanity in his world, a hideout from reality.

The screech of a radio shook him from his musings. The blare of Chinese love songs covered the quiet conversations in a variety of tongues throughout the den. The six smoking rooms were partitioned off with the colorful woven mats, mosquito nets drooping down over the open ceilings, a layer below the thatched roof. A strange set of social values reigned here. All who entered hung their street clothes and professional titles on the wooden pegs in the center room. Wrapped in Chantao's sarongs, everyone shared the common bond of the opium den. Even tonight, as Sam and Claudine were undressing before the evening's pipes, he'd bumped into the pompous French *chargé d'affaires*, a man he'd tried to interview uncomfortably a week before. Here, they were equals.

It was late. Others were leaving, their words floating under the noise of the radio. After the pipes, Sam was far from sleepy. He forced himself to stand, holding for a moment while his head searched for the walking mode. An opium high was like no other. You didn't feel bombed

as with booze, or floating as with weed. It was like peeling
back layers of the soul, both reflection and conversation
seemed to find new levels.

He worked his way through the door and down the narrow raised boardwalk that bordered the house to the tiny
dark room at the end. He took a deep breath of the sweet
tropical night air, holding it as he ducked inside. He
winced as his bare feet landed in water. He hoped it was
clean. By instinct he knew the location of the hole in the
floor with the small footpads. His lungs hurt as he finished
pissing, and there was a bit of desperation in his moves as
he dipped the gourd into the rain barrel to wash down the
area around the squat toilet.

Claudine had company when he returned. Maurice. Who
else? He'd taken Sam's spot, and they scrambled awkwardly when he returned, trying to give the impression of
normal conversation. Sam forced a smile as he moved pillows to make a new spot near the lamp. At this moment,
he was thankful for his poor command of French. Whatever the current subject, Claudine seemed disturbed. Asshole Maurice. Sam shut his eyes, not wanting to watch,
hoping that Chantao would reappear for more pipes, to
change the action.

Maurice had one of those big Froggie names that Sam
could never remember. It always made him think of cheap
perfume. He was middle-aged, ruggedly handsome, and
certainly slick. Maurice reminded Sam of his hometown
fence, Fixer Preston. Fixer, his daddy had said, would
rather make a buck under the table than five dollars across
the top. Shit, even Sam was into Maurice. He'd arranged
his first visit to Chantao's, set up an interview with the
army commander, and the President. When Sam asked
about Maurice, people would smile and shrug. He was as
much a part of the scene as Chantao. Rosen said he was
watching after French rubber interests on plantations way
the hell beyond government lines. He had his own Beech
Bonanza, which always seemed to be somewhere else when

the airport was attacked. Maurice knew everyone. Everyone needed to know Maurice. Sam suspected that was Maurice's business.

Yet if Sam wanted to be with Claudine, Maurice was part of the package. Early on, he'd made a fuss about Maurice, like a jealous lover. Claudine shut him down, the look on her face making clear that their relationship, whatever it was, would continue. At first, Sam thought they were lovers, but now, he wondered. She spent a lot of her time around Sam, especially the nights, but rarely did a day pass without Maurice popping up somewhere. Sam liked him now, but the redneck in him still bubbled up, fearing the worst. Something told him that Maurice had a hold on Claudine, and it certainly wasn't love.

Rosen stuck his head in and said goodnight. The new Swedish nurse tried to look cool, but obviously the den and the pipes had rethreaded her head. She'd accepted Rosen's offer of a ride back to the hotel. Chantao returned, giving Sam the first pipe.

"How was your trip on the convoy?" Maurice asked, just as Sam finished his smoke. He wasn't about to exhale. He just raised his eyebrows.

"There may be one, perhaps two more convoys, then *fini*. Do you not agree?" Maurice lit a Gitaine cigarette.

"Well, we wouldn't have made it without the airstrikes. Man, what will they do when the bombing ends?" Sam really didn't feel like talking.

Maurice said something in French that included "man." He and Claudine laughed softly. "I am sorry. That is not kind. I find your accent charming." Maurice watched Chantao make a pipe for Claudine, switched into Chinese, made her laugh. This time Claudine raised puzzled eyebrows at Sam.

"No problem, man. No problem." As Sam watched, he realized that Chantao was dipping from a different bottle, using Maurice's opium. Like any good merchant, she stepped on hers a couple of times. Sam could gauge her

shit, but this was Laotian Gold, a .45 between the eyes.
He felt the rush start at his toes.

"The convoys. Some truck convoys still make it through
from Battambang, and one came up from Sihanoukville
last week," he said, using the old name for Cambodia's
main port. "But that depends on the highways. Such fragile things the highways. And it takes many trucks to carry
as much as a ship. It is not good, no, it is not good. Did
you know that many of the medical supplies from your
convoy were hijacked?"

"You're kidding? When?" Pieces of scattered information clicked together in his mind.

"The day you arrived. Truckloads. It is a pity. The hospital could use the ether." Maurice looked truly disturbed,
but Claudine showed no emotion, as though to her this
tidbit wasn't news.

"So Charles was right, Claudine." Sam detected a weak
smile. "I fell into that story out around Ang Snoul. Something about a renegade battalion."

"Ah, then you know all about it." Maurice proffered
Sam a cigarette.

"I know very little. Just that the Cambodian cameraman who works for us took pictures of a hijacked convoy
and some guns or something. I didn't see them." He
leaned over the Howdy lamp to light the cigarette. "Is
there more I should know?"

"Perhaps. Many people are very upset."

"Doctors, for one, huh?" Sam was fishing.

"Yes, yes, they among others. Some in the government,
some at your embassy. Many people." Maurice leaned on
his arm and stared at Sam, like a quizmaster playing twenty
questions.

"Well, if I find the stuff you'll be the first to know."
He wasn't in the mood for mind games, but he knew that
Maurice was leading up to something. "Who else should
know?"

"Always the *journaliste*, are you not?" He used the

French, rolling the pronunciation off his tongue. "Perhaps your Colonel Reilly, for one. It was his ether. Ah, but enough. We must keep our friend happy, yes?" He patted Claudine on the leg.

"Yeah, sure. Thanks." Sam didn't like to admit that he'd get nothing from Maurice without Claudine.

"Oh, Sammi . . ." Claudine ran her finger softly down his arm, trying to change his mood.

"Well, I'll ask around," Sam said, trying to regain face.

"Sam, listen. It is good that you report on the war, tell people of the troubles here with the *communiste*. But you must not make it more dangerous for yourself."

"Look, I get shot at every day. . . ."

Maurice stopped him with a raised hand, calling his bluff. "That is true, but you must listen. Forget about the medical supplies. It is too complicated."

"You trying to stop me?" Sam's bluster was not covering his temper. He suspected that he was being prodded with a dare.

"Yes. Yes, I am. Because I like you, and Claudine likes you, and these people don't care about that. Go to the highways, do your stories, but leave this alone."

"Go on, Maurice. Be like everyone else. Blame it on the Chinaman." Sam couldn't resist.

"Oh, that is much too easy. No, we must blame it on the times. People do not care for other people. They just look out for themselves."

"That sounds like the Chinaman to me."

"Sam, you must be careful what you say," Maurice chided. "You are not talking about Saint Nicholas."

"Santa he ain't. Do you think there is a person, a real breathing body, that's the Chinaman?" If anyone knew, Sam figured, it had to be Maurice.

"I know that many things that are attributed to him are fact, that under his name things get done. Both good things and bad things."

"Tell me some good. All I ever hear is the bad."

Sam had been bothered by everything being blamed on the Chinaman, but now he found himself using the same excuse.

"Your car, for one. Do you like your car?"

"Sure. And I keep buying back the same goddamned headlight lenses and Mercedes emblem." They were ripped off weekly from the car when it was parked down the street from the den. Sam really suspected Driver Joe.

"Ah, yes . . ." Maurice chuckled. "But please, my good friend Sam, please be careful who you talk to about the Chinaman. It could do you harm."

"Did he arrange the convoy?" There I go again, Sam thought, talking about him as a real person.

"Yes. Without the Chinaman, nothing that large could occur."

"Why does he care about the supplies? Why not leave it to the Americans or the French?"

"Ah, Sam, you miss the point. You think he is not Cambodian?"

"Shit, I don't know. I don't even know if he exists."

"Think of him as a real person, and you will be much better off." The firm look on his face indicated that this was the end of this line of conversation. "I think you are very brave, Sam Michaels, but sometimes you are *stupide*."

"Thanks." Sam fumed.

"Ah, a bad choice of words. Not quite the meaning you think."

"Sam. Maurice. Stop." Claudine rolled on her back, letting the sarong slip enough to change the subject.

"When I was in Saigon, I saw a good poster." Sam waited while Maurice translated "poster" for Claudine. "It showed a guy with a M-60 machine gun facing down a half dozen Viet Cong. 'Come on,' the caption said, 'make my whole day.' I guess I feel that way about those bastards out there who rip off medicine." Sam was talking with more bravery than he felt.

"Yes, that is one way of thinking. But I believe we are only observers, that the same things will happen whether we are here or not. I have watched the dying for many years now."

"I'm going on three, and sometimes I can't remember what it was like before I started chasing wars. India, Bangladesh, now here."

"Ah, but you love the wars."

"Love. Bullshit."

"Yes, the wars. You may not like to hear these things, Sam, but it is true of you and the others. That is the only reason you go out there. Not for money. Not for fame. You are not known here. It is for the love. And I am afraid it is true for our friend here as well." He mussed Claudine's hair with a playful touch.

"I don't want to think about it." Sam eagerly accepted another pipe. He felt more relaxed now, less threatened, but the thought nagged him that Maurice was right.

"I see my first dead person when I was three, four." Claudine didn't open her eyes as she softly talked. "It is one of my first memories. A bomb destroyed a building on our block. In Dresden. Do you know Dresden?"

Sam nodded yes.

"Americans should know Dresden."

"You know that Claudine's mother was French. Her father German." Maurice played with the tail of his sarong as he talked. "They lived with her grandparents when her father went to the Eastern Front. He didn't come back."

Claudine stared at Maurice for a long moment, then talked. "Mother knew the war was *fini*, that we must go back to France. We started walking. I was five. My little brother three. The first night, I danced on a stone wall as I watched the huge fires in the city. I thought it the most lovely sight I'd ever seen. Then I look at my mother. She is crying. She know Grandpa and Grandma are in the flames."

Sam wanted to apologize. He'd visited Dresden once, walked the modern streets of the new state. Everyone said go to Kraków, in Poland. There, you would see how Dresden once looked. The combined U.S. and British air raid had leveled the city. First the napalm to start the fires, then the high explosives to feed them. A firestorm consumed the city, crammed with refugees from the Russian advance. The Germans still claim there was little of military value in the city. Just a little experiment at the end of the war to see how it would work. It worked fine, but the atomic bomb made the tactic obsolete within months.

Maurice stood up, chatted with Chantao for a moment, then turned to Sam. "It is easy for us to, how do you say, 'gang up' on you. We French have our sorrows. But it is best we do not forget."

"But why do we live on other people's sorrows?" Sam asked, more of himself than the others. Opium raps tended to go this way.

"You know the answer, Sam, even if it is not a nice thought." He turned his back to dress, then said over his shoulder, "Here, the sorrow has only begun."

"Maurice. *Halte*. It is too depressing. One minute you laugh, the next you talk of these things." Claudine pushed up on one hand. "Do not listen to him, Sam. He wants us all to be like him." Maurice grinned and blew her a kiss.

"Does that mean I get an airplane?" Sam kidded.

"You like to fly? Yes. Then someday you must fly with me." He'd almost finished the buttons on his silk bush shirt.

"Sure, any time. I have a license, but a Bonanza is a little out of my class." He did like the idea.

"Ah, airplanes are like women. You handle them well, they will fly, my friend. Will you see Claudine back to the hotel? I must go the other way." He shook hands with them once firmly, in the French style, and left.

Sam wondered where in hell "the other way" was. He could think of nothing good out there, not at night. "War lover. Bullshit." Sam was feeling upstaged, a real countryboy. Now, too late, the answers came.

"He is correct, you know. I, too, was angry when he first said it to me, but I now understand. So will you."

"No, Claudine, I'm not sure that I ever will." Sam shut his eyes and thought. "And even if I did, I'm afraid war loving will have to go into the same category as beating your meat. It's something you like a lot, but an impossible subject with your mother."

"Meat beat?" Claudine asked, a half grin showing she knew it was funny, but not catching the slang.

"Pud pounding. Chicken choking." He made a crude gesture with his hand. She laughed loudly.

"The masturbate!"

"You got it. The masturbate." That's what you and this war are doing to me, he thought. Jerking off my mind.

"This is nice, Sammi." Her eyes were again closed, the Howdy lamplight playing on her long body. The sarong, nothing more than a couple of yards of green-patterned cloth sewn in a loop, was tucked into the cleavage of her full breasts, the hem not reaching her knees. One tug, Sam thought, and pay dirt!

Chantao returned and knelt by Claudine's head, whispering in French. There was a closeness between the two women, both competing in a man's world. She was more animated with Claudine, giggles and nudges punctuating their conversation, sidelong glances at Sam making him feel uncomfortable. He first thought that he was the subject, but now he realized that they were cooking up something that didn't include him.

Sam studied Chantao's face, wondering for the hundreth time how old she was. When they first met, he guessed fifty, but her now pregnant belly suggested a younger woman. She winked at him, giving his sarong a playful

tug as she moved to the bamboo door and left Sam and
Claudine alone again.

"She likes you, *M'sieu Moustache*." Claudine laughed
as she used Rabbit's name for him.

"I like her, too. Sometimes when it's quiet out here,
I'll bring extra candles and read. The other night she came
to my room, smiled, curled up on the mats and went to
sleep."

"The baby come soon . . . she is tired." Claudine sat
up and looked at Sam. "You get massage from Rabbit
sometimes?"

"Yeah . . . I could use one tonight."

"Sometimes, special massage . . . like this?" She made
an up and down motion with her cupped hand.

"Sure, when she's got time. Why?"

"They have a special way for ladies. Chantao, she know
I want to show you tonight."

"You're joking. Why tonight? Why me?" Sam wasn't
sure what was happening, but it intrigued him. The conversation had the blue clarity of opium. Sam was hesitant
to ask Claudine to explain, afraid he might kill the mood.
One wrong move, a misunderstood inflection in his voice,
and he might bring the mysterious eroticism of the moment to a grinding halt.

Rabbit, the masseuse, slipped into the room. She
brought a bottled Pepsi for Sam, a pot of tea for Claudine.
She was slender and small, the root of her nickname. The
historic Indian strain that made the Cambodians distinct
from other ethnic groups in Indochina was in her dark
features, the fullness of her face, the big dark eyes. She
fascinated Sam. He never knew her real name, probably
never would. His only communication with her was in
broken French, when he'd ask for another Pepsi or a rub-
down. When she gave a massage, she found parts of Sam's
body he didn't know he had. She was a master at her
skills, carefully trained by Chantao to serve.

Sam shifted deeper into the darkness, propping up on

several of the oblong pillows in the corner of the little room. He hoped to become invisible in the stillness, to find a position he could hold comfortably for a long time without moving.

Rabbit placed a long cloth bundle beside the lamp. She locked her fingers together, giving them a loud snap, then turned her attention entirely to Claudine. The massage down her long white limbs was slow, deep, deliberate. Sam recognized the same kneading, the same pressure of Rabbit's palms from massages of his own body, but he sensed something was different now, Rabbit's strokes meant to do more than relax Claudine's body. They seemed to draw it open, to coax her physical sensations into the same plane as her mind.

He lost all track of time, of his body. His mind became totally immersed in each small revelation as Rabbit worked her limbs and the sarong slowly disappeared. Claudine was completely passive, yielding to Rabbit's touch. At first, small flickers of pain crossed her face as a tense muscle recoiled from the strong fingers, but any discomfort soon passed. She looked asleep.

The massage over, Rabbit carefully unrolled the cloth bundle and produced a small bottle of brown liquid and two identically shaped, well-polished sticks, one twice as large as the other. As she covered each of Claudine's nipples with the dark oil, they in turn took on a soft brown glow in the lamplight. Her clitoris was next: Rabbit sprinkled an extra drop or two of the mysterious liquid there.

Rabbit shifted back, next to Sam. Neither made a sound, taking the moment to appreciate the beauty of Claudine's body. There was none of the apprehension he usually felt when confronted with a woman's naked body. Nothing was expected of him, nothing wanted. He didn't have to perform, satisfy, push.

Claudine took a deep breath, her chest rising once in a sigh. With the short stick, Rabbit gently began touching her nipples, drawing them out farther than Sam imagined possible. Claudine's breasts seemed to be reaching out for more from the stick while the rest of her body remained still. As her breathing caught up with the movement of the stick, she parted her knees slightly in invitation. Rabbit repeated the slight, circular motion across Claudine's clitoris, establishing a rhythm that seemed to make the two women one in the soft blue light. He started to understand. Instinctively, Rabbit knew the exact motion, the touch, that turned Claudine on. He hadn't known it was possible for someone to sense the perfect moves of pure sex for another person. Rabbit was doing a better job of exciting her than Claudine could do for herself.

Gradually Claudine's entire body picked up the rhythm, her muscles pulsing, fingertips pressing into the mats, spreading herself, ready for the next step. Rabbit manipulated both sticks now, slowly, slowly entering Claudine's body with the larger. Never was the motion or the contact lost. Sam expected Rabbit to shift to a thrusting motion, use the large stick like a penis, but it never happened. As her excitement climbed, he found himself following the pattern of her breathing, pulling out of his mind the sensations she must be experiencing. He wasn't erect; that part of his body knew it was unneeded.

Claudine's breathing took on tone. It was a steady, low sound, coming from some place deep, paced with the sticks. The first climax seemed to ripple her from head to toe, each part of her body giving in to the next in waves, again and again. Rabbit, like a runner who helped others find the perfect pace and stride, quickened the movement, as though they were trying to win a race. Claudine's body arched into the air, supported only by the balls of her feet and head. The hum from her throat changed tenor until coherent sound was gone. The room seemed alive, to spin. The lamp seemed brighter.

She came. Her body sustained the rhythm without Rabbit's sticks. In his mind, Sam came too, knowing that at that moment the three of them were one, each putting energy in and taking pleasure out. Long minutes passed before Claudine stirred. Again Sam and Rabbit were careful not to break the mood.

"Did you like?" Finally Claudine opened her eyes, trying to focus on Sam in the dark corner.

"Yes, very much." Sam's voice was no more than a whisper.

She talked to Rabbit for a moment, a little giggle ending the conversation. "Rabbit say too bad Sam a man."

"She may be right." Sam smiled, appreciating the two women's sense of having shown him something he could never have, yet aware that he wasn't threatened by their desires. Rabbit touched Claudine's face, tied up her sticks in the bundle and slipped from the room, leaving them alone.

"Do you want Claudine now? Would you like to make love?" She was still spread on the mats.

"No." Sam spoke softly, not wanting her to feel rejected by his reply but letting her know how much he'd gotten off on this, that she did not have to satisfy him further. "I am very happy like this."

"That is good. I wanted this to happen this night, like this." She studied his face for a moment. "Sometimes, Rabbit is my lover."

"That's not surprising. You seem comfortable together."

"Does that upset you?" Her eyes were shut now. Sam felt like he was being tested. No time for another strike.

"No, no it doesn't. The way I figure it, if it turns you on, do it." Could she tell that he meant that?

"One boyfriend, he became very upset when I told him I like women. He forgetted I also like the men." She reached over and placed her hand on top of Sam's, tracing the veins and bones.

"Just about the time I think I know you, you come up

with something like this. You are a very complex lady."
Sam was wide awake, wanting to know more.

"That may be true, but I am like the other ladies. Perhaps I say more, do more . . ."

"That's an understatement. . . ."

"Men, they like me, then they go pfooof. . . ." She flicked her free hand.

"They fall in love with you." He sensed they were picking up an earlier conversation.

"Yes, then they want me to stop taking the pictures, stop the roadrunning, sit in the hotel and wait for them. They are crazy. You never ask me that, Sam." She rolled toward him, played with the hairs on his chest. "Maybe we should not fall in love."

"I'll try my best," he whispered, without conviction. Sam remembered the story of a local who'd fallen in love with Claudine. She broke it off, he took it poorly, and one evening he slashed his wrist in her hotel room. She handed him a towel and told him that if he moved quickly, he'd make it to the hospital before passing out.

"We keep things as they are, Sammi. That is the fun with you. When we are together, we find new things. Many things we do not know. Some people, they have entire lives without knowing these things. Sometimes I think they are lucky."

"Not knowing about this?" Sam grinned, but saw where her mind was going.

"No. These things, Chantao's and Rabbit, they make the bad things better. But no matter how we like Chantao's, we must see war to come here. You understand?"

"You mean with the good comes the bad. You are starting to sound like Maurice. But that's not the only reason we're here, is it? We came here for the war, Chantao's is only an escape. I damn near got us killed by a sniper, yet I still saw it as a great element for a story. How's that for getting your priorities fucked up?"

"Maybe, but you take the pictures, tell the world what

is happening. If we not here, it still happens. Then nobody knows. I saw that many times when I was a child.''

Sam realized he'd underestimated her age by a good five years. Knowing her was like looking into a diamond with a thousand cuts and facets.

"Three, maybe four. I'm an old lady, Sammi.'' She smiled, gripping his hand.

"I like older women. . . .'' He leaned over and pecked her on the forehead. He wondered where she found the stamina and guts to survive. "Why do you come back to another war? Wasn't the first one enough?''

"I do not know. I do not think much about that. I am more alive here than in Paris. In the desert, in Cambodia, I am alive.''

"So am I, and sometimes that bothers me. I like it here, I'm happy, and I don't think I should be. I think I should be overwhelmed and horrified by what I see and do, that it should be all bad. It doesn't come out that way.'' He leaned over the lamp, lighting a Salem from the flame.

"Why did you come here?'' She took the cigarette from his fingers.

"It just happened. I couldn't stay in India, and I didn't want to go back home. I'd met a lady there: you'd like her, named Suzanne, and she got thrown in the Delhi slammer courtesy of yours truly. I'd probably gone home with her if she'd asked. . . .''

"Did you ask her?'' She let the smoke drift from her mouth, suddenly interested in this other woman.

"No. Things were too fucked up.'' He tapped the Howdy bottle with his nail, rocking the flame. "A truly class woman. Just a little thing, she was.''

"But why do you come to Cambodia?'' she said, handing over the Salem.

"The network needed a stringer here, so I took the job.'' He took a pull from the cigarette, looking at the patterns of the mats on the wall. "You know what's funny? I shucked and jived for four years in the Air Force, making sure I'd never be sent to Vietnam. Now I'm in the middle of the fucking war as a civilian. Strange, no?''

"What do you want? The big staff job?''

"No, I don't think so, although sometimes I wonder when I say yes to convoy trips. I never thought I'd get with the networks, so this job is really a bonus. Look, I went further in my life by the time I was twenty-five than I'd ever expected to go. Whatever happens now is gravy, a free ride. I'm not selling insurance, not riding a desk in some fucking office, not working for some asshole. That will come soon enough.'' Sam had thought of this before, but he'd never spoken the words aloud.

"I do not understand . . .''

"What I mean is that I'm not tied down, don't have to work just for the money. I guess I'm lucky. I know I'm lucky.''

". . . and you come here to test the luck?''

"Yeah, in a way. This time last year I was sitting on a mountaintop in India, chasing gurus. I found it difficult to believe that someone else had the answer for me. I only learn by doing, by being involved. I know myself pretty well, and I'm not unhappy with who I am. I respect people who search for the truth, but for me . . .'' He burned the Salem up in the lamp, letting his thoughts drift.

"Perhaps that is why we make the pair, Sammi. We both must do, how do you say, for ourselves. It is not good enough that others have done it. That is why we are survivors, Sammi.''

"Survivors? No, you're the survivor. I never had to survive anything. Maybe that's what brought me here, to find out if I could survive.''

"No, you are survivor. The others, they stay behind, never find out for themselves. You are a brave man, but you must know that. You must prove that.''

"To whom? I'm not brave. Dumb, stupid maybe, but not brave. What makes life good for others is absolutely boring for me. One thing from life I never want is boredom.''

"Boredom?'' She did not understand the word.

"Unhappy, *ennui*. Nothing to do. Everything done for you. Split-level houses, two cars, a boat. That's the most boring thing I can think of.'' Sam rubbed his face with his hands. He wanted to quit thinking of boredom. He would be faced with it soon enough. He knew this, here, wouldn't last forever.

"Then, you must not be bored with me.'' She played with the new word as she spoke it.

"I certainly don't see that happening.'' There was a discreet knock on the door. Chantao slipped into the room in a baggy dressing gown, carrying the pipe. Sam shifted on the mats, watching her, reflecting on how much he'd learned about himself tonight. He was starting to understand this world and its people. Now his problem was ever giving it up, letting go, returning to the old world. He pushed the frightening thought from his mind.

Howdy, pipe.

XI.

Renegade Coup

THE ROOM WAS hot and crowded. Soldiers with rifles pushed up the steps, none wanting to miss the meeting. General Chandaran sat on the edge of a bed, talking heatedly with two sergeants. Eng looked at the men closely, men he'd led for three years. Since the hijacking, a new attitude had come over the Ninth Brigade, and Eng didn't like it.

It was an exaggeration to call the Ninth a brigade. Much of the Cambodian army was only on paper, the units small by western standards. There wasn't a full platoon left, and the lines of command that had started to fade on the mountain now seemed to disappear altogether. Three officers remained, a handful of NCOs, the bare bones of the headquarters staff, and the remnants of two ragged companies. Half the men were left on the mountain or had simply gone home, leaving the war to prepare for the uncertain peace.

Many of the soldiers shed their uniforms, opting for civilian dress. The way they slung their M-16s at the ready showed their training, but the arguments and hard looks told Eng that the men were not happy, that Chandaran was fighting to hold the brigade together until the Chinaman finished the deal. He'd seen the same nasty reactions the day the men killed the paymaster and ate his liver. He'd begged Chandaran to punish those responsible, but the general laughed it off, saying the army got what it deserved, that the men were now bonded together, bonded to Chandaran. But the same men were now turning on Chandaran.

When the raid was planned, they'd figured the situation would be resolved within a few days, a week at the longest. But as each day passed, the secret was harder to keep, the men harder to control. Eng wanted to include only the most trusted men, but Chandaran had insisted that all the Ninth be included, a reward for their loyalty and service. Now they had 130 men, most of them upset, demanding action.

Chandaran explained for the tenth time why they had to wait, that the next move was up to the Chinaman. Only the officers knew his master plan. They'd use the gun, hit the city as it had never been hit before. That would put pressure on both the government and the Chinaman. If that didn't work, they'd take out the lab, buying more time for themselves.

But most of the men just wanted money, and wanted it now. When? When? The same questions flew at Chandaran, never letting up. Eng pushed through the door, down the steps to the ground, getting away from the words and the heat. Under the house and at a table nearby, the men were drinking strong rice wine from clear glass jugs, building their courage. One soldier shoved past him, showing Eng that rank meant nothing to him now.

After the meeting at the lab, Eng was certain that the Chinaman would compromise, that some arrangement would be made. But they'd heard nothing, the Frenchman hadn't shown for the next meeting, and one of their spies at the lab said that it was running, with enough ether for a few days' processing. Did the Chinaman have another source? Could he afford to wait them out? This was a time for patience, for standing firm as a group, but Eng felt control slipping by the minute. Men who'd followed him into battle time and again now shrugged when he gave orders. They were now a mob, Eng thought, not a military unit. It was time to retake control.

The voices in the house grew louder, the others yielding to the sergeant. Then there was silence. Eng waited a moment, then trotted back up the stairs, pushing past the others, forcing his way into the room. The sergeant stood behind the bed, his M-16 barrel waving in the air. He kept shouting at the General, demanding to know when they would be paid.

Suddenly, men grabbed Eng's arms, pinning them behind his back. He heard a round snapping into a chamber, the cold touch of a barrel on the back of his neck. No one spoke for a minute, the tension suspending conversation. Again, the sergeant demanded money from Chandaran, who explained in a resigned voice that the money was in the bottles on the trucks, that they had to wait for the Chinaman to pay.

The sergeant's eyes swept the room, carefully checking each man's expression. Most were smiling, the pent-up tensions of the past days and the normal animosity toward officers coming out. Why must we wait? We must put on more pressure. We have listened to him long enough. Eng started to speak, but his arms were jerked farther up his back, the shot of pain cutting off his words. The sergeant signaled Chandaran to stand and pushed him toward the door with the barrel of the rifle. We must take action, he said, whether you want to or not. At the door, Chandaran turned and spoke quietly, saying that they were fools, that none of them understood the plan. As he talked, his hand slipped slowly up his back to his belt, where he had tucked his pistol.

The flash of the muzzle stopped the talk; the impact of

the bullet melted the sergeant's head. His body slipped
backward beyond the steps and landed on the packed dirt
with a thud. Eng broke loose and pushed to the General's
side to close ranks before taste of blood overwhelmed sane
thought. He stood with his .45 drawn, lending authority
to the General's stand.

The corner was turned. Those who'd backed the sergeant were out, and they knew it. One by one, men left
the house, calling to their backers. It is all over, they said,
it is time to go home. Finally, a handful was left. Chandaran had stood his ground. Now they were few in number, but a much more practical group.

Chandaran moved into action. Plans had been made.
The sergeant in control of the 105 was ordered to get ready
for an attack. If they couldn't force the Chinaman to yield
to their demands, he explained, they could create enough
havoc in the city, and President Prek would make him pay.
If the Chinaman wouldn't give them what they asked, then
they must capture the lab. Chandaran then explained that
none of them knew how to make heroin, how to sell it,
nothing. They must listen to him. He had the plan and it
must be followed. Don't be like those fools walking down
the road, without money and without their old unit. We
will capture the lab as well. That would definitely up the
ante.

Isn't it too late for talk? another sergeant asked. No, the
General said, we will continue to talk. But now the talk
must be coupled with action. We must all work harder.

Chandaran ended the meeting, and Eng led the way out
the door. The sergeant's body lay contorted on the ground,
two drunk soldiers trying to pour wine from five feet into
the dead man's mouth, frozen in mid-word. The General
struck the nearest man with the pistol. He hadn't wanted
to kill the sergeant, but there was no choice.

They walked toward the middle of the clearing. Eng
counted as the men took sides. Many had left, but those
who'd fought hardest and believed in their leaders stayed.

Some had trouble keeping their feet after the orgy of wine, but they'd be OK. Two dozen. Not many, but a loyal, leadable group. Maybe it was loyalty, Eng thought, but he knew the men could count. If they succeeded, there would be more for each of them now. He looked back at the sergeant's body. The confrontation was over, and he had lost. But Eng felt a moment of strange envy. For the sergeant, it was over.

XII.

Sam's Buddha

BOYS WITH SHAVED heads filled the musty room, their saffron robes adding color to the heavy smell of incense. Sam wondered how many of the boys used the razor and robe as their ticket out of the army. He sat cross-legged on the floor of the Wat, his long limbs uncomfortably tucked under his thin body. Sweat collected on the back of his workshirt and the seat of his jeans, adding to the humidity in the crowded temple. His head was still light from the late night at Chantao's, but Sam decided against taking the red bandanna from his neck to wipe his brow.

Sophan was by his side, intensely staring at the big Buddha that dominated the rough yellow altar. Glazed pots decorated with bright colors held fresh-picked flowers from the hillside. Other Buddhas rested on small shelves and in the niches of the stone walls of the inner room.

They left at dawn, and slipped from the sleeping city into the murky world of the countryside. Sam decided as he climbed into Sophan's classic Mercedes to give this day to him, to go native. Breakfast cooking fires sent white plumes skyward from the small villages in the trees along the highway. They sped along, westward, toward the Cardamon Mountains. They passed the sites of old roadblocks and battles, stories from other roadrunning days. Sam was relaxed, seeing the countryside from another perspective. This was a special day. Sophan was taking him to get his Buddha.

They all sat on the hard dirt floor, made marblelike by centuries of sweeping and the packing of bare feet. Three old Bonzes sat nearest the altar, their bodies only a few slow heartbeats away from the stillness of the big Buddha. Outside, a gong softly gave beat to the chanting of the young boys. In Sam's mind they were light-years away from the highways, the war.

An old Bonze dipped his fingers in an ornate bowl, the jasmine petals swirling away from his touch. Sam concentrated on the top of the old man's bare skull, tracing the purple veins that looked like a road map on his skull. Instinctively, he lowered his head as the Bonze completed the libations.

The water was warm on his head. The Cambodians increased the volume of the chant, the beat unchanged. A few years ago he would have felt out of place here, the recipient of this mysterious blessing. But two years in India had taught him that appreciation for another's beliefs didn't necessarily mean understanding them. He'd seen people walk on live coals, lie on nails. You weren't supposed to be able to do that, but they did. Just knowing what was going on didn't mean you understood what was happening. He had the same feelings about combat.

"You wear this, Sam," Sophan said softly, a small jade Buddha suspended from a gold chain draped across his dark hands. "Now you have bulletproof Buddha. It brings you beaucoup luck." Sophan grinned as he spoke of the bullets, but there was nothing playful about the ritual or the war.

"Will it tell me things, like yours?"

Sophan covered Sam's hands with his own, in a soft grip. *"Sok sabai,"* he said in lyrical Cambodian. "Good luck."

The Bonze took the little jade figure and shuffled toward the large Buddha, its placid face obscured by the clump of joss sticks smoking in front.

"What's he doing now?" Sam asked.

"He say all things Buddha do for Sam." Sophan placed his palms together in front of his round face and bowed from the waist toward the Bonze. Sam followed.

The old Bonze turned, signaled Sam to move forward. He got up on his knees and leaned toward the monk, the chain holding the Buddha tickling his neck as the Bonze fumbled with the clasp.

"This man, he give me Buddha," Sophan said, looking at the Bonze. "Now, when Sophan gone, Sam have own Buddha." He smiled again, pleased that Sam now shared his power.

"I'd rather have you around, ol' buddy," Sam said, putting his arm around Sophan's shoulder. It was a moment of complete, honest emotion. Yet Sam knew there would be a day when he would leave Cambodia and Sophan would stay.

"You never forget Cambodia, Sam. Everybody, they want to come back here."

The two men rose, their arms around one another.

"I think you're right. Please thank the Bonze for me." Sam watched as Sophan and the old monk smiled and chatted, punctuating their words with frequent bows, touching their lips with prayerful hands.

"Bonze, he say you lucky man, Sam." Sophan listened again, then became shy.

"Go on, what did he say?" Now Sam was grinning.

"He say Sophan have special power." The little man giggled. "He say that because he one who pass it on to me."

"You don't have to deny your powers with me." People

weren't supposed to have powers, either, but he'd seen them in Sophan.

"He say someday, when war end, Sam come back here and live. He want you to come here, stay with him at temple for time."

"Tell him I'd like to do that. I really would." The idea struck Sam. He'd lived in ashrams in India, spent weeks in meditation retreats. But here, he'd be entering a different level, accepted as more than another truth-seeker.

The old monk nodded in agreement, and smiled. "Sophan come too, OK?"

Sophan bowed again to the Bonze, as did Sam, before they worked their way toward the pile of shoes on the woven mat. His chappals, or Indian sandals, stood out, twice as large as the others. He fished them from the stack with his toes, slipping the leather thong between his toes. They walked out into the harsh light of the morning, Sam ducking his head to pass through the doorway.

$$\oplus \qquad \oplus \qquad \oplus$$

Sam sat on the edge of the seat, his arm propped up against the door of the Mercedes. Three days ago, this place was nothing more than a crossroads. Now it was a full-blown refugee camp. Sophan worked his way through the buffalo carts, talking with people, trying to find out why they were running.

Refugees were the key to what was really going on in Cambodia. When villagers were under fire, or the situation started getting out of hand, meager worldly goods went into two-wheeled carts pulled by water buffalo and they would hit the road.

"He say the armed men, they come and take over their village," Sophan said, signaling toward an old man sitting in the shade under the cart. "He say village over there, about two kilometers."

"Well, I don't think we'll be going 'over there' anytime

soon," Sam said as he looked down the road where Sophan was pointing. Fighter bombers were still pounding a
target beyond a clump of trees, acrid black smoke rising
like a marker on the horizon.

"He not know why they come. He say they try to be
happy with everyone." Three children played at Sophan's
feet, a yellow mesh network film bag the toy of the day.
He had a real attraction for children, and he seemed to
give off an aura which told them they'd found a friend.

"Well, check it out, and maybe we can make it down
there tomorrow and see what's going on." Sam didn't
really feel like working today, the building heat and humidity doing nothing for his head. After the visit to the Wat,
Sam was ready to get back to the hotel. He wanted to meet
the flight from Hong Kong, to catch the "pigeon," a passenger who'd agreed to bring in a bag full of mail, supplies
and money, the latter unknown to the traveler. They had
another hour to kill, and Sam thought they might get more
information on the action out here.

Under trees in a clearing, a group of men were going
through a Chinese fire drill trying to get a large tarpaulin
to stay up, a cover for a crude portable kitchen. The church
relief workers had arrived at about the same time as Sam,
and after a heated discussion with the village headmen,
they realized that the refugees weren't willing to go the
extra couple of miles to the established camp. These people had been on the road before, and felt they were better
off on their own, just that much closer to home, where
they'd go once they felt it was secure.

Refugees were another weapon in the Khmer Rouge inventory. Force them toward the city, and put even more
pressure on the government to feed them and find room
for them. When the wagons were headed toward Phnom
Penh, things were going poorly. When they headed out,
things were looking up. This was not a good day for the
government.

"My boy, I don't have a thing in my kit that will help

you this day." Sam was surprised to hear the rich Australian accent of Dr. Jake. The tall doctor had slipped up from the other side of the car.

"It would seem to me that since you caused the illness, the least you could do is provide a cure." Sam grinned, but he knew his condition was obvious. The Foster's beer he could handle, but when the doctor broke out the vodka, Sam should have declined. The evening at Chantao's had been enough, but the group was still by the pool when they returned. Sam reminded himself for the hundredth time that morning why he should stick to smoking weed and opium: no hangovers.

"Medical research, my boy. Find out how much abuse the human body can take." Jake showed no signs of the vast amounts of alcohol he'd consumed the night before. "Why do these people stop here? The Catholics have quite a nice setup for them near the Russian Hospital."

"They know better, Doc. Once you get into one of the regular camps, it's hard to pull up and go back to the village. The longer you stay gone, the less there is to go back to. Here, they can just boogie a couple of klicks and be home." More than a million refugees were thought to be living in camps around the city, and these two hundred or so wanted to go back home. "What brings you out on the road? Thought you specialized in the carriage trade?"

"Little Miss Big worked her wiles on me, and I agreed to come out and look at these blokes. Besides, I got a few hours off. I needed a vacation."

"That's a fuckin' joke, Doc. This whole place is a vacation." Sam gave an exaggerated grin, knowing that Jake worked seven days a week at the hospital, doing dozens of operations a day. So he gets a few free hours and comes looking for more. "Other than feed them, what can you do?"

"Not a lot, but it's the thought that counts." Jake had wandered over to one of the unhitched carts nearby, looking closely at a large picture of a Buddha in a gilded frame that sat on top of the pots, pans and other personal belongings.

"Turn it around. . . ." Sam watched Jake's expression when he picked up the picture and saw an ornate photograph of Sihanouk on the reverse side.

"What's this?"

"When they are headed toward the government lines, they show the Buddha; when they head back toward the insurgent lines, they show Sihanouk. No dummies here, my friend."

"I'll be damned." He carefully replaced the picture when he saw Miss Big walking toward him. She was a relief worker who stayed in the field most of the time, to the distress of those with a fondness for full-bodied ladies with white skin. Sam wondered how far her dedication to the church really went, whether she turned to people like Dr. Jake for a little comfort now and again. Why should she be any different from the rest?

"Doc, we're seeing the eye problem again with the children. Do you have any of that salve?" Lyda, who was from New Zealand, had never acknowledged the nickname. She smiled at Sam but didn't let herself be drawn into their conversation.

"Not for the past few months. 'On order,' I think they say. I do have some drops in my bag that might help."

"Anything for now." Lyda walked away, Jake in tow, and Sam decided to follow. Without Chan and the camera, he was just another tourist. Besides, he might find something in Jake's kit for his hangover.

Under another tarp was a clinic, mats spread out on the swept ground, a couple of portable gurneys filling in for examination tables. Mothers sat holding their babies tightly in their arms, smiling weakly toward Jake and Sam, hoping for help. Flies swarmed around the children, and several of the kids made a feeble effort to swipe them away, giving up when they realized the action only stirred them up more. The secretion from their eyes seemed to be the main attraction for the flies. Isolated from the rest were a dozen people wrapped in bandages, waiting for Jake to come pick out the shrapnel or treat their burns. It hadn't been quiet in their village.

"Mate, make yourself useful. Hold this chap's leg." Jake was examining a young boy, who'd been peppered with tiny shards from a grenade explosion. Sam's job was to take the place of any painkiller, holding the limb still while Jake probed around the wounds, digging for the little hunks of metal.

"What you need is some of that ether that was stolen from the convoy." The boy was strong. Sam used both hands to hold the limb still.

"What are you talking about?"

"Well, that's what it said on the bottles. I was down in the hold of the ship and saw all these bottles in crates."

"Well, first, Sam, I haven't seen much ether around here lately, and second, I doubt it was intended for the hospital."

"You're kidding. . . ."

"You don't know what it's used for?"

"To knock folks out . . ."

"Yeah, that, but I suspect it's headed for a lab somewhere."

"Lab? In Cambodia?" Sam knew he was missing something.

"Heroin. You need it to process the opium paste." Jake smoothly picked out two lumps of metal and dropped them into a ceramic bowl.

"Wait a minute. That's Laos, Thailand, Jake, not here. They don't make heroin here."

Jake stared over the top of his half spectacles, making Sam feel like a mere student. "It is coming apart up there, and I wouldn't be at all surprised to hear that the operations have moved to Cambodia. Where there is demand . . ."

"Opium, yeah, I understand that. But skag. I didn't think there was a market for it here."

"Sam, Sam . . ." Jake stroked the child's head, gave him a gentle pat on the leg and helped him off the table. "In Asia, it is all the same. The market isn't here. It's in Saigon, New York, Paris, hell, even Sydney. You can't even imagine the profits with heroin."

"Sure I can," Sam said with more confidence than he felt. Jack had just handed him some puzzle pieces. He'd heard all about the Golden Triangle, talked with people who'd visited the poppy fields, who'd traveled into Burma with the Chinese who controlled the trade. But there were things that were nagging Sam, things he couldn't quite finger. Jake might be wrong, but it was worth checking out.

It took another hour for the doctor to work his way through the waiting patients. Young girls in labor, children with eye infections, a few more injuries. Hanging outside the tent was another group, trying to decide if they wanted the white man's medicine. Finally, Jake went back to the hospital, and Sam wandered the camp, searching for Sophan. He found him squatting under a tree, laughing with a couple of Bongs.

"These old friends. We were boys together." Sophan and Sam bowed and headed back toward the highway and the car. A truck loaded with food crawled past, a young guard sitting on the tailgate, rifle cocked.

"Man, it's saying something when you have to guard the supplies like that." The trucks broke free, picked up speed, and headed on down Highway 4 toward the smoke.

"When war start, people stand in line, wait for food. Now, people shoot for the food." Sophan smacked the dash of the Mercedes, as though that would help the glow plug on the diesel to work.

"Get that damned thing fixed, Sophan. I have no desire to sit around and fuck with that plug when we need to get away."

Sophan looked crestfallen, and Sam felt bad for his outburst. There was little Sophan could do about the plug until someone sent one in from out of the country. He'd asked Sam to get one, and he kept forgetting.

"Shit, man. I'm yelling at myself."

It took ten minutes to reach the airport, and they arrived just as the passengers were clearing customs. Sam spotted a church worker with the yellow network shipping bag, gave him twenty dollars for the effort, and headed back to the car, idling outside the door.

"Home, Sophan, and through the park," Sam said, putting on airs. "Get me back to the hotel so I can read my bills." Sam thumbed through the stack of letters, trying to decide which to read first. There was a package from Steve Chan's wife, probably a resupply of the chili peppers that kept him going. He picked out one from his sister. Nothing like news from the East Tennessee hills to help him escape from the heat that was building by the minute. He tucked a letter from his lady friend from India into his shirt pocket. They were infrequent and special. They were read in private.

Sophan threaded the car between the little two-wheeled taxi carts towed by Hondas, and the bicycles. Sam pulled out a carefully taped envelope, opened it, and counted five thousand dollars, or "green stamps." He found a note from the Saigon Bureau, saying that their missing gun story had run on the Evening News. There was a tightly sealed envelope from Tom Rider, which Sam split open on the end. Said that he wanted to come over for a few days. That was nothing unusual, Sam reminded himself. Rider liked to just visit, and it had been a couple of months since his last trip.

Sam admired the stamps on a letter for Chan, apparently from his daughter in Canton. She'd gone there to visit her grandmother, just before the Cultural Revolution, and had been stuck in China since. Chan had given up his U.S. passport in his efforts to retrieve her. Sam wondered what six years in China had done to her head. He pictured a young woman dressed in gray, holding a little red book.

"Sam. Maybe next time in Hong Kong you get Sophan new glasses," he said, tapping the frame on his shades, held together with gaffers tape.

"No problem." Sam wished for something cold to drink, to cut the taste in his mouth. He started to complain, then remembered his new Buddha. "I really appreciate this," he said, holding it away from his chest. "I'll never take it off."

"That good. You wear Buddha, you be OK. Just never forget, because Buddha get unhappy when left behind." Sophan laughed as they turned into the hotel parking lot by the pool. "You leave Buddha, and Buddha will get even."

"I get the point. You keep wearing yours, because I don't feel like testing mine."

"You safe now, Sam. You don't need Sophan for Buddha anymore." A crowd gathered around the car, word spreading rapidly that they had mail from Saigon. The long limbs of the Weeping Tree blocked the sun, the red flowers the color of blood. Sam watched as Sophan walked away with his friends, pointing at Sam and his Buddha. I hope I don't test it soon, Sam thought. I'd rather have Sophan than the Buddha.

XIII.

Market Attack

SAM FELT LIKE a player on the day of the big game. The artillery shells started falling fifteen minutes before the white Mercedes screeched to a halt at the edge of the Olympia Market, on the south end of the city.

"Let's move," Chan barked, mentally counting off the time between blasts. "We've got fifteen seconds." The rounds were landing at that interval.

"You're dragging the mike, Sophan," Sam yelled as he caught up with the other two.

"We're going for that wall." Chan led them toward the smoke boiling up from behind the row of grass-thatched houses raised on stilts just ahead. This was the kind of story television thrived on . . . fire and brimstone, one that could make New York forget about Watergate, at least for a day. Sam's main job came later, when it was time to set the scene told by the pictures.

The crew crouched by a white concrete wall and waited for the next explosion. "Thirteen, fourteen, fifteen," Sam was counting out loud. Nothing. They waited for another minute. "Ain't getting shit here, Tiger. Let's *didi*." Chan took off again, jerking Sophan along behind him on the end of the cord that ran from the camera to the soundbox.

They pushed against the fleeing Cambodians, dodging the tables, chairs and beds being salvaged from the fire. At the next corner, the crew hit a paved street that cut back to the market center. A shell had landed between the concrete buildings and fragments fanned both sides, skipping off the sidewalk and catching everything within fifty yards. In the doorway of one building, an old woman sat rocking on her haunches, her hand covering her mouth. She stared into the dark staircase in disbelief. Chan dropped to one knee and turned on the camera.

"Back off, you're in my light."

"Sorry." Sam swung around the men and moved to the edge of the sidewalk. He slipped, the treaded sole of his jungle boot losing traction in a puddle of blood covered by the fine white powder of blasted concrete. Sam heard the clicking of a Nikon behind him, Sy Rosen taking pictures of the doorway.

"Looks like we've found the missing gun," Sam said, his breath coming quickly, the chewing tobacco like straw in his cheek.

"No, the gun found them," Rosen replied, pointing toward the doorway before he disappeared down the street. Sam saw it for the first time. Five people had taken shelter on the concrete stairway inside the door, ten feet from the impact point of the shell. The explosion had molded their bodies to the shape of the steps.

"Jesus fuckin' Christ," Sam whispered, more of a prayer than a curse.

"These people sure know how to throw a barbecue." Chan didn't miss a beat, but panned the camera slowly up the stairwell. "Bet the bastards won't use this shot," he said, moving for a side angle.

"Probably right," Sam answered. He pulled his narrow reporter's notebook from his hip pocket to make a shot

sheet, listing the order of Chan's pictures. This helped him
later with the script, and told the editor where to look.
They never seemed to use the stuff that was hard to get or
hard to look at.

The crew rounded the corner. A small girl, her dark
sarong and brown skin covered with white powder, ran
toward them. Her mouth was open in a soundless scream.
She saw Sophan, a fellow Cambodian, and dived into his
legs.

"Is she hurt?" Sam jumped out of the way as Chan
focused the camera on the pair.

"She OK. She just scared." Sophan stroked the top of
her tangled hair and talked softly to her. Sam took the
microphone from the canteen case holding the tape recorder and tried to pick up her sobs as background for a
radio spot. As quickly as she had grabbed Sophan, the
little girl broke away, and the crew lost sight of her in the
crush of sarongs and cycles heading away from the flames.
Sam checked the dials on the soundbox, then looked at
Sophan.

"This bad. Very bad. They are not soldiers." Sophan
shook his head, looking around. "I have little girl. . . ."
The Buddha around his neck bounced as his head turned.
Sam checked to make sure his was still there.

"Got it, let's split," Chan said, getting to his feet.
"Shit, just like south L.A., man. Goddamned glass everywhere." Patches of blood were seeping through his
bush pants at the knees. He'd been kneeling in broken
glass.

"You'll live. No R&R for that one," Sam said, man-
aging a quick wink at the cameraman.

A billow of smoke engulfed them, filling their lungs and
burning their eyes. "Let's get down there. We gotta get
some of that fire." Chan tugged Sophan into action.

"Fire, hell. That's a firestorm." Rosen had doubled
back to meet them, and now trotted alongside. Beyond the
buildings, a fireball roared toward the smoky sky fed by

dry thatch roofs of stilt houses that were going up like tinderboxes.

"Sam, radio . . . ," Sophan yelled, slapping the canteen case on Sam's belt.

"Yeah, right . . ." Sam checked the mike and pushed the buttons on the bouncing machine and started talking as he ran. "Radio . . . radio . . . Michaels . . . Phnom Penh . . . An hour ago, this was a busy, crowded marketplace in the capital, now it is an inferno, the target of an artillery piece only a few miles from here. . . ." He thought about alluding to the captured One-Oh-Five, but considering the shit it had caused, he decided to stick with what he saw, which was plenty, with the massive cloud of smoke and the flames. The crew was now on a dirt road running through the heart of the fire, a residential track behind the market. Sam's foot dug under a fire hose that snaked down the road and he went sprawling into the gutter. He thrust out his hands and felt the slick mire of days-old garbage running through his fingers.

"You OK?" Sophan saw him fall, but still trailed after Chan, who was now duck-walking among the houses, getting an angle shot of the people streaming down the road.

"Yeah, yeah . . . I'm OK." A large water pot sat under the raised floor of the nearest house. Sam stuck his arms in the jug to the elbows and quickly rinsed off the stinking muck. The water was heating up as the fire moved closer.

"Sam, keep your eyes open. Don't let the fire get behind us," Chan yelled. Pictures like these were rare, but not worth being roasted for. Chan's mind focused totally on the inch-square image in the camera viewfinder, composing shots, looking for sequences.

Sam wiped the crud off the mike and talked again. "We're on the edge of a firestorm. . . . It's jumping the road." An arc of flames leapt from the burning houses on the right, engulfing those on the other side. The heat lifted the smoke, giving Sam a clear view for several hundred yards. He shifted farther away from Sophan and the television mike. He could feel his throat tightening, his voice rising. "I can see far down the street now; the smoke is cleared by the heat and flames . . . a half-dozen people are running toward us, trying to escape. . . ." He stopped, unable to believe what he was seeing.

One after another, the runners dropped to their knees, then crumpled to the ground, some grabbing for their throats as they sank. A pall of smoke covered them, then lifted. Sam spoke slowly into the tape recorder, almost choking. "You see things that are almost impossible to describe. Those people running are still now, lying in the road . . . probably dead . . . a hundred yards short of safety. The firestorm has taken the oxygen from the air. . . . They crumpled into the street. . . ."

"You gonna do something on camera?" Chan lifted his head from the viewfinder.

"Yeah, I'll do a bridge. . . ." Sam stepped over the hoses and debris toward the front of the camera, taking the television mike from Sophan. He tried to run his hand through his hair and realized it was coated white, just like the little girl's. He wondered how bad he looked.

"No fuckin' good to anybody if you stand in the middle of the best shot." Chan didn't smile. This was business, and like most cameramen, he doubted a reporter's ability to understand what he was trying to do, what he was trying to create in the camera.

"You tell me where, and I'll do it. . . ." Sam spat the wad of tobacco on the ground and ran his tongue around his gums to get out the stray strands. He wiped his mouth off on the tail of the bandanna, hoping to remove any traces of juice.

"To your right . . . a little more. . . ." Chan was framing him in the viewfinder, signaling with his hand.

"Sam . . . wait . . ." Sophan ran up to him with a comb and handkerchief. Sam bent toward the small man who made a couple of passes at his tangled hair and wiped the white dust from his face. "Now you pretty," he said with a grin.

"Mother would be pleased to know I'm being looked after, " Sam replied, mussing Sophan's hair. About a minute in this position was all he could stand.

"Rolling . . ." Chan twirled his finger in a circular motion in the air. The lens looked cold to Sam.

"This is bridge . . . bridge . . . market attack . . . Phnom Penh . . . Michaels / Chan / Sophan take one. . . ." Sam hesitated when he caught a flash of Larry Moss' blond hair, saw his crew cross the road.

"Do it man. . . ." Chan was tired of balancing the camera in this awkward position. He had to compensate for the difference in his and Sam's height by holding the camera a little off his shoulder.

"Picking up . . . Throughout the war, Cambodians have seen Phnom Penh as a haven from the fighting. Now the war has come to the capital, and these thousands of homeless people have nowhere left to hide. . . ."

"Sounds good, Tiger. . . ."

"We got company," Sam said, waving his hand at Moss, who returned the gesture. "Wonder how long they've been here?"

"Don't worry about it, Sam. We're all even now. Our job is to get this stuff out of here." Chan looked tired now, letting down his guard just a little bit.

A siren moved up the side street. Chan propped the camera against the stilts of a house, following the ancient French fire engine as it labored toward them. A bicycle was caught under the engine's frame and clattered as it was dragged along. Two other television crews appeared, everyone taking the same shot. Sam recognized the German crew, but he could only guess who Clive Allen, the Australian freelancer, was working for today. He was a one-man band, working alone, doing it all, selling his film to the highest bidder.

"Hey, Sam . . ." Ty Stoneman ran around the truck, a

necklace of Nikons around his neck. "You gonna try to ship today, man?"

"You know it."

"Would you throw some stuff in the bag for me? Get it to AP." He dug through the pockets of the combat shirt, pulling out silver canisters of film.

"Hey, I don't know where it's going yet. Probably Hong Kong." Sam knew that Air France was slipping in earlier and earlier, and he wanted to get it on that flight. They didn't have much time. No matter how good their pictures, they were worthless if they missed the plane. The network wanted the film to go to Hong Kong, where they had a full staff and satelliting facilities. A story like this would always make the satellite, or "bird," regardless of where it was shipped. But a marginal story could lose out if the network had to spend money to send two people to Bangkok to edit and feed the satellite. Even if Sam was on the New York shit list, they'd have to use this one.

"Anywhere, man, anywhere. Just get it to AP. The fuckers will have to buy this stuff. . . ." Ty grinned, knowing that if Sam could get this photographs in the right place, he'd make some money.

". . . Stoneman . . . wait a minute. . . ." Rosen headed toward them. "What you got?"

"Two rolls. Fireballs, bodies, the whole shot. . . ."

"I'll buy it. . . ."

"How much?"

"Hundred a roll . . ."

"Two hundred . . ."

"Hey, who's the Jew in this deal?" Rosen smiled as he stuck out his hand for the two rolls of film.

"No skin off your ass, man." Ty had the backs open on two of the Nikons, expertly threading fresh film into the cameras. "You need anything else?"

"Get me some people stuff, and I might buy it. . . ." Rosen was taking his own pictures, but he couldn't touch Ty's skills.

"Put my stuff in with yours. When are you shipping?" Rosen asked, inching back toward the corner, out of the direct heat of the fire.

"Air France, this afternoon . . ." Sam watched as a screaming woman was restrained by her friends, keeping her from running back into the fire. Ty's camera whirred as the motor drive spun through the frames.

"You'd better get a move on. They're probably running early again today."

"That's what I figure. Did you share that tidbit with Moss?" Sam arched his eyebrows, trying to cover his concern.

"Who's Moss?" Sy winked back then headed down the street looking for more action. On another street leading into the fire, Sam saw Claudine's red tee shirt as she pushed through a crowd. She hadn't been right there when they ran from the hotel, and Sam wondered if she was pissed at being left behind.

"Let's get this stuff out of here," Sam said.

"Where's Moss?"

"Still around the corner. I've got enough. Let me change magazines." Chan walked across the road, sat on the curb and flipped open the side of the camera. In a moment, he slipped out the used magazine and snapped a fresh one onto the top of the camera. Another twelve minutes of film if they needed it. Sam shoved the exposed magazine into the canvas map bag slung over his shoulder.

Sam led the way, skirting the fire and heading in the opposite direction from where their car was parked. He didn't want Moss to know they were leaving early, and the detour might throw him off, or at least that's what he hoped.

Driver Joe wasn't fooled. The Mercedes sat with two wheels on the curb, less than a block from the side street. He'd guessed where they would come out of the maelstrom. Sam felt the urge to yell at him for leaving the agreed upon rendezvous spot, but so far, Driver Joe had always been right. With his silver hair, horn-rimmed glasses and a Mercedes, Driver Joe looked like a diplomat visiting hell. The trunk was open, the ice chest full of beer, clean face cloths chilled on the ice. At two hundred dollars a day, service went with the car. "Grab one for me. . . ." Chan called out, unhooking the camera and soundbox, getting into the back seat with Sophan.

Sam pulled three Export 33 beers from the case, wiping one of the bottles across his face to catch the icy water. He followed with the cloth, instantly turning it sooty. "Tell me what you remember," Sam said to Chan, handing back the beers as he climbed into the passenger seat.

"You got good shots of the people on the steps, the guy from the cyclo. I'd open with the people running. You could see all that fire behind them."

"What about Sophan and the little girl?" Sam fiddled with the air conditioning as he listened. He turned it on full blast, aiming one of the side ports at his face.

"Yeah, use it if you want. But there was nothing around the kid that said what was going on. An editor will go nuts trying to cut to that shot." Chan spoke softly, not wanting to force his point, because he knew that Sam would yield to his judgment.

"You're right, but it's a shame to dump it. . . ."

"Do what you want, but do it." Chan handed him his battered Olympia portable typewriter, the cracks in the plastic case patched with gaffers tape and shipping labels.

"Jesus, Chan, we just got to the fucking car. . . ." Sam grinned to take the bite out of his comment and popped the cover off of his typewriter. He fished around in the glove compartment for six-ply carbon paper, used for television scripts. He balanced the machine on his knees, spun the paper in and started to write.

MARKET ATTACK . . . MICHAELS / CHAN / SO-PHAN . . . he wrote across the top. He reset the left margin to the middle of the page, leaving the left half for editing notes and identification names. Sam shut off the

chaos around him, tried to ignore the bumps as Driver Joe
steered the car over the curb, horn honking, trying to get
the dazed people to move, to give them a path. Posses-
sions saved from the fire were in piles on the streets and
sidewalks. Escape had taken all their energy, their will.
Now they just sat and stared blankly at the creeping car.

Just short of the open road, a water buffalo pulling a
two-wheeled cart had frozen, refusing all efforts by a
stooped old woman and two children to get it to move.
Sophan leaped from the back seat and wrapped a bandanna around the animal's eyes to calm it. Slowly, the
beast moved. The cartwheels creaked; it gave them just
enough room to slip by, then Sophan jumped back into
the car.

Chan yelled at Sophan in Chinese, and everyone but
Sam laughed. He had to wait for Driver Joe's translation.

"Chan kid him about how that the way the water buffalo
stand still for sex . . . when Sophan a boy in countryside." Joe chuckled, watching the road as the car picked
up speed. They hit the main road to the airport, ten minutes away. Time was running out for Sam.

IT WAS JUST AFTER LUNCH WHEN THE FIRST
SHELLS HIT. . . . THE REALITY AND HELL OF
WAR HAS REACHED INTO THE HEART OF THE
CAPITAL. . . . He stopped, picked through the hour's
events in his mind to decide which ones to include in the
two minutes allowed him on the news shows. He skipped
the girl, stuck with the fire and running people. Typing
quickly, he'd finished SAM MICHAELS, PHNOM PENH
as they turned into the airport.

"Just five more minutes, baby . . . just stay five more
minutes." Chan talked as he stared at the blue and white
Air France 707, engines running, looming over the small
terminal like an impatient eagle.

Before the car stopped, Chan handed Sam the mike.
They parked near the curb. And Steve went outside the
car with the camera; if left inside, the motor was too noisy

to do the voiceover. The windows were up, the car motor off, and the heat inside built by the second, making the script slippery in Sam's sweaty hands.

"VOICEOVER . . . VOICEOVER . . . VOICEOVER . . . MARKET ATTACK . . . MICHAELS . . . CHAN . . . SOPHAN." He said, reading from the script, putting the voice track on the audio strip of the remaining unexposed film. He made it through the whole thing without a fluff, unusual for him. Chan opened the door, grabbed a black film-changing bag to unload the magazines. Sam hunted for an envelope for Stoneman's film but couldn't find one, so he scribbled a note on his pad instructing his people to get the still film to the paper and credit Ty. Chan handed him a large yellow mesh bag with the film cans inside, taped together, the folded script sandwiched between the cans. He dumped in Ty's stuff and the note, pulled the drawstring on the neck of the bag, twisted the neck and taped it tightly with silver gaffers tape.

"Let's go . . . let's go . . ." Chan left Sam's door open as they both ran into the sleepy terminal, which to Sam had the feel of a small town bus station. The dank room reeked with the stale sweat of generations of travelers. Sam held the bag high so the customs man could see, and they cut through the exit of the customs room pushing through the arriving passengers. He could hear the scream of the jet turbines start to rise as the pilot anticipated departure.

Sam jumped the low luggage counter and ran onto the hot tarmac. He could feel tar sticking to his boots. The ramp was an antique plane buff's paradise. The 707 looked like a spaceship next to it.

He ran toward the plane, waving the bag over his head and whistling through his teeth to catch attention above the engine's wail. The ground crew was pulling the steps away when he reached them, but he ran up anyway, forcing them to stop moving. He leaned out at the top to bang on the door of the jet. It opened with a gush of pressurization and the steward looked at Sam.

"Take this film to Hong Kong, please. . ." He knew the steward by sight; he only hoped the steward remembered him.

"Is it the fire?"

"Yes . . . yes . . . you'll be met . . . a bottle of whiskey . . ." Sam smiled, waiting for the man to say yes.

"I will take it. . . ." He reached for the bag, dropped it on the floor inside and slammed shut the door with a thump. Sam gave the surprised Cambodians at the foot of the stairs a slap on the back, relief and joy sweeping his body.

"Tiger, we did it. . . ." Chan was waiting for him at the edge of the tarmac, a grin breaking through the grime on his face.

"You bet your sweet ass we did, Wetback." They hugged, the horror of the day overwhelmed by the thrill of doing their job while sticking it in the competition's ear as well. The jet made a quick turn on the runway, gathered speed and slowly climbed back toward the smoking pyres of the city. It was the last plane leaving Phnom Penh. His company and Sy's had the only same day pictures. Sam could feel the sunshine, see the breakfast smiles. He dug into his pocket and pulled out the Levi Garrett tobacco pouch, tore off a plug and stuck it in his cheek, watched the plane for a moment, then headed back inside the terminal. Not a bad day for an old country boy just tryin' to make it through.

XIV.

Reilly's Gun

"I WANT THAT fucking gun," the Colonel yelled. He slammed his fist down on the desk, knocking over the miniature flag stand that held his nameplate. COL. HOBART G. REILLY, read the gold letters standing out from the black lacquer dragon. Reilly seemed worried. Hell, he was furious.

"Sir, if the Cambodians have a fix on it, at least the general area, we can call in spotters." Maj. Larry Bishop answered his superior firmly, but with respect. The row of ribbons about the left breast pocket of the Colonel's neatly pressed uniform attested to his record of military and political survival in three wars. Reilly, Bishop knew, was under the gun himself. Now he might find out why.

"Cambodians, shit." Reilly rubbed the craggy skin around his closed eyes and slowly shook his graying head. "Do you know what this all means, Bishop?"

"It would appear . . ."

"It would appear that we have a major fuckup on our hands, son."

The Major felt his throat tighten and sweat began to pour down his legs. Bishop had been warned about Reilly before he started this tour. Watch out for him, they said, look out for those steely ball eyes. The Smiling Cobra, they'd called him in Saigon. The Smiling Cobra was smiling now.

"Should I ring up MACTHAI for an airstrike on the gun, Colonel?" The air conditioner in the embassy window began to rattle, drops of water dripping off the grill to the bucket on the floor. Reilly turned toward the noise, then swiveled back to Bishop.

"If there's any talking to be done with those assholes in Thailand, I'll do it, are we clear? Ask those bastards at the Military Assistance Command Thailand for the time of day and they'll take over the entire operation. The less they know, the better."

"Intelligence didn't report any lost weapons this morning, sir." Bishop was bluffing. He hadn't read the traffic cables.

"We must be reading different pages, Bishop, because my overnight file is full of it. Jesus.

"Look, the last thing we need on top of everything else is some crazy bastard cranking off rounds into the city. We're not talking about an army here. A dozen half-naked Cambodians and a thick rope, that's all you need. They've had days to hide it."

"Yes, sir." Bishop could feel the heat. He wondered what the real story was. He'd also been warned of Reilly's problem with the booze.

"While you're catching up on your reading," Reilly said with a tight grin, calling Bishop's hand on the cables, "you might like to read this one." Reilly shoved the red-bordered telex across the desk. "Seems that gun, and a bunch of medical supplies, popped up on television in the States the other night."

"Sir? I don't understand."

"Sam Michaels did a story about it. Now I have half of Washington crawling down my back."

"Well, this is a war, and supplies do get lost, captured." What in hell was the man talking about? He'd been through several senseless harangues with the Colonel, but none like this. And how in hell did Michaels get pictures of hijacked medical supplies and a lost gun?

"OK, look. I have information to indicate that the convoy wasn't captured. It's being held by some outlaw government troops."

"They looking for a pay hike?" Bishop regretted the joke as soon as he said it.

"Get serious, Major. Right now, helping the government get this stuff back is our top priority. Understand?" Reilly took a deep breath, gathering his thoughts, "Bishop, let me tell you about this war. I mean the truth about this war. I want you to understand a basic fact of military life. Your future is keyed to my getting out of this place without dropping the ball. And that fucking gun out there is a dropped ball. Understand?"

"Yessir." Bishop wondered who dropped it. Reilly?

"Your friends at MACTHAI are good at blowing things up. That's not what we need here. We've got to recover the gun and those supplies intact. That's the way the Cambodians want it, and that's the way they get it. That's something we must live with. This isn't our war. It isn't Vietnam. We're propping up this army, trying to keep the wolf from their door. These losses are bad for morale.

"As long as we have the air support and the B-52s, we can save the Khmer Republic's ass. But in a few weeks, who knows. Then they'll need every gun they can get." Reilly leaned back in his big leather chair, hands behind his head, getting into his lecture.

"We can only hope those bastards hold on until you and I get out of here. But right now, today, I want that gun. Is that clear?"

"Very clear, sir." Bishop leaned toward the desk. "It's

all very clear.'' Now Bishop understood. The Colonel was making the One-Oh-Five his responsibility, and he probably felt he should go down the highway and drag the gun to the city with his bare hands.

"Settle down, Major." Reilly could read his thoughts. "The last thing I need is for a field-grade officer in the U.S. Army to get his West Point ass killed in the field. I want the Cambodians to get that gun. We gave it to them, they lost it, now they can get their asses out there and get it back."

Reilly got up and walked over to a large briefing map tacked to a three-legged stand. His eyes leveled on Phnom Penh, parked on the west bank of the Tonle Sap River, at the point of its confluence with the Mekong. The problem area was half jungle, half paddy land, a no man's zone to the south of Phnom Penh. The gun was down there somewhere. Red grease marks formed squares, circles and diamonds across the map. No matter what the shape, they all meant the same thing—in enemy hands. Reilly had little doubt that someday the whole map would be red; his main concern was leaving before it happened.

"Bishop," he continued, "that convoy might as well have docked on the moon for the amount of stuff that got to the right place. You're the intelligence officer. How do you explain that?" Reilly stood at parade rest. He was not a tall man; he compensated in other ways. Parade rest was one of them.

"That is difficult, Colonel. We didn't set up this convoy, local civilians did. I don't see how lost supplies from those ships could be our responsibility." Bishop knew he was pushing, but he wanted to know what he was being dragged into.

"You're about to blame it on the Chinaman, right? Every fucking thing in this country is blamed on the Chinaman."

"I'm not sure there is a Chinaman, Colonel. I suspect he is a handy excuse to cover their mistakes."

"Look, this is going to sound strange," Reilly said, taking a step toward Bishop. "It doesn't matter whether there is a real Chinaman or not. He could be one or fifty people. The fact is, 'the Chinaman' makes things happen here, and we have to live with it."

"Yessir." So it was the Chinaman turning up the heat. "Wasn't Michaels aboard that convoy? Couldn't that be the pictures they mention in the cable?"

"Listen to this," Reilly said, grabbing the cable. " 'Evening News showed numerous trucks loaded with medical supplies, shells, and One-Oh-Five artillery piece. Soldiers dressed in bits of government issue. Very relaxed, proud of their prize. HOW PLEASE SOONEST!' "

"Fine, sir. And what would you like me to do?"

"First, I want you to get to Michaels and find out where the gun is located. How he got the pictures. I've already responded to the cable."

"You have?" How, Bishop wondered.

"I said that the story was staged, that the pictures were of regular army troops, that Michaels lied."

"And now we must make that come true? Correct?" Bishop didn't like this at all. Reilly had made him part of the lie, and he was to be the front man.

"If that's the way you want to look at it, yes."

"Why do you think the Pentagon will buy it?"

"Michaels is a stringer. Not staff. They don't really know him back in New York. I've dealt with these people before. Who are you going to believe? Some kid that popped up in the middle of nowhere, or an army colonel?"

"That's obvious, sir." Bishop answered without conviction. He remembered a class at the Point, where the professor challenged this very point. They just might believe Michaels.

"Another thing. This map sucks. We're guessing where the gun may be located, but this map tells me nothing.

What do these marks mean?'' Reilly demanded, pointing to the area around the river.

"It means the sectors are fluid, sir. Those grids are based on the best intelligence we can gather. The rest is just supposition.''

"The only thing 'fluid' about this sector here, Bishop,'' he said, his eyes still fixed on the map, "is the river. I don't like that word, Bishop. Don't bullshit me. Even if you only suspect the Khmer Rouge have it, I want to know about it. Let's get one thing clear, Bishop, and we won't have any problems. I don't like surprises. So let's get this map in shape, all right?'' Reilly was smiling again, the upward turn of his mouth making his lips even tighter.

"That's fine, sir. I'll put it all on the map for you. Is there anything else?'' Maybe this was his chance to get out of the Colonel's sight for a while.

"Yes, there is. How much time did you spend in Nam, Bishop?''

"Two tours. Infantry line officer the first tour and division headquarters the second.'' He wondered what was coming.

"Bright boy, aren't you, Bishop? Quite a jump in responsibility. I like bright people.'' Reilly was still smiling. He looked out the barred window, down on the main gate of the embassy. "The American war is over in Vietnam, Major, and we're the only thing left. Those pilots out there are the last Americans fighting in the world. You know what that means, Major?'' Did he detect some discomfort, a little tightening of asshole by one Major Bishop?

Bishop wiped his brow with his kerchief. "We're being closely watched?''

"Precisely. We're in a fishbowl here, the only game in town. I think you know my feelings about the press. Do you like the press, Bishop?'' Reilly thumped the front panel of the air conditioner to stop the vibrations.

"I try to avoid them, sir, unless ordered otherwise. A television crew spent some time with me in the highlands on my first tour, but in Saigon we just tried to stay out of their way.''

"Well, you have a new job. Michaels and the others have the information we need, and you must get it. They know the gun is out there, and we'd better get our ducks in a row before someone starts counting shells." Reilly stared at the map again. "We'll let our Cambodian friends help you do the talking on this. I want you and Colonel Rang to work together. I'll try to calm Washington down. Do you understand?"

"I understand." Bishop was stuck. "Will that be all?"

"That's it, Bishop. Oh, and Bishop, you look like Captain America in those tailored fatigues. Get an issue pair. We don't need to advertise."

XV.

Truth or Consequences

"TIME NOW FOR Cambodian Truth or Consequences!"
Larry Moss jumped up on a chair, unplugged microphone
in hand. "I'm Bob Barker, one of America's ten best-
dressed men, and we're here to play. Sam, who's our first
contestant?"

"Well, Bob, our first lucky contestant is Hung Saprim,
a truck driver from Battambang."

"Not old 'Shakes' Saprim?" Rosen joined the game,
signaling the waiter for another bottle of wine.

"One and the same, sir, one and the same. Now we've
asked Shakes our fun question for tonight—what's the half-
life of plutonium 235—but the answer just slipped his
mind. You know what that means, don't you, Bob?" Sam
dropped his voice an octave lower.

Moss raised his hand to the crowd. "Yes, yes, we all
know, don't we kids . . ." In a drunken chorus, those
around the table shouted: "He must pay the consequences!"

"And that's not all! We've invited Shakes' three wives,

twenty-seven children and his girlfriend to join us tonight, while he has his fun.''

"And what would that be?" Sam was getting stoned.

"Ah, this is our best yet! He gets to drive his truck with the family in back from here to Battambang . . . at midnight!" Whistles and cheers rang out from the gathering.

"Now, what Shakes doesn't know," Sam said, his voice in a stage whisper, "is that the road has been freshly mined, and a full Khmer Rouge division is hidden just around the first curve. Let's watch the look on Shakes' face when he realizes he's in the middle of the minefield! Better yet, let's see the look on the wives' and kiddies' faces in the back of the truck when they see the Khmer Rouge!" Sam was laughing now, ducking napkins thrown at him by some of the drinkers at the table.

They'd pulled two long dining tables from the restaurant onto the patio, taking over the hotel pool for the afternoon. As the others drifted in from the market, word spread about Sam's getting the film out. Moss was ready to reap the losers' benefits. The winner bought the wine on a story like this. Today Sam was buying.

Claudine looked at him from the end of the table. Hans Schecter, a Prince Charming-type German photographer who'd just returned from home leave, seemed quite happy to see her. Sam wasn't jealous; he just wanted to throw the Kraut into the pool, see how long he could tread water.

"You know, one of these days a consequence will come true." Rosen was staring closely at the wine in his glass, his horn-rims at the tip of his nose.

"Just hope I'm not on the truck." Sam eyed the fresh bottle of wine being brought to the table. He wondered how much the dust on the bottle ran up the price. There was still fine wine and Iranian caviar at the hotel. But the water was a little iffy. . . .

"Samuel, good fellow." Rosen struck the pose of a pukka Britisher from the Raj. "Would it be indiscreet of me to inquire about the chap that seems to be propelling himself around in my wine glass?''

Sam leaned over and peered at the glass. ''I say, I think you have got something there, my good fellow. Do they charge extra for the little wings?'' Rosen was another Delhi veteran, and they both enjoyed mocking the British.

''Neat backstroke, don't you think?''

''Oh, certainly, my good Michaels, certainly. Olympic hopeful for sure.''

''Yes, we've been looking for swimmers since the entire National Aquatic Team swam across the Mekong, never to be seen again. Sad day, that.'' Sam twicked the bug with his finger. ''Did you order him with the wine?''

''Heavens, no. Bloody *wogs* don't know any better. No, I was going to wait for appetizers, but I was so busy looking down Claudine's blouse that the waiter might have misunderstood.'' Rosen twirled the stemmed crystal in his fingers, studying Sam's face for a reaction.

''One of my favorite pastimes,'' Sam replied, ''but a little hard on the old ticker.''

''You know, mate, that's a half-decent wine you've got there.'' Dr. Jake had joined them after running out of lights and blood at the Russian Hospital. ''Now, that's not to say Australian wine is not just as good. . . .''

''Anybody who drinks Foster's beer warm and eats vegemite can't complain about the wine,'' Byers muttered. Sam had damn near choked the first time he tried vegemite, the unusual yeast paste from a jar that's a staple in Australia.

''Hey, Moss . . . try this one.'' Sam turned back to the game. ''Our next contestant is Hobart G. Reilly, colonel, U.S. Army.''

''. . . and his trusty sidekick, 'Starched Drawers' Bishop, major, USA.'' Rosen was picking this one up fast.

''They were unable to name the winners in last year's Ugandan International Film Festival, so they must suffer the consequences.'' Sam was on a roll now.

''And what would that be, Sam?''

"They can't find the fucking convoy. . . ."

"Hear, hear," whistling and applause greeted the idea.

"We'll send them in a Day-Glo armored personnel carrier. . . ."

". . . at midnight . . ."

"With loudspeakers playing 'Country Joe and the Fish . . .' "

"Well it's one, two, three, what are we fightin' for . . ." A half-dozen voices joined the song. The tune had been an anthem among GIs during the sixties in Vietnam. Laughter ended it at the second line. Claudine shook her head from side to side and frowned. Hans was still working on her ear, oblivious to Sam's stares.

"I think we should start a pool." Byers was never one to miss a wager.

"What kind this time?" Sam had lost fifty bucks in the "end of the bombing" date pool.

"Nearest shell or rocket to the hotel. Fifty bucks. I'll hold and we'll make a deadline."

"From the pool . . . the hotel's too big." Rosen gambled too, but he was always clear on the rules.

"May the ladies play?" asked the Swedish nurse, Rosen's friend from Chantao's.

"Lady, you can play on credit." Byers tried to suck in his belly, take away the toll of tropical sunlight and pastis on his face.

"Watch him, he's sneaky. He'll try to collect in trade." Rosen gave her a little wink.

"I'm a big girl, Mr. Rosen. . . ."

"I'm well aware of that. . . ."

". . . and I can take care of myself." She smiled, her face that of the classic Nordic blonde, much too pretty for this place. She was tall, well built, with long hair that almost touched her waist. She'd arrived the week before, joining one of the United Nations medical teams.

"OK, OK . . . we'll make it August 15th . . . last day of the bombing. . . ."

"Midnight, August 15th . . ." Rosen was now quarreling for fun.

"Dammit, OK . . . midnight. Now where's the money?"

"Put it on my account. . . ." Sam wasn't touching one that involved betting on things that could land on your head.

"You guys always back out. Looks like you and me, sweetheart." Byers drunkenly leered at the nurse.

"Wrong, Mr. Byers, wrong." She leaned over and patted him on his flushed cheek.

Sam pushed to his feet, a nature call pressing through his stoned mind. He stood carefully, letting his head catch up with the increased altitude, then worked his way past Claudine. Hans was sitting back now, in temporary retreat.

"Sammi, you are funny. . . ." She took his hand and squeezed it.

"How did you do today?"

"I get good pictures. Chan says you ship story already. Is it true?" Her eyes peeked over the top of the big sunglasses.

"Yeah, that's right. You know me; never let the facts get in the way of a good story." He circled through the bar, into the toilet, to the urinal. Moss was already there. They shared the long trough.

"How did you know about Air France?" Moss had no animosity in his voice.

"Just lucky, Larry." Sam didn't want to admit it was sheer luck, something that seemed to be in short supply these days. He stared at the old green tiles on the wall, wondering how many kings, ambassadors, generals and rogues had studied the same insignificant spot.

"My luck seems to be running a bit thin of late." Moss looked at Sam. "But the war ain't over yet."

"Nope, not by a long shot. I got a little surprise for you. Tom Rider is coming in for a visit."

"Yeah, I know all about Rider's visits." Larry zipped his pants and turned to leave. "Ah, Sam . . ."

"Yeah?" He was ready for another funny shot.

"I snuck a call through on the Tiger line to Saigon today, trying to get them to lay on a charter." He seemed to wish he hadn't started the conversation.

"And the cheap bastards wouldn't buy, right?" Sam tried to be loose, but he sensed something here.

"You got that right. I think you should know that there's some shit coming down in Saigon with your name on it, and I think that Rider's coming over for more than a social call."

"What kind of shit?"

"Can't say. They didn't want to talk much on a line they knew was tapped, but they did say Reilly is after your ass. But what else is new?" He smiled, then punched Sam lightly in the gut. "Probably just your bar girl pregnant with twins."

"Yeah, probably." Sam laughed and waited for Moss to leave. He wondered what this was all about. Maybe Reilly was really turning up the heat. The booze and weed in his brain slowly took over, pushing the bad thoughts down for another time.

Sam thought how good something as simple as pissing felt when you've had a good day. He was pleased at how well he and Larry could compete without letting it affect their friendship, how they protected one another, handled the situation like grown men. As he walked back to the table, he could hear the laughter and feel the wet on the cuff of his jeans. Moss had pissed down his leg.

"Piss poor loser, that's all I can say. . . ." Sam was laughing, happy with the bad pun. He retook his seat, signaled the waiter for service.

The old man trudged toward the table, wine bucket in hand, towel neatly folded across his left arm. Sam sniffed the cork, tasted the wine and proposed a toast.

"To Cambodia . . ."

"To Cambodia . . ."

". . . and to the poor bastards who got zapped to-day . . ."

". . . and to Hobart Reilly, who now has found his gun."

". . . hear, hear . . ."

". . . and to Tom Rider, who is arriving soon to shush out the truth in this dirty little war." Sam smiled, but Moss looked away. He'd kept the information to himself.

". . . to Tom Rider, finder of truth . . . ," Rosen chimed in.

". . . groper of little girls . . ."

". . . a true friend of Cambodia!" Sam was starting to see the good side of Rider's arrival, realizing he might need help.

Rivulets of water poured down the waiter's face, the white jacket hung limply from his thin bones. He tried to ignore these people, these journalists, who seemed to have no respect for what the hotel had once been: the bastion of French culture in Cambodia. He held his place behind Sam, refusing to give him the satisfaction of taking cover. Not only were they crazy, they were uncultured. How could they let the hotel's finest wine overflow from the glasses, mixing with the pouring rain? A soggy piece of wirecopy stuck to the fine linen tablecloth, the English words that he couldn't read bleeding into the cloth:

PHNOM PENH: AT LEAST ONE HUNDRED PEOPLE DIED IN A MASSIVE ARTILLERY ATTACK ON THE OLYMPIA MARKET. THE SHELLS STARTED LANDING DURING THE PEAK OF BUSINESS, KILLING AND WOUNDING . . .

XVI.

Couscous

"WHAT DO YA mean ya don't like couscous; your father was weaned on the stuff." Byers grabbed at the dark, tall woman who spun away from his grasp. She spun again around the open deck of the houseboat, so that each man got a quick flash of her smooth, chocolate skin. Thirty people crowded the long table running the length of the houseboat deck, scooping food from the huge bowls placed every couple of feet, washing it down with wine and gin, passing joints with greasy hands.

Sam took another bite of the sticky ricelike couscous, tasting the heavy concentration of dope liberally cooked into all dishes. He kept glancing at the Stateside crew which arrived with Tom Rider, a surprise to Sam. They'd been "bigfooted." Now Rider was expected to do the big stories, leaving Sam's crew with the crumbs. He wondered how long it would take for the dope in the food to hit them. The big cameraman from Texas missed his mouth with the spoon, and great globs of couscous ran down the front of his bush shirt. Welcome to Cambodia, asshole.

The houseboat was tied to the shore of the Mekong, two miles from the edge of the city. Sam had wanted to pass on the feast, but Rider would have none of it. From the moment Sam met them at the airport that afternoon, he knew that something was wrong. Rider tried to make light of it, but Sam wasn't having any. You can't bullshit a bullshitter. They'd met with Rosen for a drink by the pool, satisfying Rider that Sam was on firm ground with the missing gun and medical supplies. Rider told them the Pentagon claimed it was a government convoy, that Sam had embellished the story. Sam's exclusive on the market attack should have relieved some pressure, but there was more. Sam just knew it.

The meal was laid on for one of the old-time French journalists returning for a visit, and the chatter along one end of the table was in machine-gun French, friends playing "top this." The dancing lady was only part of the program. Outside on the deck, Sam could hear the giggles of Cambodian girls getting ready for their performance. At one end of the room a fortune teller had set up a small table. At the other, a lone musician tapped a flat, stringed instrument with sticks as three others tuned up for a concert.

"You look unhappy." Claudine touched his cheek with the tips of her fingers. "You must not let these things make you unhappy."

"I'm OK." Sam forced a smile as he fished a Salem out of his pocket. "I just need to sort a few things out." He watched Rider, who'd joined a heated argument with the French.

"Please, be happy. For Claudine." She gave him a peck on the cheek, then turned to join the discussion. Sam felt isolated by language, his feeble French too primitive to follow the conversation. The Cambodian family who ran the restaurant cleared the table, swiftly removing plates before they became part of the evening's entertainment. Sam had bought a few plates himself the last time they dined here. He'd wanted to demonstrate his stone-skipping skills on the placid waters of the Mekong.

A double hit from a fat joint went straight to his brain.

Pierre, their host and *L'agence France-Presse* bureau chief, pounded on the table for attention. Claudine offered to translate the toast, but Sam shrugged her off, concentrating on smoking the Salem and thinking.

Somewhere back there he'd crossed the line, one he couldn't see. He took inventory. Right now, it was clear that Reilly was pissed, the network was getting heat, and that he'd been benched. He'd broken the rules in his eagerness to get on the air, using the stringer film at face value, blending it in with his story. Yet events seemed to prove him right, and even Rider said that the Pentagon didn't get twisted unless you hit where it hurt. Sure, he'd covered himself, and no one had questioned that part. But that's what bothered him. If he's covered on the story, as Rider contends, then why the visit, why the other crew? Right now, he thought, a mountaintop in Nepal is appealing.

"Sammi, they talk about you!" Claudine gripped his leg as Sam tried to focus on Pierre. "He say you win the prize for best story, how do you say, storytelling." A burst of laughter followed. Pierre held his glass toward Sam, giving him a chance to reply.

Sam chose to toast with the joint. He pushed back the chair and stood, unsteady. He waited for his head to clear, for his mouth to start moving.

"I would like to announce the opening of Sam Michaels' Rent-a-Story," he said, surprised at his own words. "Fifty bucks and we'll ride down the roads and find whatever you like." Most laughed, but it seemed a couple of the European reporters took him at his word. "Hear, hear . . ." rang around the table.

"That was very silly. . . ." Claudine nudged him as he sat back down. He felt like making a shitty reply, but held his tongue. If he had any allies, they were right here, at this table. As the toast continued, he mulled over his reaction, why he wanted to yell at those who cared. Like his friend Graeme, an Australian diplomat whom he'd met in India and had shown up in Cambodia at the Australian Embassy, complete with his orange Morgan 2+2 sports car. He'd broken the rules for Sam many times, and came tonight just to be with his friend.

Chairs scraped as they were pulled away from the table, making way as the proprietor pushed the tables against the back wall. The lone player had been joined by others, each tuning up and joining the next. Sam grabbed a cushion and propped it against the bamboo wall, creating a backdrop. As they all settled down on the deck, the dark woman again appeared, this time wrapped in veils. Sam watched.

"She is *pied-noir*," Claudine whispered to Sam. "How do you say, black foot?"

"Damnedest Indian I've ever seen," Rider muttered, obviously happy to be back in Phnom Penh. The woman spun down the length of the room, the North African music strange and out of place on the Mekong, especially to the musicians who were far beyond their depth.

"*Non, non!* Not red Indian." Claudine took a friendly swipe at Rider, who ducked his head and laughed. "Her father was the African soldier, her mother French."

"Well, that sure makes more sense." Sam wondered how many of the people on the houseboat counted Algeria as one of their stories. The older French reporters for sure, maybe even a Rosen or two. Claudine, with her husband in the desert, knew well that part of the world. Sam remembered it from his traveling days, more of his time spent combing the casbah in Marrakech for great hash than studying the local culture.

Pierre knelt in front of them. "Do you want a chance on the lady?" He nodded toward the dancer. "She is very expensive, but very good."

Sam glanced at Claudine and smiled. "No, I think I'll

dance with who I brung.'' He could see the others going for their money, thousands of riels going into the pile.

''Why, yes, yes,'' Pierre said, not quite understanding Sam's colloquial expression. ''Everyone should have the chance, that is all.'' As he spoke, the music peaked, then shifted to the atonal sounds of Cambodia. The dark woman was lying with her face to the floor, the thin veils spread around her like a fan. They cheered, called for more. As she slowly rose, the Cambodian girls slipped into the room and started their dance.

''You do not like?'' Claudine opened her eyes wide in mock amazement.

''Ah, very much, but not tonight.'' Sam watched as Claudine slowly took in every inch of the prostrate woman.

''Sure you don't want to buy a chance?'' Sam gave her arm a squeeze.

''*Non.* That I do not buy. Men or women.''

''I can see why.'' The dancers with the bright sarongs and conical hats were a sharp contrast to the exotic work of the *pied-noir*. Those in the pool carefully counted the money, arguing over the final sum. The Chinese fortune teller shuffled a deck of cards, dealing them with a flourish to the circle of bettors. Byers cursed his five of hearts and returned to his drinking. Pierre smiled broadly, holding his card against his chest. Rosen showed no emotion but, still in the game, carefully watched the cards turn over.

''Not a bad scam when you think about it,'' Marty Satterfield said, sliding toward them on the floor. ''Dance an hour, grease the wallets, then take home the loot and the winner.'' He'd passed as well. Pierre put down the queen of hearts; Rosen topped it with a king, looked around the group for a trump, then smiled. Graeme spun his three of spades into the river night.

''He's one lucky bastard,'' Sam said, watching Rosen gather up the money and approach the woman, presenting the wad of bills to her with a great flourish. She smiled tentatively. He spoke to her softly in French as the losers cased the room for a suitable second prize.

Rider nodded to Sam, and they walked to the bow of the riverboat, looking at the moon cut a silver path across the Mekong. They were loose enough now to talk, and whatever Rider had to say could not wait.

"I take it that the Reilly hassle isn't the sole reason for your visit." Sam lit another Salem.

"Part of it. That story really got everyone going." Rider watched as Sam's match slowly floated away. "Nothing like a little controversy to whet New York's appetite."

"Then what are you doing here? Have we missed something?" Sam wanted to get to the point.

"Quite the contrary, my friend. You've been on the air more than most, and you certainly haven't been beaten on anything major."

"Then why are you here?"

Rider looked at the moonbeam on the water, then turned to Sam. "In the film bag with the supply story were three film cans of heroin."

"You're shitting me?" Sam was stunned.

"I think I have the lid back on, but good buddy, we got to get this straightened out between us. What I need to know is how it got in there." He looked Sam straight in the eye.

"I don't know . . . ," Sam replied without conviction. Suddenly things fell into place, and he felt completely deflated, used.

"It's Claudine, isn't it?" Rider was no fool.

"You said that . . ."

"Come on, Sam. You've been shipping her stuff for months." Rider fished out another rum crook and lit it. "The wire service thinks it's Stoneman."

"That comes as no surprise. Does Byers know?"

"No. Our shipper brought in the bag, pulled out the 35mm film cans and turned them over to the wire. Guess he mixed in one of the cans with Stoneman's rolls." Rider turned to Sam with an ironic grin. "Want to hear the kicker?"

"Yeah . . ." Why not, Sam thought. Couldn't get any worse.

"The lab guy dumped one can into the developer. Cost me a thousand bucks to buy him off. The Saigon wire guy said that he would sit on it until I got back to him. I should fire Driver Nga. I think he's been the Saigon contact. But if I do that, everyone will know."

"Who knows now?" Sam was ready to contemplate the losses.

"The wire chief, Nga, the lab guy. They know about this batch for sure."

"This batch?"

"Look, Sam. Someone here has been shipping the stuff out through us. There's not been enough to get excited about, but now the cat's out of the bag. The embassy in Saigon talked to me about it months ago, but they thought you were clean."

"And you?"

"That's why we're having this conversation."

"Right." Sam knew Rider wasn't convinced.

"Look, Sam. You pop up out of nowhere. You're fresh off the Hippie Highway, and your taste for drugs is no great secret."

"My tastes are recreational, and if I wanted to deal, I wouldn't shit in my own mess kit."

"I hope not. Look, this is hot gossip all over Saigon and Hong Kong. A couple of people in New York have heard the rumors. This added to the flap with Reilly is pushing your luck. We've got to do something to get you out from under this."

"Like what?" Sam was at a loss.

"Like, I don't know." The laughter from the party behind them was a counterpoint to the conversation. "What about Claudine? Did you know?"

"Hell, no. I was just helping a friend get her film out. We all do it."

"You're pretty tight with her, aren't you?"

"I was until about two minutes ago." Sam gave a tight grin and they both laughed to relieve the tension.

"Talk to her and find out what's going on. We can hold this off for a couple more days. I feel like I own half of Saigon now, and buying a couple more folks won't hurt."

"You know, I was right about the supplies and that gun. I think there's a connection with the convoy stuff. It's a hell of a story if I can just get some proof. I think there's a lab around here somewhere, and I think the Chinaman is the key."

"Ah, yes. The Chinaman." Rider took a long pull from the cigar. "I appreciate you wanting to recoup, and I'm not going to stop you. But remember, one more slip, one more piece of evidence against you, and the game's up. There's nothing I can do if the embassy puts your name on these cans."

"Understood." Sam felt that Rider was behind him, but what to do about Claudine. He'd have to work that out for himself.

"As to the gun and supplies. When I found you in India," he said, referring to when he hired Sam, "I knew you would work out fine. But they shot you right into the big leagues, Sam, and you've still got to learn to hit the New York curve. Your field work is good. You're almost there. Let's just make sure that Reilly doesn't strike you out."

The music grew louder as the yelling and laughter at the party increased. They worked their way back through the crowd, Sam forcing a smile for Claudine. Satterfield gave him a long look, that of a savvy field commander who knows when his troops are out of sorts. Sam's mind raced with excuses and plans of retribution, the party atmosphere counter to what he felt.

"Sam, you must have your fortune read. The Chinese,

he is very good.'' Claudine tried to drag him off the cushion toward the man at the table.

"No, no,'' he protested, staying put. "I think I already
know what my fortune is going to be.''

⊕   ⊕   ⊕

"It is all true,'' Claudine whispered. She sat on the edge
of the pool with Sam, her feet dangling in the water. "I
have the habit. I cannot stop.'' She started to cry. Sam
wanted to put his arm around her, but couldn't bring himself to it. He felt betrayed.

"It is how I get my drugs. It seemed so innocent. Just
send out the samples.''

"For whom?''

"The Chinaman.'' She looked at him.

"Ah, fuck the Chinaman, Claudine. That's all I ever
hear around this place.'' He took a deep breath and lowered his voice. "When I was a kid, I had an imaginary
playmate named Johnny Renna. Sam never did anything
wrong. Blame it all on Johnny Renna. That's what you're
doing with the Chinaman.''

"Sammi, listen. They leave the samples in my room,
along with a gift for me. In the last weeks, they wanted
more and more of the drugs tested.''

"And you put them in my shipping bag, right?''

"Yes. I am sorry. That is all I can say.''

"Is that why you took up photography? So you could
use fools like me?'' Now he was angry.

"No. No.'' Now the tears came. "I take the pictures to
get away from all that.'' She paused, wiped her eyes with
her blouse sleeve to stall for a moment, then continued.
"Before, I would carry it out on my person. I thought if
I could be free of the people, I could be free of the drug.''

"Guess it doesn't work that way, does it?'' Sam mulled
over the conversation. "It's Maurice, isn't it?''

"What?''

"Maurice. He's your source, isn't he? He's the China-man."

Claudine said nothing, showed nothing in her face. Sam was certain he was right, but he wasn't going to get it from her.

"Sammi, I am sorry. I want to correct the mistake. Give me the chance."

"How?"

"Give me the chance," she said, standing up and reaching down to give Sam a hand. "Just give me the chance."

Sam thought for a moment, then agreed. "I don't have much time. Rider needs an answer."

"If we could find the lab, the gun. That would help?"

"That would be good for starters. Yes, that would be good."

"Sam, maybe it would be better if I just talk to Rider, tell him everything. I have been very bad luck to many people." She put her arms around Sam, holding tightly.

"Back home, they have a name for this," Sam said in a low, monotone voice. "Call it gold-digging."

"I do not understand. . . ."

"Getting whatever you can from a relationship." He didn't return the hug. "Claudine, I don't really care about the fight with Reilly, that will blow over. And I can understand the thing about your habit. What I don't like is being made the fool."

"That was not my plan, Sam. I want to be someone, I want people to know Claudine as a good photographer. I have hurt myself as much as you." She let him go and walked slowly toward the hotel steps.

Sam wanted to yell something after her, but he could think of no words to express the way he felt. He'd been thinking with his dick, and the time had come to pay up.

XVII.

Pao's Run

EVERYTHING WAS COMING apart. Pao felt the tension build in the village, could see that he was trapped here, in the lab, because of the missing ether. The process was running, the heroin pure, and there was nothing left for him to do until the bottles arrived. He busied himself with the pipes and tubes, checking each connection, making measurements that meant nothing. He didn't want the Chinaman to know that he was finished.

He'd made a plan to escape. A weak plan, but it was all he could work out now. He'd hidden some chemicals, and when the time was right, he'd douse his thin cotton mattress with the fluid, slip out of the house in the dark, and hope that the chemicals would ignite, giving him a few minutes to run while the guards fought the fire. But run where? He knew that if he followed the dirt road, he'd hit Highway 4. But then what?

The shouting in the village had increased when the thump of artillery shells could be heard and the heavy smoke started rising from the city. Were the Renegades carrying out their threat? Was this the attack they'd promised the Chinaman? All doubt ended that night when the Frenchman returned and called together the guards and others. There was little discussion. He simply told them that they must wait, that the rebels were falling apart, and that the ether would be found by friends. They would not be threatened by thugs, he'd told them, that they had friends as well.

The Frenchman came into the lab, inspected the setup with an experienced eye. Pao realized that he knew the lab was finished, but his fiddling about was buying time for the Frenchman as well. He tasted the latest batch of pure heroin, smiling as Pao ran a crude purity test that showed it above 90%. They were interrupted by a guard, who told the Frenchman that the American had arrived.

Pao tried not to listen, but the Frenchman did not attempt to hide the heavyset American. Instead, he seemed to be drawing him further into the conspiracy by showing him the lab in detail. The man looked scared, sweat pouring through his ill-fitting bush shirt, his wrinkled tan slacks and black shoes pegging him as a military man, just like the thousands Pao had seen in Hong Kong.

With every new face he saw, Pao's anxiety rose. The more people who knew him, the slimmer his chances for escape. Last week, it was the beautiful woman. Now the American, the last thing he needed. It was one thing to be involved with Orientals, but a frightened American officer was a real danger. He'd spent his career as a master chemist making certain that he didn't know the people further down the pipeline, so he wouldn't find himself in this position.

The two men left to continue their conversation, and finally Pao heard the jeep crank and leave the village, followed shortly by the Mercedes. Now it was too quiet. The usual night sounds of dogs and the low voices of people were stilled, letting the mind fill in the blanks with the most paranoid thoughts. Pao tried not to listen to them, but he did move the chemicals next to the bed as he lay down to rest.

His dreams were jumbled, one nightmare following the next like a horror parade. He dreamed he heard drunken voices, men yelling and laughing in the night. He rolled over in hopes of shifting the dream when the first rifle opened fire.

All hell broke loose in the village. Bullets slapped through the walls of the lab, glass shattering as the fighting picked up. This was his chance. He soaked the mattress then crawled toward the lab, taking a deep breath as he reached the door, chemical smells from the broken beakers causing his eyes to tear. He gathered his courage and crawled rapidly through the room, ignoring the slivers of glass in his hands and knees. In the front room he bumped into the body of one of the guards sprawled in the doorway. He paused, thought a second, then pushed the lifeless form down the steps, to see if it drew fire. Nothing. He slid down the ladder, hit the ground running and headed for the edge of the village, away from the shooting.

Just then the lab blew up. Pao wondered for a moment if the mattress had set it off. He realized that his back and legs were stinging, debris from the blast blowing him to the ground. He pushed with his feet and elbows, every inch feeling like a mile, until he rolled into a ditch. The smell told him it was a sewer, but he didn't care. He could no longer see the muzzle flashes, he was out of the line of fire. He could go no farther, not now.

He heard women scream and children cry. The firing became scattered, the drunken voices louder. A woman screamed and screamed, until a single shot silenced her voice. The glow of the fire was bright, and Pao slowly crawled down the ditch through the mire, until he was hidden by an overhanging bush. He heard two men cursing, coming toward him. As he held his breath, they fired a clip at random into the place where he'd first hidden, ten feet away. Someone else shouted from the village, and they turned back, leaving Pao buried in shit.

The pain increased, pushing him into action. Soon, he knew, he'd pass out, and dying in a ditch full of shit was avoidable, he thought, even if he died elsewhere. Foot by foot he slid down the ditch, the evil laughter and the screams slowly falling behind him. Finally, he could see the berm of the dirt road. He rested a moment, heard Cambodian voices whispering frightened words above him. A water buffalo roared, unhappy with the night's bedlam.

Pao knew he could go no farther alone. He crawled up the bank, toward the family trying to push the buffalo cart faster down the road. A child started to scream when she saw him, but was hushed by the father. They lifted him to the back of the cart, on top of the pots and pans and bedding, and as the wheels creaked over, Pao called to the man in Chinese and French.

Pao started blacking out, giving in to the pain and exhaustion. As the blackness came on, Pao knew it might be death. He was at the mercy of these villagers, but he knew they were running, too. His clothes were stiff with the drying shit, his body aching and his mind screaming. There was another explosion from the village, as the bottles of gas heated in the fire. Pao reached out and pulled the man toward him. His last memory was the man nodding yes, he knew the place Pao repeated again and again.

XVIII.

The Groaning Board

"HERE COMES CAPTAIN Video," Larry Moss muttered under his breath. "Check the sunglasses."

Capt. Kew Son, the Cambodian army assistant press spokesman, came striding across the drive toward them, the legs of his fresh tan uniform bloused into spit-shined jump boots and a pair of aviator glasses wrapped around his small head, the latter picked up by Sam in Bangkok in return for a story tip.

This was what passed for the morning press briefing, reporters and photographers gathering in the garden of the old French villa that was Rang's headquarters. A parachute shaded the small restaurant that survived on the drinking habits of the foreign press. The journalists sat on small stools and picnic benches along metal tables covered with drinks, cameras and tape recorders. Bicycles and mopeds leaned against the trees and walls of the grounds. A large shipping crate stood on end, providing shelter for the bar and the small hot plate that served as the kitchen. A neatly lettered sign above the square hole cut into the box that hung down as a counter proclaimed the place as the "Groaning Board." Twice a day they would come, to socialize and to read the single sheet of lined school note paper Kew Son tacked to a nearby tree. Today, Kew Son was nervous about his mission. Colonel Rang told him that he planned to come, to pass the word. That was easy enough; Son sent his aide over to the hotel to tell the other drivers.

He'd first been puzzled by the Colonel's interest in talking directly with the journalists. Rang disliked having his name read to him by the President directly from the American paper clippings. One slip of the tongue and the heat would be on. Rang soon discovered the best way to avoid that was by saying nothing at all. He learned quickly that most times the journalists knew more than he did about what was really going on. Even more puzzling were the Colonel's instructions. Rang said that Sam Michaels had used pictures of an abandoned One-Oh-Five in a story and that he wanted Son to casually mention that the Americans thought it was staged. Son was to play "Official Leak," Rang's usual way of getting his side of the story out.

Son reigned supreme inside the villa, but out here, it was a free-for-all. This must be important for Rang to risk the dangers of talking to the reporters.

"So, Son. To what do we owe your honored presence? Could it have something to do with the war?" Moss started the razzing.

"You'll be pleased to know that Colonel Rang will join us. There are several matters he'd like to discuss." Son took off the sunglasses as he spoke, carefully polishing the lenses against the front of his taut shirt.

"Like exit visas for his family?" Sy Rosen grinned, digging Son with one of the running jokes at the briefing. Son had once, during the early days when they actually gave oral briefings, presented his habitually rosy outlook on the military situation. But when the briefing ended, he took a reporter aside and said, "I've gotta get out of here," and asked for help with visas.

"Mr. Rosen, sometimes you are cruel. We are doing our best." Son walked around the table and stood next to Rosen. He did a quick head count. About fifty people. Not a bad turnout on short notice. "Why do you dislike me?"

"I don't dislike you, Son, you know better than that. And I like your country. But I do dislike being lied to and being led around by the balls." Rosen was on now, keeping the smile but making his point. With a flourish, he flipped open his spiral reporter's notebook. "Now, Son, according to my notes, your army has killed every Khmer Rouge soldier at least three times."

"Rosen, be fair." Son just wanted to disappear.

"Yeah, Rosen, be fair. We taught them to body count, remember?" Sam sat midway down the table, his boots propped up on the next stool. He was in an ugly mood, studying those around the table carefully, trying to figure how many knew he'd been had.

"Guess you're right, Sam. Anyhow, why the special treatment, Son?"

"The Colonel will tell you."

"You think we can handle a live briefing by a live Colonel? It's been a while." Sam swirled his coffee in the large glass.

"I'm confident you gentlemen can." Son had to think fast. How to bring up the convoy. Should he ask Sam outright? No, that was too direct. Perhaps he could talk with Rider, who was chatting in the corner with Clive. He certainly outranked Sam. His concentration was broken by an argument at one of the side tables.

"Dammit, Sophan. You gotta move your armies around. You can't just sit there, building up defenses. You've got to attack." Steve Chan was playing *Risk* with Sophan, a board game that divided the world into sections. Each player manipulated his own armies and the winner eventually conquers the entire world.

They played the game every day, and it always came down to Chan, the aggressive Chinese-American, gobbling up the board while Sophan sat helplessly watching his elaborate defenses crumble.

"Right, Sophan, you've got to attack, that's how the game is played," interjected Son, leaning over the table for a better look. He appreciated the irony: men who saw war every day played a war game at night. To Son, his country was like the board—simply a platform for competing armies.

"Sophan do OK, you see," he said with a grin. "Sophan do OK."

Despite his fear of Rosen, Son felt comfortable with the Americans. That's why he had this job. He looked around the group for the new Swedish nurse, who reminded him of all those blondes he'd lusted after during his four years at Florida State. Most times he wore an FSU sweatshirt, but with the Colonel coming, he thought better of it.

"Hey, Son. Where's the briefing sheet?" Bill Byers needed its numbers and incidents to fill the cycle for the wire service.

"Because the Colonel will join us, we have dispensed with the briefing sheet."

"Ah, you're just pissed off about last week," Sam shouted, leaving Son to decide if he was the culprit. On a particularly bad day for the government, someone had slugged the sheet of notebook paper *Le Menu Du Khmer Rouge*. Fitting, they all thought, for their little restaurant.

"You make light of the situation sometimes." Son tried not to smile, but he found it impossible. He liked their humor, even if he were the butt of many of their jokes and one liners. He started to ask about the nurse, but realized he'd open himself up to another round of jabs.

"You know you're fucking up old Ziggy the Pole's whole day, not posting that sheet," Moss said. Ziggy was a friendly, fat Pole who hung out with them. He'd been sent here as part of a United Nations observation team for some event long forgotten, and it seemed that the Poles had forgotten him as well. He wasn't about to remind them. But if the day of reckoning with Warsaw ever came, he was ready. Every day, he went to the American Embassy and carefully culled material from old copies of *Time* and *Newsweek*, taking special care to collect notes from the transcripts of the Voice of America broadcast. Faithfully, he recorded each word from the morning and evening briefing sheets, filing the reports away with hundreds of other unread documents.

Sam held up his glass, taking a careful look at the iced coffee, searching for signs of life in the dirty water. "You know, maybe this is what's giving me the shits." No one took notice of the comment. A solid bowel movement by anyone living here was considered news.

"I have the cure." Claudine looked up from a two-month-old copy of *Paris Match*.

"I bet you do," Sam muttered.

"In desert, my husband takes the meat of the goat. Never have the shits." They both made an effort not to let the tension between them show.

"Garçon! Garçon! A goat, please. A goat for the honkie with the shits!" Rosen was loud, a living commercial for the pastis.

"Make sure it's Kosher killed," Sam said, pleased with his response. At first, he was bothered by Sy's Jewishness, his streetwise aggressive New York manner. He felt the man was compensating for his lack of looks, his self-perceived lack of class. But Sam soon realized that Rosen was under complete control, and his voice and manner were means to an end.

"Claudine, for the life of me, I can't figure out why you're sitting next to that honkie. I mean, look at some of the talent you have to choose from . . ." Sy ran his hand through his hair, thrusting his shoulder forward, posing in profile.

"... onn-kie?" Claudine looked puzzled.

"You know, redneck."

"Red-neck?" She gave Rosen a little grin and went back to the magazine.

Son watched Sam. He always looked the same, the faded workshirt and jeans, red bandanna around his neck, auburn hair touching his shoulders, the wings curling out on the sides. He spotted a jade Buddha on a gold chain around his neck. Son knew many Sams in Florida. He knew not to underestimate them. He also knew that grin, the friendly way Southerners acted when they were mad. Certainly he knew the pressure was being put on him about the stories, but there was more. Son could sense it.

Stoneman polished off his second *croix madame*, then turned back to his puss-swollen knee, digging again for the tiny shards of metal. "My Uncle Elbert, he use to pick buckshot out of his leg like that, after he'd gotten too close to somebody's moonshine still," Sam said, watching the operation as he stuck a chew of tobacco in his cheek. "He said the whiskey killed the pain."

"Obviously, Mr. Stoneman has found a better remedy with dope," Moss said. "Where is the good Colonel, Son?"

"He'll be here in a few minutes." Son knew he was running out of time. He had work to do. "Sam, I hear you did a story on a missing One-Oh-Five, some supplies."

"Yeah, near Ang Snoul." The question confirmed Sam's suspicion that he was the subject of the briefing. Rider turned from a conversation down the table to listen. "Why, you taking inventory?" A chuckle came from Ziggy at the end of the table.

"No, but we understand that it is not quite the way you reported."

"Are you saying I lied, made it up?" Sam was more

belligerent than he wanted. He glanced over at Rider, who acted nonplused.

"We have made a most diligent check, and we cannot confirm that either the gun or the supplies are missing. It is thought that the men pictured are government forces."

Sam waited for Son to ask him the specifics, but so far he'd skated. What did Sir Charles say on that dope sheet? Sophan was listening closely from his table.

"Look, Son," Sam said, putting his feet down and leaning across the table, "there were trucks, soldiers and a gun, and they claimed to belong to a renegade group. I just know what I'm told. . . ."

"But it was there . . ."

"Yeah, it was there. You think we rented the trucks and the guns?" Daddy always said the best defense was a good offense.

"Sam, I think you are missing the point. The question is who was supposed to take care of it, and where it is now." Rosen was interested.

Son shifted nervously. "I didn't say . . ."

". . . bullshit."

"Do I hear a drip?" Sam said, cupping his ear.

"More like a leak, I'd say. Anyone for riding down there and having a look at the gun?" Moss joined the baiters. Sam cut his eyes toward Moss. That was the last thing he needed. They were heading down there as soon as the briefing was over. Claudine had come to the room early that morning with the information, and damned if he wanted Moss in on the act. He knew too much already.

"Are you saying, Son, that the convoy never existed?" Byers pulled out his pad, looking for quotes.

"Look, all I know is that we checked on Sam's story, and there was no gun or convoy. It wasn't in Ang Snoul." Son was getting in deep, but he had his orders.

"Woaaa . . . what do you mean, 'it wasn't in Ang Snoul'? Was it gone, destroyed or again raising hell with the local populace? You just claimed it didn't exist." Son obviously knew only the bare details. "You calling me a liar, Son?"

Maj. Larry Bishop had slipped in behind Sam. "No, but there are a lot of people Stateside who'd like to know exactly what you saw."

"Boy, Son, you do have the strangest friends." Rosen stared at the Major. "Well, aren't we blessed. A real, live American army major." Bishop greeted Son, then walked around the table.

"Continue, gentlemen, continue." Bishop tried to be light and friendly, but he walked tight.

"Welcome to the Groaning Board Restaurant, Major," Sam said, trying to change the subject. "It's the only Michelin Three Star in Cambodia." His kidding hid the new knot in his gut. Now what?

"Check the GI low quarters and the white socks," Moss whispered in a stage voice.

Bishop laughed but kept alert as he shook hands around the table. "So this is the press club, huh?"

"You might call it that," Sam answered. "This and the swimming pool at the hotel and the Chinese whorehouse on Monivong Road and Chantao's opium den. Our club has a number of branches. Can we guess what brings you here this morning?"

"Just a friendly visit . . ."

"To spread a little truth and light, I bet." Rosen didn't buy the friendly visit.

"No. The Colonel is perfectly capable of taking care of that part. I'm here to find out about Sam's scoop." Bishop gave Sam a tight smile.

"Which means you have nothing to say." Rosen sighed with mock disgust.

" 'At the invitation of the host government,' isn't that the phrase?" Bishop stared him down.

"Well, we're just overwhelmed you came by," Moss said. "It's been at least a year since anyone from the embassy deigned to attend our humble briefing. Guess the smoke from the market flushed them out.''

"Let's rustle up some coffee for the Major here," Sam said, signaling the waiter. A wave of sizing up swept the table.

"Ya smoke dope, man?" Stoneman was looking a little mean. He always got mean around army officers.

"No, I don't, but thanks." He hesitated. "Don't let me stop you." Bishop looked Ty over carefully; sleepy eyes, ponytail and tattered GI fatigue shirt—the antithesis of an army man, he thought.

"It never has before."

"I read in *Reader's Digest* recently," Bishop said, clearing his throat, "that marijuana could be habit-forming." He wanted to distance himself from the drugs without being pushy.

Stoneman filled another empty Salem with weed. "You know, Major," he said, tapping the joint on the table by the filter, "I've been smoking dope every day for the past six years, and I don't think it's habit-forming."

The table rocked with laughter. Bishop smiled, but he felt put down. Yet there was something about this group that attracted him. All he'd ever heard in Vietnam was his fellow officers bitching about how they hated this part of the world, how they couldn't wait to get back to the States. Here was a bunch that called Indochina home. He noticed the rubber thongs hanging off Ty's feet. Many of these guys, Bishop suspected, had gone native. But he kept his thoughts to himself. Reilly had sent him here to question Sam and discredit the story, not to win friends.

"Ah, the 'Answer Man,' " Sy said as Son ushered Colonel Rang under the parachute.

"Good morning, ladies and gentlemen." Kew Son spoke loudly, to get their attention as the group made room for the Colonel to sit among them. "Colonel Rang would like to talk about a few matters. But first, we do understand that this is off the record unless otherwise agreed?"

"Let's agree otherwise, if the Colonel doesn't mind," Rosen shot back. If the information was off the record, it couldn't be attributed to Rang.

"I'm not sure that's what the Colonel wants, Mr. Rosen."

"I think he can probably speak for himself, Son." Rosen was respectful, but his point was clear.

"Yes, Captain Son," Rang said, taking the heat off his assistant, "I would prefer to stay off the record. But the gravity of the situation is such that I will go on the record." Rang had already lost face by coming to them, but he was more irritated by Son's blundering and especially by Bishop's presence.

"Fine . . . and thank you." Rosen flipped open his long, narrow notebook looking for a blank page. No one else spoke, everyone waiting for him to open the questioning. There was a moment of clicks and confusion as others turned on tape recorders. "You're concerned about the missing gun and convoy, I suppose?"

"Mr. Rosen, did I say there was a missing gun and convoy?"

"Ah, Colonel, Son just did, and Bishop here is claiming that Sam made up the story. Just what gives?" Byers was tight against deadline.

"Here is our problem. Mr. Michaels says on the television that there is a missing convoy and gun. He says it has been hijacked by our own soldiers. We find that a very serious charge."

"He's got to be kidding," someone muttered from another table.

"All right then. Are you saying that Sam is lying?" Rider took the offensive. Not that he hadn't been accused of lying, but he was harder to discredit than Sam.

"I do not know, Mr. Rider. I will not know that until Mr. Michaels shares some details with us."

"What do you want to know?" Sam was about to run out of bluff.

"Exactly where did you see this convoy."

"The pictures were taken down Highway 4, about ten klicks beyond the airport, near Ang Snoul."

"I see. In Ang Snoul?"

"I didn't say that. Near Ang Snoul."

"And who were the captors?" Rang was now wondering exactly how much Sam knew. A lot more than Reilly had imagined, that was for sure.

"They were renegades. Maybe the Ninth."

"Renegades? I have never heard of them. And if they did exist, why would they take such things? Only one gun. Supplies for a hospital. Why? I find this difficult to understand."

"Colonel, why don't you and Bishop run down there and ask them?"

"*Pardon,*" Sophan said from the back. "You talk to cameraman, OK?"

Out of the crowd came Sir Charles.

Rang nodded. Charles was one of his best Army photographers, and he was honest. Now there was no doubt that the pictures were of the captured supplies. So much for Reilly's idea of making a fool of Michaels in front of his colleagues. He fired a few quick questions at Charles, told him he'd like to chat later, and turned to Bishop.

"Major, it would appear that there were trucks and a gun out there. As to the renegade troops, well, we have to take their word."

"Whatever you say, Colonel." Bishop had felt Sam's discomfort, and now he knew why. Sam had fielded this hardball, but Bishop wondered if he was aware of Reilly's frontal assault back home? He smiled at Sam, wondering how he drank coffee and chewed tobacco at the same time.

"Well, Major, now that Sam's hanging has been called off, is there anything else we can do for you?" Bishop stared at Rosen, but said nothing. Others shifted uneasily in their chairs.

Rang took a deep breath, then said, "You have been

most helpful, gentlemen. I'm sure this matter will be investigated thoroughly.''

"Thank you, Colonel." Rosen snapped his notebook shut. "This whole thing is absurd. First, Son slips hints about a missing One-Oh-Five, then you show up and then what you say is overridden by Major Bishop. Just what is the purpose of this briefing. Is it about the missing convoy, or is it your way of laying off a fuckup on the press?"

"We will make a special effort to locate it, yes." Rang let the sentence drop.

"Why?"

Rang didn't answer Rosen's question. Stools scraped and people coughed around the tables. "Major Bishop, is the embassy catching heat for the convoy?"

"No comment." Bishop stared straight at Rang. This whole thing was about to blow up in their face.

"Then why did Son even bring it up? Is Colonel Reilly worried about the gun?" Rosen spoke softly.

"We are all worried about the gun."

"Is it still within range of the city?" Byers continued to take notes.

"That is what we're trying to determine here. If it is the same weapon used on the market, and what Sam tells us holds, then, yes, it could be."

"And someone, either your forces or the Americans, is responsible for it and the convoy. I see Reilly's hand in all of this, don't you, Major?" Rosen stared at Bishop.

"We are always concerned about lost weapons. I don't know that Colonel Reilly is more worried about this gun than any other. But you are trying to make something out of a gun, when a terrible thing has occurred right under your nose." Bishop spoke softly and evenly, hoping he'd said enough to get off the hook.

"I can only add one and one together. You're here, Bishop, and we're drowning in leaks about the One-Oh-Five. That's why we call it Reilly's gun."

"Hey, I like that," Moss chimed in. "Reilly's gun."

"What about it, Bishop?" Rosen held firm.

"I've said all I'm going to say, Mr. Rosen. This isn't my news conference."

"Major, they're all your news conferences. You're one of ninety-nine people hidden away in that embassy, and damn near anything that goes on in this country has something to do with somebody there. And when it comes to guns, I'd say that's your department." Rosen twirled his pencil in the wire spiral.

"You overestimate my position . . ."

"No, I don't think so, Major. Someone at the embassy is worried about that One-Oh-Five, and I think that someone is Reilly. That's why I'm calling it Reilly's gun. Since it was an American One-Oh-Five, and you gave it to them, then in a way it is still your gun." Rosen leaned on the table with his elbows. "Tell Colonel Reilly that we share his concern."

"I will . . ." Bishop rose, shook a few hands, and drifted toward the gate. There was low whispering around the tables as Rosen watched him leave. Son was very nervous, a line of sweat just above his lip.

"Gentlemen, I thank you for coming. . . ."

"Oh, sit down, Son. We had to eat breakfast anyway." Moss smiled, enjoying the Captain's discomfort. "Colonel, I take it we may hear about this gun again?"

Rang was standing now, but didn't duck the question.

"Yes. Yes, I'm afraid so. But don't let this one gun make you forget about the bigger problems of the war. That is all I ask."

"Don't worry, Colonel. We won't." Rosen watched as Rang followed Son to the jeep outside the gate of the villa. He remembered three years ago when all of the journalists hit Rang's house, peppering him with questions about the secret B-52 bombing, a story that broke in Washington. Rang had dangled in the wind for an hour, because he knew nothing. The Americans hadn't warned him or briefed him. Why should he do their dirty work now?

"What do you think they're trying to hide?" Byers asked of no one in particular.

"For once, I don't think they're trying to hide anything. Only who's responsible for spiking that convoy." Rosen emptied the glass of pastis in front of him.

"Just hope they don't zero in on Chantao's," Stoneman said, straining to save his hit.

"The Colonel has a good point, you know. We concentrate on what we can see, and that gun is only a small part of what's going on here." Moss turned off his tape recorder.

"Yeah, that may be true," Rosen said. "But it is also symbolic of what's going wrong in this war. The other side is armed to the teeth with captured weapons, and now someone has one close enough to zing the city, and if Sam is right, under the control of some pissed off troops. In my humble opinion, the point of all this is to pass the blame now that the war has come to Phnom Penh."

"Well, before it comes back, I'd better file," said Byers.

People were leaving now, small groups making their way out the gate. Claudine walked with Sam and Chan back toward the hotel.

Rosen walked quickly to join them. "Sam, you'd better get your ducks in a row on this one. I can hear the heavy artillery being rolled out. Good thing Rider's here. I just hope to God you have friends in New York."

Sam felt his stomach twist, Rosen confirming what he suspected. "Sy, I know I'm solid on this one."

"Solid's not good enough, Sam." Rosen nodded back down the walk toward Rider, who was walking with another group. "Something is coming down around here, and you're the designated scapegoat."

"Well," Sam said, going against his gut, trying to lighten the conversation, "if it comes down to that, I'll just have to find old Reilly's gun."

"Right. But don't let Reilly's gun get you."

⊕   ⊕   ⊕

Sam sat on the toilet, holding the telex he'd just received
level on the tile floor with his boots. The words would
make you shit. Not being able to shit wasn't one of Sam's
problems. He read it again and again.

RIDER/MICHAELS STOP PENTAGON AND STATE
STRONGLY DENY CONVOY CAPTURED OR PART
OF INTERNAL REVOLT STOP HOW PLEASE YOU
OBTAIN FILM AND INFORMATION STOP UNABLE
ANSWER THIS END STOP UNFORTUNATELY
STORY CAUSING RAMIFICATIONS HIGHEST LEV-
ELS COMPANY AND GOVERNMENT STOP KHMER
SPOKESMAN WASHINGTON SAYS QUOTE NET-
WORK IS TRYING TO CAUSE GRAVE PROBLEMS
BETWEEN KHMER REPUBLIC AND UUSS STOP OB-
VIOUSLY WORK OF UNINFORMED AND INEXPE-
RIENCE REPORTER ENDQUOTE WHY PLEASE
NONO ONE ELSE HAVE STORY QUERY ONLY
QUOTING YOU STOP RIDER ASSUMES STORY UN-
TIL MATTER CLEARED UP STOP LITTON

Sam could see the cloud passing over his name in New
York, the sunshine dimming on his ass. He could barely
think. Now it was official. It was obvious that the heavy-
weight was in to straighten out the stringer's mess. Well,
at least it was Rider.

Sam was exhausted, tired of everything. Ten thousand
miles away, the shit was hitting the fan. There was only
one thing to do with the cable.

He used it to wipe his ass and flushed it down the shit-
ter.

XIX.

Village Massacre

"LET ME MAKE sure I understand," Chan said, popping the top off the green soda bottle with his teeth. "Pha Doh says there was an attack there last night?"

"Yeah." Satterfield leaned against the side of the Mercedes, aiming streams of brown saliva at a mark he'd made in the dirt with his foot. "The dude said he'll be here in a few minutes, as soon as he gets a handle on what's coming down." They'd been met by one of Pha Doh's men, one who knew Marty from Nam.

"Sam," Chan said slowly, swirling the drink around in the bottle. "This whole deal sucks. What makes you think the lab is there? You sure you're not trying to get it all back at once?"

"Hey, you agreed to go to the village this morning, remember?" Sam heard the edge in his voice, a nerve touched. If Chan found out about Claudine, he'd shit and refuse to go. Rider told Sam to ignore the cable from New York, that if the story was good enough, they'd have to use it.

"Right, but that was before we found out about all this other bullshit. Let's see if I have this straight." Chan was serious. "Pha Doh says his men found a foreigner, a Chinese guy, out in the middle of hell and gone."

"You forgot the middle of the night. . . ." Christ, Sam thought, I don't need this.

". . . in the middle of the fucking night. And this dude is babbling about firefights and slaughter. Right so far?" He watched as the jeep with Pha Doh at the wheel appeared in the distance.

"Look, he has no reason to bullshit me." Marty's voice dropped an octave.

"OK, then tell me why, if this Chinese guy is so fucked up, they didn't bring him into town, put him with Dr. Jake."

"He won't go. He's afraid." Sam found it hard to sound convinced on this part. It just didn't wash.

"Right. You are aware, I hope, that we are going past the last government roadblock. That is no man's land out there, Tiger."

"It's where they're staying. The road's secure up to their bridge." God, he hoped he could trust Marty.

"Sam . . . Sam . . . ," Driver Joe called out, pointing back toward the city. Sam turned to see a speeding army jeep, closing in fast. He saw Reilly hunched over in the passenger seat, and Bishop and another American hanging on to the back seat. All were in civilian clothes. They flew through the village.

"I'll be goddamn . . ." Chan's voice quickly changed tone. "They've got balls to be running out here. . . ." They all jumped back into the Mercedes, Marty signaling to Pha Doh to turn around, to follow them. Sam pressed in next to Claudine as they took off after the speeding jeep. She gave him a knowing look.

"Don't lose them, but keep back. . . ." Sam was cranking up fast. "Oh, baby, baby . . . ," he muttered, his heart beating fast as he tried to keep the jeep in sight.

Sam gripped the handle on the dash, hanging on as they sped past motorized cyclos and bicycles. They were passing refugees now, their overloaded two-wheeled oxcarts plodding down the side of the road toward the capital. This confirmed for Sam that something bad had happened, or was about to.

"There they go." Chan pointed as the jeep turned left on a dirt road, stopped briefly at a roadblock, took off again and disappeared into a treeline. Sam thought he'd seen Bishop point back at them. When the Mercedes reached the turnoff, the five soldiers waved their arms for the car to stop. They were in no mood to negotiate. They had their orders. No press.

"I know another road. One klick farther." Driver Joe waved at Pha Doh to follow and smiled at the soldiers, backed the car onto the highway and slowly pulled away. The Cambodian soldiers seemed satisfied that they'd rebuffed them. None reached for the radio propped near the sawhorse that blocked the road. The soldiers were out of sight when they turned off again.

"You sure you know where this road goes?" Chan asked. He wasn't in the mood to drive into an ambush.

Driver Joe just nodded. They ran alongside a small river, trees on either side keeping them out of sight. At a river bend, they came upon a bridge. A small, dark soldier stepped onto the roadway and signaled them to stop. He wore a US army issue shirt cut off at the elbows, a pair of shorts and jungle boots. Everything was too big, which made him look like a child playing soldier. But the way the M-16 hung over his shoulder and the ammo clips stuck in every pocket indicated that these were his tools.

The soldier saluted smartly as Pha Doh swung from the jeep to the ground in a graceful move that did not betray his forty years.

"We must take jeep. Car cannot make road." He made room in the jeep while the crew got the cameras and spares out of the car. Marty trotted down to the camp and ducked into a tent. This Montagnard camp was somehow different from the Cambodian camps. Same tarps strung over holes, cooking fires burning around the lean-tos, women and children mingling with the soldiers, but everyone seemed alert. The soldiers kept their weapons slung or propped up near them; the mortar tubes glistened from cleaning, the shells were neatly stacked, ready to go. It would be hard to catch these people by surprise.

"Sam, grab the ditty bag. . . ." Chan tossed him the green map case, which held spare film magazines and batteries for the camera. Chan and Sophan hooked up, testing the camera and recorder. Claudine dropped a handful of film cans into the bag, hung an extra camera around her neck. Sam checked the batteries in the tape recorder stuck in the canteen case.

"You want some heat?" Marty held out a spare M-16. Slung over his shoulder was a Swedish K light machine gun.

"No. Allergic to those things." Sam started to ask Marty not to carry a weapon, but stopped himself. He wasn't part of the crew, and what he chose to carry around was up to him. American civilians weren't supposed to be around, but Marty was in deep enough shit not to care. But Sam did feel he should add: "Remember, Reilly is over there."

Marty just shrugged. "What do I care?" He took off his hat with the medals and jammed a battered jungle hat on his head. "Let's move."

Sam gave Claudine the front seat and squeezed into the back with Sophan and Chan. Marty sat on the right front fender. Pha Doh jammed the jeep into gear. They bounced across the bridge, down the dirt road for a few hundred yards, then took a hard left down a cow path that crossed the paddy dikes. Marty scanned the trees for snipers, the Swedish K across his forearms. Sam noticed a pair of fuzzy dice hanging off the rearview mirror. He nudged Chan and smiled.

"All he needs now is a stuffed dog with blinking eyes for the tailgate." They both chuckled, trying to break the tension of the ride. Sophan obviously coveted a pair for his old Mercedes. "OK, OK, I'll get you some." Sam had no idea where to find them, but he'd try. Sophan slapped his leg and grinned. The jeep roared, fighting to pull such a heavy load as the track turned to mud. They could see a thin wisp of smoke beyond the trees.

"Look. There." Pha Doh pointed with a stubby finger. Through the trees they could see Reilly's jeep. Sam tapped Pha Doh on the shoulder to stop. Chan was the first to hit the ground and head for the Americans, more than a hundred yards away. Just as he dropped to his knee to film, Reilly looked straight at them and barked a command. Within seconds, the jeep sped out of sight.

"Mother fuck . . ." Chan hadn't even had time to focus. He jumped up, towing Sophan along behind, and headed into the village. Four armed men moved toward them, M-16s pointed at their feet, fingers on the triggers. Claudine drifted off to the right.

"Heads up, Chan . . ." Sam and Marty moved out toward the soldiers. Pha Doh swung the jeep past them and cut off the soldiers. They saw the major's insignia on his tiger fatigues and threw a sloppy salute. He started yelling at them in a mixture of Vietnamese and Cambodian. They obviously had orders to keep people out of the village, but Pha Doh outranked the officer in command. The crew was able to move quickly through the trees. In the clearing, nothing was left of the burned huts but the stumps of base poles. Sophan and Chan went to work. There was another jeep on the far side of the village where a soldier held a radio headset to his ear, watching their every move.

"Sophan, I want you to find somebody who knows what's happening around here. Give me the soundbox." Sam took the wide leather strap off Sophan's shoulder and slipped it over to his. He glanced at the dials and shook his head. He was reminded how little his soundman knew about sound.

"Sammi, come here . . ." Claudine's voice called from behind a hedge row. The crew pushed through the bush and stepped over a low fence. In a ditch lay a woman. A dark trail of blood up the front of the sarong thrown over her body marked the path of a bayonet that had ripped her from crotch to throat. Two feet away, impaled on a fence, was the nude body of a little girl. The top of the stake protruded from her neck, her legs dangled on both sides of the wood.

"Mother . . . of . . . God . . ." Sam could hardly believe what he was looking at. Chan carefully shot the bodies from an angle so the pictures wouldn't make everyone blow their dinners. Indirect shots would tell the story by suggestion. Then he backed off and took a long, wide shot.

"This should wake the fuckers up in New York. . . ." Chan had long since forgotten the bitchy cable from his wife, but he never forgot his running war with New York.

They heard a moan. In a clearing ten yards away a young woman sat rocking on her haunches, a ripped piece of cloth covering her shoulders. Sam spotted the rope burns on her wrists and ankles, Chan started to film her, calling from behind the camera in a soft voice that it was all right, that he wasn't going to hurt her.

"Find out what happened," Sam whispered, pointing the shotgun mike toward her face to pick up the moans.

"Don't need to ask . . . she was gang raped." Four stakes lay on the ground nearby, lengths of nylon rope tied to the thick end. They formed a square in the grass, the impression of her body still there, the knee prints of her attackers making deep dents in the lower part of the square.

"Sam . . . Sam . . . ," Sophan called from far away. They headed back through the ashes of the huts, to where Sophan stood talking to an old man in a white shirt and a sarong. As they walked, the government soldiers jumped into the remaining jeep and headed down the road. They were now alone with the surviving villagers. Pha Doh sat in his jeep, defiantly staring down the road as they departed.

"Soldiers tell Pha Doh to leave. Pha Doh no want to leave," said the Major with a grin as the crew walked by. He'd kept the soldiers occupied, giving them time to shoot the story.

"This is headman," Sophan said, putting his hand on the old man's arm. "He say bunch of men come about midnight, they all drunk, attack the village. They have big fight over house over there. They take men from houses, say they communist and shoot them, burn the houses. The house over there, he say that where the Chinese man stayed. He say it blow up, big!" Sophan threw his arms out wide. The headman started babbling again to Sophan while Sam and Chan filmed the interview. "About an hour later, other men come. They shoot some drunk soldiers. They take some things from the big house." Sophan paused in the translation to ask more questions. Sam adjusted the sound level. Sam still wasn't positive what was going on, but he had a hunch that Claudine was keeping her promise, and he wanted to make certain he had the headman's version on film, a record of what happened, one that would stand up with Rider and in New York.

Sophan put his arm around the headman as he started to cry. "He say then first men come back, looking for something more, find nothing. They very angry. They rape women, kill children . . ." Sophan's voice trailed off in sympathy.

"Get down here," Marty called from down an embankment, "they're trying to hide some of the bodies."

"Find out all you can, Sophan, and see if he knows why Reilly was here," Sam called over his shoulder as he followed Chan. On the edge of the village nearest the highway, a ditch was full of bodies wrapped in sarongs, interspersed with brown burlap bags. There was no bier, no monks to do the final rites. He suspected the soldiers had been waiting for a truck.

"Keep up, dammit . . . ," Chan barked at Sam and broke into a trot, pulling the umbilical cord tight.

There were eleven bodies in the pile, mostly men. Chan panned down from the faces of the men looking at the pile of bodies. At least two had smashed skulls, probably beaten to death with rifle butts. Sam suddenly realized that the three men standing by the bodies, the injured woman, and the headman were the only people around. Everyone else had either left or was dead. Now he really wanted to talk to the man Pha Doh's people had found.

"Just a couple more shots . . . think about a close . . . ," Chan whispered as he worked. Claudine went back to the jeep for more film. Sam stared at the rubble of the nearby house. Sticking out of the ashes were a half-dozen tall bottles, like the ones he'd seen on the ship. Could this have been the lab? "Right . . ." Just as Sam answered, three sharp *chunks* rang out from somewhere beyond the treeline. Chan dived into the ditch next to the bodies, Sam landed on top of him.

"Fuckin' M-79s . . . ," Marty yelled as he hit the ground. Grenades had been launched from M-79s, stubby sawed-off shotgunlike weapons. One round exploded in a tree. Another landed behind them.

Sam knew Sophan was hit from his cry of pain. Chan pushed Sam away, swung the camera back toward the clearing just as the third round exploded. Through the grass they could see Sophan rolling over and over, his hand in his crotch. The headman lay limp as a rag beside him.

"Drop the box . . . get to Sophan . . ." Chan reached for the soundbox and put it next to the camera. Pha Doh tried to reach the crew but his jeep stalled, and he cranked for what seemed like minutes. Sam ran on by the jeep down the road toward Sophan. His heart banged inside his chest.

"Sophan . . ." Sam rolled him over. His sunglasses had smashed into his face, covering it with bleeding cuts. But that was the least of his problems. The grenade had sprayed his thighs and crotch, and a patch of fresh, dark blood spread across the front of his tan slacks.

"Move . . . Sam . . . move . . ." Satterfield pulled him away, reached for Sophan's belt and roughly ripped off his pants. Blood spurted wildly from the inside of his thigh. Sam looked around. Pha Doh checked the headman, then let his body roll to the side. He unwrapped a compression bandage as he ran toward Marty.

Sam wanted to throw up. Sophan's blood was spurting across Sam's chest. The Cambodian's eyes were glazing as he lapsed into shock.

"Let's get him to the jeep. . . ." Pha Doh had his hand clamped inside Sophan's thigh to stop the squirting blood. The bandage was on the other leg. They hoisted him into the passenger seat, Pha Doh twisting to keep his hold while they moved. Everyone else hopped in as Marty pointed the jeep down the road.

"We have to go back to Driver Joe," Sam said, gripping Pha Doh's arm to keep him from falling out. They bounced back toward the bridge, the jeep loaded like a tiny circus car. "What about the Chinese man?"

"We'll grab his ass and take him with us. They'll find him out here." Marty blew the horn, letting the alert Montagnards know they were returning.

Driver Joe opened the back door of the Mercedes, and they laid Sophan across the back seat. Claudine and Pha Doh knelt uncomfortably on the rear floor, keeping the pressure on his groin, trying to comfort Sophan. Pha Doh's medic broke out compression bandages, gave him a shot of morphine, then shook his head.

"Who did it, goddammit . . ." Sam was on the verge of angry tears.

"Who do you think? Reilly is well known as a consummate asshole. It doesn't matter, man. We got to get him to a good cutter, quick.'' Marty had seen his people fall before. For Sam this was a first he could do without.

Two Montagnard women slowly led a Chinese man from a tent up to the jeep. His body was covered with a yellowish salve, bandages over part of his face. As they put him into Pha Doh's jeep, he protested in Chinese and English, calling out a name.

"You guys get Sophan out of here. We'll take care of this dude.'' Marty tossed his weapon to one of the soldiers.

"We're taking him to the Russian Hospital . . . Dr. Jake's over there.'' At least Sam was thinking straight.

"No. Take him to Calumet. We'll find Dr. Jake.'' Chan was thinking straighter. Calumet, the French hospital, was much cleaner. Even with Driver Joe's skill it would be thirty minutes before they'd get to the hospital, so Sam forced himself to work. He pulled the Olympia from its battered case, found some copy paper and wrote a script. He played it straight, trying to stick with the headman's story, not blaming anyone, wondering what brought it on. He glanced up, looked at the speeding jeep ahead, and for a moment thought of asking Driver Joe to stop them, let him talk to the Chinese man, find out what he knew. He thought he knew the reason for the attack last night, and maybe the Chinese guy could confirm it. There was some good reason this place was wiped out. Things were starting to add up. Now he needed proof. As for Reilly, that could wait. Sophan was jerking from rushes of pain. He worked in the shaky shot of Reilly and Bishop, hoping that it would show enough to prove that they were there.

Sam studied the script. Reilly and Bishop either showed in the shot or they didn't. This one was too strong, showed too much of Sam's feelings, but he was in no mood to change it. The words told what the pictures were about, but didn't describe the pictures. He'd give himself an *A* for writing and a *C* for objectivity. It would have to do.

Besides, they probably wouldn't use the story, not with this latest layer of shit.

Sophan's low moans pulled him back to reality. Ordinarily Sam would have stopped at the airport to put the film on the first flight to Bangkok or Hong Kong, but he knew that Sophan couldn't stand the wait. He decided to voice the story later, let someone else worry about getting the film on the airplane. He could concentrate on getting Sophan patched up and out of here.

"Sammi, he is resting . . . ," Claudine called in a soft voice. She held her hand out toward Sam, showing him the small vial of morphine. For once, her habit had helped a friend. Sam's heart raced when he looked back at Sophan; he looked dead. Sam saw his eyes moving inside the lids. Thank God, he thought.

When they reached the outskirts of the city, Marty waved and turned toward the Russian Hospital to fetch Dr. Jake. The Mercedes turned onto Monivong Boulevard. They had made it this far. Sam found himself praying that they could get him patched up and into a decent hospital. Sophan began moaning, struggling. Sam watched as Pha Doh unbuttoned his shirt to cool him off. There was nothing on his chest. Sophan wasn't wearing his Buddha.

XX.

Sophan's Balls

"I SAID PUMP the bloody thing . . . pump, man!" Dr. Jake reached over Sophan's head with a blood-spattered glove and pressed down on his assistant's hand, flexing hard the rubber bladder that controlled the anesthesia. Sophan stirred on the table, the anesthesia giving out. Some of the gouges in his groin and thighs were clean now, but there was more digging to be done.

"I swear to God . . ." Dr. Jake said, wiping his forehead on his shoulder then going back to work. "OK, Claudine, get ready with with light." Sam stood across the operating table, rubber surgical gloves pulled to his elbows. He did whatever Jake told him to, handling instruments, holding clamps, probing for pieces of shrapnel. Claudine stood next to him with the portable television light. At least the Calumet was clean, but the facilities were as overspent as the country, the huge operating light over the table doing little more than illuminating the room, the generator incapable of powering it properly.

"All right, mate, this is the tricky part. I'll need a

steady hand here." They'd been operating for more than an hour, all of them completely soaked in the wet hot air of the surgery. Dr. Jake led Sam's hand under what was left of Sophan's testicles. The scrotum was shredded, but his balls were still intact. "Hold steady up there, and I'll try to sew around your fingers."

"If you save his balls, will they still work?" Sam felt his own tighten.

Dr. Jake peered over the top of his half-framed glasses. "Doubt it. I'm even doing this against my better judgment. He might lose them later on. But I'll leave that decision to someone else. Here . . ." Dr. Jake pointed to several entry wounds to the side. "I'm afraid the real damage to his love life is in there."

"Can he travel? I want to get him out of here." Sam swallowed hard, the blood oozing over his gloved finger.

"He shouldn't be moved, but that's irrelevant. Forget today. I've got to get him stabilized. See what you can do about tomorrow morning." Dr. Jake's huge hands wove the tiny needle and fine thread with skill. "Someone must go with him."

"Can you?"

"Sam, I see a hundred patients a day. You expect me to leave them?" He shot Sam a glance without stopping his work. "Light, please, Claudine." She turned it on, holding it on the area between Sophan's legs. It was starting to dim, only a few minutes to go on the last battery belt. "Look, I need the break, bad. I'll go, but we'd better take that Chinese guy out too."

"Shit, forget all about him. Is he here?"

"No, I looked at him in the jeep. They took him somewhere else. Bloody bastard is scared shitless." Sam watched as Dr. Jake pulled the skin back together and made some sense of the bloody mess. Sam swallowed hard, felt tears welling in his eyes for the second time that day. "Just be glad we're only worried about Sophan's love life. He's a strong man. He's brought himself this far."

Dr. Jake moved Sam's hand, nodded to Claudine to kill the light and stood back. "That's the best I can do."

Sam carried the plasma bag as they moved Sophan to an already cramped room down the hall. He was obviously in agony. Dr. Jake had somehow scrounged the plasma, but painkillers were out of the question. The last batch had never made it from the airport to the hospital. "Claudine, can you get more morphine?" Sam whispered the question.

"Yes." She gently stroked Sophan's head, giving Sam a glance of resignation over the surgical mask.

"I've got to find Kip, get a plane," said Sam. "I'll be back here later." Once they settled Sophan in, the crowd descended on the room. The two wives acknowledged one another with their eyes and took positions on each side of the bed. Ming stood in the hall, within sight of her lover. Carefully, Sam walked down the hall, the exhaustion of the day setting in. Rider cut him off just outside the hospital door.

"They closed the fuckin' telegraph office. I argued that it was two hours early, but they said they had their orders. No telephone, either." Rider and Rosen had shown up as soon as the word on Sophan hit the hotel. Sam had filled them in on the details of what they had seen down the highway and what happened. He'd given them a copy of the script.

"Did any of the wires file it?" Sam felt the uneasiness return. A chopped up soundman, a dicey story, Reilly. This was getting out of hand.

"No," Rosen answered. "Byers tried to get down Highway 4, but they have the road closed now beyond the airport. Claim the Khmer Rouge have cut the highway." Rider wiped his brow with a handkerchief, then flipped through the notes he'd taken from Sam. "You sure that was Reilly out there?"

"Yeah, it was him all right. We have it on film . . . a little out of focus and range, but it's on film. Maybe Claudine got something.'' Sam sat down on the steps of the old colonial building. ''Nothing I can do about that now. I've got to get Sophan out of here in the morning.''

''We're working on that,'' Rider said. ''Kip's willing to fly him to Bangkok. Does Sophan have travel papers?''

''I doubt it. He went to Hong Kong last year when he was hit in the leg, but they only gave him a temporary passport.'' Sam rubbed his face in his hands, the smell of dried blood flooding his nose.

''Guess he'll need a 'greenback visa,' so take some money with you for Kip.'' Rosen got up. ''He's at his bar. I'll give you a ride.''

''I'll keep an eye on Sophan,'' Rider said. ''Should have brought boxing gloves for all these women.'' He squeezed Sam's arm and went back inside.

Sam didn't speak during the ride, closing his eyes and trying to sort out events. The Khmer Bar was so dark that, even coming in from the unlit street, Sam had to wait at the door for his eyes to adjust. Sam spotted Kip's blond hair. He was at a table in the corner. Rosen stayed at the door.

''Hey, appreciate you lining up a plane. Did you get the DC-3?'' Sam pulled a chair up to the round table. It was packed with pilots and their collection of women. Country music drummed from an old Wurlitzer in the corner, the dull needle pulling sound from records for the thousandth time. From behind the back door, Sam caught a strong whiff of opium.

''Yeah. It's the only plane old Mama-san's got with papers for Thailand.''

''Good enough. Dr. Jake is going with you. Sophan's in lousy shape. Speaking of papers . . . I don't think he has any.'' Sam eased into the problem.

Kip looked at Sam and took a long draw on the cigarette. ''They'll hassle him in Bangkok. But if you have an ambulance to meet us, they'll release him to the hospital and your people can fight the paperwork later on.''

Sam was relieved that Kip didn't see it as a problem. "OK, in case things get squirrely, here's some bread." Sam handed Kip five one hundred dollar bills. "Just as backup."

"Right, that could help. I've got to have the bird back early, so I want to take off at seven." An attractive lady sat down by Sam, looking for a date. Kip said something sharply to her in Chinese and she left, pouting.

"Fine. We'll be there." Sam gripped his hand and held it for a moment. He didn't know Kip that well, but at this moment he was coming through like a friend. "I'll try and return the favor."

"You'll probably get the chance. Seven o'clock sharp." Kip squeezed his hand and turned back to his beer.

Sam followed Rosen out the door and back to the car. They drove down the road toward the hospital as the town got ready for curfew.

"Funny thing. I always thought it would be me who got zapped. Not Sophan." Sam lit a Salem and leaned against the window.

"Sam, you keep this up and it *will* be you. Ease up. You act like you've got a tiger on your ass. You're trying to win every point and either you're going to burn out or make a bad mistake." He wasn't lecturing Sam, just talking his mind. He paused, wheeled the car around a bicycle, then picked up speed. "What made you go out there?"

Sam told him about Pha Doh, about the mysterious man, but he didn't mention Claudine. "Guess I fucked up, huh?"

"Today wasn't a mistake. You were right in going, right in following Reilly. Who do you think fired on you?"

"Well, the last soldiers had been gone about five minutes. It sounded like it came from the east. Your guess is as good as mine."

"I'm almost afraid to guess." Rosen drove on in silence until he reached the hospital parking lot. He turned to

Sam, then sighed. "It was because of Claudine, wasn't it?"

Sam didn't answer, covering the silence by lighting a cigarette.

"Rider and I are old friends, Sam. He had to know whether it was you or Stoneman. You're clean, right?"

"Yeah." Sam felt deep exhaustion sweep over him. "Did you know?"

"I suspected as much. It could have been me at one time. I sent out a lot of her stuff in my pouch. I got lucky. She nearly OD'd in my room one night, and Chantao filled me in. Guess I should have told you, but she seemed to have cleaned up her act."

"Is Chantao part of this?" For a journalist, Sam realized he'd missed the obvious.

"No, not part of the operation. She's very attached to Claudine, and keeps her supplied during tough times." Rosen took the cigarette from Sam and took a pull. "Couple of years ago, Claudine tried to go cold turkey at Chantao's, but it didn't work."

"I pick 'em good, don't I?"

"Hey, don't get down on yourself. Just remember, if it comes down to you or her habit . . ."

"Bet on the habit . . ."

"A pisser, but true. How did she get you in this mess?"

"Said she would show us the lab, or at least where it's located. I think she wants to get out of this, Sy. I really do." Sam flicked the cigarette out the window.

"Yeah, I hope so. Reilly has a massive hard-on for you, and it would appear you are now fucked with the Chinaman."

"Maurice?"

"You said that, I didn't. Remember, you have no proof."

"Well, Sy, I can't see any way out but forward, that is if I keep the job that long." Sam opened the door and started to get out.

"Maybe you should go to Bangkok with Sophan, give things here time to settle down." Sy touched Sam on the arm. "Just free advice."

"Much appreciated, but I think I'll stay." Sam got out, shut the door and waited for Rosen to walk with him into the hospital. "Besides, my ol' daddy always said, 'Don't let the bastards get you down.' "

"This time I just hope your old 'daddy' is right."

XXI.

Reilly's Balls

"I CAN DO it myself," Reilly heard himself say, pulling his body step by drunken step up the stairs of the villa. The houseboy stayed one below, ready to catch the staggering colonel. It was a drill he'd learned from the former houseboy his first day on the job.

Reilly got out of his pants and shoes, banged into the shower stall in his undershorts, socks and shirt and turned on the water. Two days had passed since he'd showered or slept. He slowly slid to the tile shower floor, letting the cold water pepper the top of his head.

Until two hours ago, Reilly had done OK, at least by his standards. But the visit from Rang was the final blow, all it took to pop the cork out of the bottle. He had no desire to sober up, or for that matter, to live. The tiger had jumped up and bit him; the East victorious once again.

The market attack. The village massacre. The Chinaman. The gun. The pictures. Each event carried its own name in his mind, any one capable of driving a man over the edge. But he'd stood up to each one, dealt with them, then was hit with the next. Towns got hit, that was all, and he was unlucky enough to be the overseer. They made it look like the work of the Khmer Rouge; they'd come up with the bodies to prove that. Not exactly the sort of thing he wanted, but one he could explain.

The market attack could fall under the same alibi. How many people knew about the gun? Even the reporters wouldn't go that far out on a limb, claiming it was the same gun. But it was, and it would hit again, he knew that.

Reilly rolled over onto his knees and dry heaved into the drain. As he shook his head to clear it, the memory of the village rushed in. His mistake was going back out there. But what choice did he have? His motive was clear enough; there was a message from the Chinaman. The Frenchman was smooth, making Reilly hate him more. He'd shown him the lab as though he were on a school show-and-tell trip, explaining the process to the smallest detail.

Reilly crawled out of the shower, through the bedroom to the bedside table, and fished out the quart bottle of gin. A long hit settled his head, the warm rush soothing his frazzled nerve endings. He pulled the cover off the bed to cut the draft on his wet body from the window air conditioner.

That wasn't the message, however. The Frenchman didn't drag him that far into the boonies at night to give him a lesson on heroin processing. No, he wanted him to have a long look at the pictures. There were an even dozen, all enlarged, showing him in numerous sexual positions with the boy, recognizable in all. He knew others were missing. His days in intelligence had taught him that there had to be at least one roll, thirty-six frames.

That's why he went back this morning, to find the pictures. The big house was in shambles, the lab burned to the ground. He couldn't tell Bishop why they were there, other than to investigate. And the soldiers had gotten it all wrong. He'd ordered them to keep Michaels from filming, not to open fire. Now the soundman was full of holes, and he knew his name was all over the story. In two days he'd have to explain; the ambassador was returning from Washington. His inquiry cables already loaded Reilly's desk.

He'd handled all these things, or at least had beaten them back. But the visit from Rang took him out at the knees. The lab was gone, Rang agreed. The Chinaman would make other arrangements. The ether bottles were moved again two days before, when the renegade soldiers turned on their mastermind and killed him. None of the pieces would fall into place.

There was one more matter that Reilly needed to be aware of, however. Rang's formal style made Reilly even madder. The pictures.

What about them, he'd asked.

Well, I've brought the prints. The Chinaman is an honest man, Rang had said.

And the negatives?

They're gone.

Gone?

They're with the Renegades, they took them when they attacked the village. Turns out one of our men, who ''unfortunately'' died this morning, was playing both sides, telling the Renegades about our ''understanding.''

Where are they now?

With the gun. With the Renegades.

Reilly tried to throw up, stopped gagging, turned the bottle of gin straight up and watched the bubbles as he poured it down his throat. He had forty-eight hours before the ambassador returned, forty-eight hours to clean out his rice bowl. No one knew that better than Rang.

Well, he could drink now, because he'd already set the wheels in motion. He'd see to it that the gun, and the Renegades, were destroyed.

XXII.

Midnight Message

"WOULD YOU SHUT up and listen, man?" Satterfield slumped down in the seat of the Mercedes. "I'm just the messenger boy on this one."

"I've got enough coming down tonight without this." Sam had just left Sophan at the hospital, the past two hours spent feeding him opium and morphine for the pain and watching his wives and girlfriend cut one another up with dirty looks across the bed. Marty had been trying to talk for the entire five minutes they'd been in the car, and Sam couldn't stop babbling.

"Claudine told me to get your ass to Chantao's. She wants the Chinese dude to go out on the flight." Marty had brought the morphine over from Chantao's for Claudine.

"What does she think this is, a fucking airline?" Sam was at the end of his rope. He'd finally gotten through to New York on a terrible phone line to tell them about Sophan, and all they wanted to talk about was the story. Someone was trying to steer them off of the village massacre, even before they'd seen the film. Said they wanted Rider to do the story.

"Take a little advice from your one-balled friend. You're sweating yourself into a Court Martial. What's done is done, and tomorrow ain't here yet. Stay loose." Marty took another pinch from the Levi Garrett pouch he'd stolen from the glove box.

"Look, I can handle somebody getting zapped on a story, but this sucks, man." Sam crammed the struggling Mercedes into a lower gear and threaded the next road-block at high speed, the tires squealing. "That should wake them up."

"Yeah, just enough to squeeze a trigger." Marty slid lower in the seat.

"I'm sorry, but it seems to be coming in from all sides."

"You're blaming yourself. You've never lost anybody in combat, have you?"

"No, and I didn't plan to, either." Sam gave Marty a tight grin, acknowledging the stupidity of the statement. "And of all people, it had to be Sophan, and on this story. . . ."

Marty held up his hand to stop Sam. ". . . let me tell you about the first troop I lost."

"Yeah, OK . . ."

". . . I'd been in-country for about two days, hanging around Pleiku. They'd set up a little night ambush near a village about twenty klicks out, then the platoon leader comes down with the terminal shits. They packed my green ass on a chopper and sent me in to lead." Marty spit out the open window, then looked straight ahead for a moment. "That was a fucking joke."

"And . . ."

"And, we got out to the ambush site, set out a few Claymores, and here I am, doing things by the book. These dudes trusted their lieutenant, and unfortunately, had the same trust in me. They lay back from the trail the way they'd been taught, but I had to show them how smart I was, so after we'd been in position a half hour, I crawled around and moved a couple of them, just like in the book." Marty pointed ahead, at a sleepy sentry with a rifle held loosely in his hands. "Keep an eye on that dude. . . ."

"Right." Sam slowed, making sure the sentry saw they were westerners.

"Funny, I haven't told anyone this story in years. Anyhow, about ten VC came boogying down the trail, and we got 'em cold. You could hear them for a mile, talking and thrashing through the brush. The first three caught a Claymore in the chest, three more were dropped on the spot, and the others ran."

"Sounds pretty good to me."

"Yeah, except for the guys I moved. One of them popped up, and three of his own people cut him in half. They didn't expect him there."

". . . because you moved them?"

"Brilliant deduction, Watson." Marty shifted the tobacco from side to side in his mouth, looking for moisture. "Worst part is that none of them blamed me. I expected the roof to fall in when we got back, and the old man just shrugged. 'That's why it's called on-the-job training,' he said."

"Yeah, that's tough." Sam turned the car down the side street near Chantao's, heading for his usual parking spot. Was Marty trying to make him feel better, or tell him he'd fucked up the same way with Sophan? He jerked the steering wheel hard, barely keeping the car out of the deep sewer ditch.

"Jesus, Sam."

"Sorry." He pulled back in, edging close to the ditch to clear the road. "I put it in there one night. Cost me fifty bucks to get it out and fixed. The Chinaman is picky about his cars."

"I really don't know whether I should be saying this," Satterfield muttered, watching Sam turn off the lights.

"Oh, God. Mystery time." Sam really couldn't handle

much more. All he'd wanted to do was get to Chantao's
and have a couple of pipes, give his mind a rest. Now
Chantao's was getting complicated.

"I think we should go find the gun. . . ."

"You what?"

"Pha Doh says he can take that gun." ·

Sam turned in the seat. "Reilly's gun?"

"None other . . ."

"Where?"

"Somewhere south of town. They move it around every
day. If they fire it off again, we should be able to run it
down."

"What makes Pha Doh think he can find it?"

"Look, once you know the general area, and what they
have in mind, you can pretty well draw an arc on the map
and figure out the location."

"Well, I don't know . . ."

"If you want to go on a little spontaneous operation
with the Montagnards, it can be arranged. You'd be going
with them, not the other way around. They don't care
much for the chappies who are running this scam."

"Scam?"

"I'm filling in the blanks like everyone else, but I can
confirm this much. They're the remnants of a battalion
that's decided to fight their own war. Same ones who
shelled the market. Pha Doh hears they are the ones who
ripped off the stuff from the convoy."

"This doesn't make sense. Why would they want to
shell the city?"

"To let folks know they're serious."

"You mean the government."

"Not necessarily."

"Who?" Sam tried his best to follow the logic.

"Well, Pha Doh says the stuff belongs to the Chinaman."

"The stuff from the ship."

"Yeah, but there's a lot more to it than that. He did some checking on that village."

"And . . ." Get to the point, Sam wanted to scream.

"That burned-out house was a heroin lab."

"I thought so." Sam flashed on the bottles sticking out of the ashes. Did they have Reilly in the pictures? God I hope so, he thought. "The Chinaman's lab."

"The man has a claptrap mind . . ." Marty started to open the door.

"And Reilly wasn't out there for his health . . ."

"You'd never be able to prove that . . ."

"I know. I'm just trying to find the pressure points."

"I've known a hundred Reillys. He's just trying to survive, and maybe he got sucked up in this thing. Could be money, pussy, God knows what. But you'll never prove it."

"You think he's the one jerking my chain."

"Who else could do it so fast? He got on the blower to the Pentagon, and they leaned on your foreign desk. It makes sense, you know."

"Well, maybe I'll never get to put the wood to Reilly on the village, but I like the idea of getting his gun."

"Once we figure out where it is. If we get lucky, and it's still in Pha Doh's sector, we should go."

"Guess it would help if we knew the exact location?" Sam knew it was a stupid question.

"Yeah, it sure would. Let me think about it."

"Think about it?" Now Sam really wanted to scream.

"Look. It's bad enough to have civilians along on a deal like this, without one swearing vengeance. Those kind tend to wind up dead."

"I'm cool. I just want pictures of that gun."

"OK. This time you are with us. But our rules."

"OUR rules?" Sam dragged it out.

"Yeah. Mine and Pha Doh's." Marty got out of the car and started walking down the dark road. Dogs started barking, first one, then many. Sam locked the car and jogged to catch up.

"Thanks for the talk. I needed it bad. If we do the trip, we'll do it your way."

"Yeah, I figured as much." Rabbit was at the gate to meet them, alerted by the dogs. They were silent until they entered the den, the bare bulb over the refrigerator hurting Sam's eyes.

"Ah, Sammi." Claudine held open the beaded curtain that led into Chantao's living quarters. "Please, come."

"I don't like this," Sam muttered to himself as he followed. She entered a small room, where the Chinese man they'd picked up in the village lay on a cot, his body covered with bandages. Chantao sat on the edge of the cot, talking softly to him in Chinese.

"He must go too. He cannot stay here." Claudine held Sam's arm tightly as she whispered.

"Claudine, I'm putting Sophan on a plane without papers. I figure Kip can talk him into the country. But there's nothing I can do about this guy. Who is he?"

"Chantao's cousin . . ." Chantao looked up at Sam as Claudine spoke.

"First cousin, third cousin, what?" Sam had long since learned about Chinese family ties. They were endless in the western mind.

"You must not ask such things." Claudine was getting angry. "He has papers. You must do this for Chantao."

"Tell Chantao that I'll get him on a commercial flight tomorrow, I promise."

"No. He must go on your airplane."

"Why?" Sam watched Chantao turn away, rejected. She knew by the tone of his voice that he objected.

"Sammi, I do not think you want to know."

"He rides on my flight, I have a right to know."

"He is in trouble with the Chinaman."

"Shit. Just what I need. What kind of trouble?" Sam was dying for a pipe, the smell of opium filling his nose.

"That I cannot tell you. Just take him out." She looked him full in the face. "I know you do not feel good toward me now, but for Chantao, you do this thing?"

Sam detected desperation in her voice. "Well, if he has a passport, I guess he can go. Can Chantao get him to the plane? We're taking off at seven."

"That has been arranged." Claudine switched to French, telling Chantao that Sam had agreed. Chantao stood and embraced him. She took him by the hand to the front room, dug through a wooden box, and pulled out two ampules of clear liquid.

"More morphine," Claudine said from behind him. "For Sophan."

"Merci," Sam said, smiling at Chantao. Inside, his anger built. He wanted to scream at Claudine, say that she has no right to ask more of him, but he couldn't. His head wanted a pipe, but he knew every minute he stayed here, Sophan would suffer. As though she were reading his mind, Rabbit came into the room with two loaded pipes and the Howdy lamp and set them on the floor. He felt strange lying on the floor in his roadrunning clothes and boots. He told Claudine to fetch Satterfield for a smoke. He really felt out of place when Marty came in wearing a sarong. Between smokes, he filled Marty in.

"I'd do the same thing, Sam, but I think you should know this is hot stuff." Marty nodded toward the room where the man lay.

"Right now, I don't want to know why."

"Ah, you're getting into the program." Marty grinned as he picked up the pipe.

"Ignorance is bliss," Sam said, feeling the first rush.

"Do you mean the 'ignore'?" Claudine tried to translate the word.

"Yeah, ignore the obvious."

"There is a time you must be true to your friends, Sammi. This is one of the times." Claudine nodded toward Chantao.

"Yeah, and ignorance of the law is no defense," Sam muttered, remembering his brief prelaw days.

"There ain't no law here, Sam. You just make it up as you go along."

"Yeah, you be sure to tell that to the Chinaman." Sam let the rush take him away, but not so far that he couldn't come back and finish out the night. The knot in his stomach eased, his neck snapped like a whip when he moved it from side to side. Right now, he wanted quiet, not people, but that wasn't going to happen.

XXIII.

Bangkok Flight

"A DEAL'S A deal, Mama-san." Kip towered over the old lady, watching as Sam Michaels and his friends gingerly loaded the injured Cambodian into the DC-3. She'd tried to double the price the moment she saw the stretcher, and now she wanted him to take more passengers.

"No, no. This international trip. Need more money. Must pay in Thailand." She clutched at the wad of money inside her blouse as she talked.

"They'll take care of that. Look, we'll be back here by one, two o'clock. We'll make another flight for you to-day." You can rob those folks, he thought.

"You take other passengers. Beaucoup room. You take!" She shuffled back toward the shed that served as an office. Kip stood on the ramp, cleaning his sunglasses and looking at the airplanes. He was always impressed by the collection. A man could start an antique aircraft museum from the birds squatted in front of him. Just about every prop transport built since the thirties was there. The tired old iron had found its way here, just about the last

place the planes could legally fly. Mama-san even had a
Boeing 307 up in Battambang, awaiting an engine. Shit,
that's the old passenger version of the B-17, the same bird
Howard Hughes flew to set a coast-to-coast speed record
before World War II.

"The passenger is all strapped in," DeRosa said, talk-
ing as he walked toward Kip. "The doctor says he's stable.
Sure hope so." DeRosa remembered another flight to
Bangkok a couple of months before when the patient died.
They had a bitch of a time leaving the stiff in Thailand.
The police acted like they'd killed him.

"Well, we have more passengers. Let's load them and
be off."

"Not yet. There's one more litter."

"As long as we don't go over gross, it's her airplane to
fill up." Kip led the way back over to the Gooney Bird.

"They were asking if there was room for another
stretcher." DeRosa definitely wanted to shift this decision
over to Kip.

"I thought only one guy was hurt."

"Yeah, well, so did I." DeRosa busied himself with the
preflight as Kip called Sam out of the plane.

"Who's the other patient?"

"Don't rightly know, Kip. Doing a favor for a friend.
He's Chinese, but he does have a passport and papers for
Thailand." Sam looked exhausted, still wearing the clothes
he'd had on in the bar the night before.

"Anything else about him I should know? The Thais
are curious people."

"Don't think so. He's burned pretty bad, but he's in
better shape than Sophan."

"That's not saying much," Kip commented as he
watched Dr. Jake through the window hovering over the
injured man.

"There's our boy. Right on time." Sam nodded toward
the domestic terminal, where he could see Pao, Rabbit and
a Cambodian man working their way toward the plane.

Pao had on fresh clothing, the long shirt and pants covering most of the bandages. The other two discreetly held him up by his elbows, his feet barely touching the ground.

"Just hope Mama-san doesn't see that he's hurt. She's already tried to jack the price because of your man." A half-dozen people were pushing past Mama-san, heading for the aircraft. Several carried large wicker baskets crammed with produce. They never miss a chance to wheel and deal, he thought.

"Let's give them a hand," Michaels said. They eased in behind the three, trying to block the bandaged man from Mama-san's view. At the door of the plane, they lifted Pao up. He almost passed out from the pain, but Kip could tell that he knew he had to carry out the ruse. Kip sensed that the extra passenger was a problem for Sam as well, but he wasn't going to ask why.

"Mate, I don't know if this boy can handle this flight sitting up." Dr. Jake was helping him into a canvas seat.

"Look, if I ask Mama-san for a stretcher, she'll know." Kip looked around the ramp, then said, "I think I have the answer." He headed toward the domestic terminal, into the small room the pilots jokingly called the "Ready Room." He rolled up a thin cotton mattress from one of the two bunks, grabbed a GI blanket from the corner. He made it back to the plane without passing the Chinese lady.

"That will help a lot. Thanks." Kip pulled himself through the oval doorway and secured it behind him. He stepped around the Chinese man now lying on the floor, checked the positions of the other passengers and slipped into the pilot's seat. Outside, Michaels was trying to talk with the two people who'd brought the Chinese man, language an obvious problem. Sam looked beyond tired, the wrinkles on his face deep. He had more on his mind than just this flight. How lucky I am, Kip thought. I suck up the wheels on this baby and for an hour or two, I'm out of all this. Reporters were certified crazies in his mind. In

his Air America days, he'd flown photographers and reporters into places people wouldn't believe. That's why he
liked them.

"Let's crank . . ."

"OK," DeRosa said, sticking his head out the window.
"CLEAR . . . CLEAR . . . ," he yelled. The old radials
ticked right over, the gauges looked good.

"Phnom Penh tower, 78 Zulu, taxi, takeoff . . ." Kip
stuck to the old Navy phraseology, even though half the
time Phnom Penh tower never answered back. Let's make
this look as normal as possible.

"Seven-eight Zulu, roger," the controller said, speaking the English words by rote. "Runway 18, wind two-
two-zero degrees at five."

"I'd like a midfield departure," Kip said. The plane
didn't need all the runway, and this way they could take
off from the edge of the ramp. The tail bounced as they
taxied toward the runway.

"Roger. Approved. Cleared for takeoff." Out of the
corner of his eye he saw Maurice, the Frenchman, standing next to the wing of his Bonanza, talking heatedly with
Claudine Peirpoli, the same sweet French lady he'd seen
hanging out with Sam around the pool.

"Pressure is OK . . ." DeRosa twitched the switches,
mouthing the checklist.

"Fine, I've got it." He eased the plane toward the left
side of the taxiway, made a wide turn onto the runway and eased in the power once he'd established it on the
centerline. Once the tail lifted, things smoothed out. He
let the aircraft fly itself off the runway.

"Wish we could overnight in Bangkok," DeRosa said,
his eyes still on the gauges.

"You're the mechanic. Let's have a little problem."

"Gotcha . . ."

The lush green rice paddies unfolded below the wings,
the aircraft strong on the climb in the cool morning air.

Nothing to do now but let it fly and think about a night on Patpong Road.

"You got it," Kip said. He glanced back at the doctor and the passengers. He started to change the frequency on the radio when he heard another voice.

"Phnom Penh tower, Bonanza 33 Whiskey, taxi and takeoff for Bangkok. . . ."

"Now what? If ol' Sam had of known, he could have gotten them on with Maurice."

"Ah, you know those Froggies," DeRosa said, lightly touching the trim wheel for the climb. "They don't want to help nobody."

"My, what an un-Christian attitude you have."

"They speak just as highly of me. . . ."

"I know, I know . . ." Kip glanced back through the door to check on the patients. Dr. Jake sat next to Sophan's stretcher, monitoring his pulse. A couple of the men who'd boarded late played cards. When they reached cruising altitude, Kip slid down in the pilot's seat and tried to catch a nap. Even DeRosa can find Bangkok, he thought.

"Kip, my God. Kip!" Dr. Jake was screaming from the back. As he jerked around, he caught the side of his face on the barrel of the pistol held to his head. One of the men who'd lugged on the produce stood in the door, holding the gun. Beyond the man, he could see a scuffle and then he heard the moans.

"What the fuck . . ."

"Only a hijack," DeRosa said, trying to imitate Kip, but the tension in his throat made his voice squeak.

"Where to?" Kip looked at the hijacker.

"Fly." The man pointed the barrel of the gun directly ahead.

"Roger that."

"Kip! They're beating the Chinese fellow!" Dr. Jake sounded desperate.

Kip could see the flash of the gun as the other man pistol-whipped Pao. The plane dipped as Pao's limp form banged to the floor. The second man headed for the cockpit, no emotion on his face. He talked quietly to the first gunman, then pulled a chart from his pocket. He thrust it in front of DeRosa and said, ''There. You land there.''

It looked like no more than a long jungle clearing, but he'd seen worse. There was a quiet tension as Kip searched for the landing spot and set up for the landing. He could hear one of the passengers sobbing as he dropped the gear, skimmed over the trees and touched down.

They rolled out, the bouncing aircraft throwing the gunman forward, the pistol banging against Kip's head, opening a cut. When they stopped, the men left the cockpit and headed for Pao and the door.

''Kip, you may think I'm crazy, but I've had about enough of this shit.'' The stocky Italian pulled himself from the right seat and headed toward the back. ''Keep the RPM's up.''

Kip wiped the blood from his eye with his shirttail and watched through the door. One of the gunmen was already out the door, the second was pulling the unconscious Pao toward the opening. DeRosa worked quickly through the overturned produce and the stretcher, lunging the last couple of feet at the gunman, leading with a tight right fist. The man's head bounced off the top rim of the low door, but before he could fall, DeRosa pulled Pao away and kicked the gunman in the gut, out the door.

''Go, go, go!'' DeRosa and Pao fell back as Kip firewalled the throttles and let go the left brake. The big bird turned on the locked brake, the whack of the prop blade through the gunman's head barely heard above the roar. A streak of blood and brains coated the window on the propline. Kip heard the pop of the pistol as he let go the brake and rolled back the way they'd landed. He jerked up the tail, hoping to build airspeed on the rough grass, before the treeline ahead. Suddenly he knew it wasn't going to work, the pilot's survival hunch. Chopping the throttles, hitting the brakes, he slowed enough to turn just before the first bushes.

"Jesus, man, what now?" DeRosa grabbed the right seat as they turned. His knees bumped the big yoke as he clambered into the seat. "Oh, lordy, look at that."

Midway down the strip was the surviving gunman, crouched next to the body of his friend, pointing the pistol straight at them. Kip didn't answer as he built up speed. He felt terribly calm, not feeling the pain of the cut or the danger of the bullets. A bullet shattered the side window, spraying glass on his shoulder, but he didn't flinch.

There were two more flashes from the gun before the man stood to run, but it was too late. A scream started from his throat just as his face was wiped down the bottom of the plane.

"Holy God." DeRosa was stunned. The plane climbed smoothly past the trees, the old engines sensing their need.

"Is Sophan all right?" Kip yelled, turning to the rear.

"Yes. But God, get us out of here." Dr. Jake was very shaken.

"You better get back to the doc," DeRosa said, trimming up the bird as they gained altitude.

"It's not that bad." Kip just stared out the window for a long moment, surprised at the depth of his anger, his lack of feeling for killing two men. "What you think we should paint on the side? Little men?" It was time to get back to the real world. He wasn't about to show DeRosa what he felt.

"God, you're a sadist." But DeRosa grinned as he spoke. "But you're right about one thing. You just can't beat flying these trucks."

"Trust me, DeRosa, trust me." Kip pulled himself up and realized how exhausted he was, the adrenaline rush all gone. He headed toward Dr. Jake to get his head fixed. The passengers were sitting in stunned silence.

DeRosa called Bangkok approach, declared a medical

emergency and got priority in the pattern. He just hoped the gunk on the side had dried enough to look like mud.

An ambulance was sitting on the ramp, waiting for them. The Thais didn't put up much of a fight; a few hundred dollars greased the way. As Dr. Jake crawled into the back with the two injured men, he waved, the sign of a survivor.

"We'll be at the Montien," Kip yelled. No way they were going back today. Not after this. They tied down the plane, gave the authorities a song and dance about a bad compression problem that wasn't far from the truth, and headed for immigration.

"Funny thing," DeRosa said, speaking for the first time since they'd landed.

"Yeah. What?" Kip was in no mood for trivia. The only place he'd get this trip out of his system was in the hot baths at Caesar's Palace massage parlor.

"That Frenchman never got here. He should have beat us by a good half hour." They looked at one another knowingly, sure of their hunch that the Bonanza was involved in this somehow.

"Too bad. He might have bought us a drink on Patpong tonight."

"After what we did to his friends?" Every day DeRosa got more like Kip. Thought like him.

"Probably. Because if there's one thing folks like that hate is people who fuck up." Kip eyed the immigration counters, looking for the shortest line.

DeRosa fell in behind him. "Yeah, but there's one thing I hate even more. People who fuck with me."

XXIV.

Rice Run

"OPEN UP, MAN, open up. . . ." Sam pounded on the heavy metal shutters of the rice shop with a wrench. "I know you're in there," he said, laughing at his poor Jack Webb imitation. The hammering on the folding shutters sounded like prisoners banging on cell doors with tin cups. He and Moss spent a half hour trying to find a place that sold rice, not the easiest task at midnight when all the shops were shuttered until morning. But they had to get some rice. Stoneman was getting married.

"You see anybody yet?" Moss asked as he stood anxiously at the street corner, keeping an eye out for the curfew patrols. The whole city was on edge, and the last thing they needed was to be mistaken in the dark for burglars or insurgents and be shot on the spot.

"Yeah, there's a light inside. . . ." The sleepy Chinese shopkeeper pulled back the metal shutter a couple of inches and gave Sam a puzzled look. "We need rice . . . white rice . . . *riz blanc*. . . ." Sam optimistically shook his head yes and waved a couple thousand riels in the man's face.

"No open . . . *fini* . . . *couvrefeu*. . ." The shopkeeper pointed to the deserted street. Sam spotted what he needed behind the man, a half-filled sack of white rice.

"There . . . that . . . *ici* . . ." Sam dug in his pocket for another chunk of money. The shopkeeper was waking up now. He smiled, nodded yes and fetched the bag. Sam pulled it through the crack, gave the man his money, about ten times the going rate, and slung the bag over his shoulder. He felt like the Huck Finn of the Orient. Moss had his car running by the time Sam got to the corner.

They were the rice detail; others at Chantao's were sent to find champagne, cake and assorted trappings for a western-style wedding. It was a surprise to all, Stoneman's announcement that he wanted to marry Choe. They'd appeared at Chantao's just as the curfew siren blew. Choe was the first Cambodian woman Sam had seen in the den as a guest, Chantao's way of approving of the match. Getting ready for the wedding was just what Sam needed. He was in sore need of an attitude adjustment.

"Let me see if I have this right," Moss said as the two Americans made their way back to the opium den. "I'm competing with two crews, right?" He drove slowly, keeping the dome lights on so the patrols and roadblock sentries could see in the car.

"That's what the man said." Sam still had the latest cable in his pocket. MICHAELS STOP FURTHER EARLIER ADVISORY STOP RIDER AND CREW REMAIN PHNOMPERS STOP RIDER TO ADVISE FURTHER SOPHAN DEVELOPMENTS STOP MARKET ATTACK MADE EVENING NEWS STOP LITTON.

"You're still making air. It can't be all that bad. But someone has a hard-on, from all the heat you're getting." Larry looked at the road, but kept his head turned toward Sam.

"Yeah. Then I turn around and get Sophan blown away.

That didn't help." He felt he had no control over what happened here or in New York. He could plead his case with them only via cables because the telephone link sounded like a tin can hooked to a taut string. Rider was his only hope. New York wasn't convinced, too many heavyweights whispering in their ear. Sam pointed to a soldier leaning against the wall in the darkness. Moss flashed the headlights and the soldier waved them on by.

"Look, Sam. Rule one of the gospel according to Moss. When you see what someone doesn't want you to see, they're going to do their damnedest to prove that you can't see. . . ." He got tangled on the "sees" and both men laughed.

"I admit the 'seeing' part gets a little tricky." Sam wished he'd never heard of the gun. "Why do you think Reilly is screwing me?"

"Oh, come on. Reilly is taking a beating now, between the gun popping away and the market attack. The ambassador is due back in a couple of days and he is tight-assed. Let's see. Add the bombing halt, missing convoys, and revolts in the ranks, and you have the ingredients for 'scapegoat stew.' You're not the first one around here to get the full Reilly treatment." Moss doused the headlights and turned down the dirt road that led to Chantao's.

"What tightens my jaws is that I know he tried to get us wiped. You'd think *we* were the enemy, instead of the Rouge."

"Sam, in Reilly's mind we all are responsible. He's one of the old school who's convinced that things would have gone fine in Vietnam if the press hadn't been around."

"Well, I don't know what he's telling Washington, but it isn't true." Sam felt some release by talking it out with someone who understood.

"Sam, Sam. You remember the old tale about Lyndon Johnson, where he told his aides in a close election to spread the word his opponent liked sex with pigs? When they protested that it wasn't true, he said yeah, but let him deny it. That's what Reilly is doing. Forcing your company to deny that you lied.''

"And they don't know me well enough to go all the way to the wall. . . .''

"Ah, the man sees the light! Well, the good news is that your fellow travelers here are behind you. Rosen drilled him yesterday on the gun. Front page story, two columns, above the fold. . . .'' Moss pulled the car off the road around the corner from the den. Chantao didn't like fancy cars in front of her house. "Think the headline read, 'Khmer Government Can't Find Phnom Penh Artillery.' ''

"Now if I'd done that story . . .''

". . . you'd be shoveling shit against the north wind.'' Moss chuckled as he got out of the car. He waited for Sam to walk around in the dark. In a low voice he asked, "Is there anything to that bullshit about junk in Saigon?''

"You know?''

"Know enough. Just give me a yes or no.''

"Yes, it was in the bag. No, I didn't put it there.''

". . . and Moss can fill in the blanks.''

"Right.''

Somewhere a dog barked, adding to the sinister feel of the night. Another car turned the corner and pulled in behind them. It was Byers, with a passenger.

"Hark, who goes there?'' Sam whispered as he slung the rice bag and moved down the dirt road.

"The fat man and a spy. . . .'' Byers had to suck in his stomach to get past the steering wheel. Sam looked twice at his passenger before he recognized Bishop.

"Boy, you pop up in the damnedest places.'' There was no humor in Sam's whisper. Being near Bishop made Sam's gut knot. As a Southerner, his reaction was to kill the son-of-a-bitch, and then compromise. Was he also pulling Sam's string? What a difference a few days made. Sam remembered the old Air Force expression, that there was only a thin line between a Court Martial and a Medal of

Honor. And standing in front of him now was one of the people Sam figured was trying to push him over the line.

"Figured you'd love to meet me in a dark alley . . . ," Bishop said.

"Alone, my man, alone. . . ." The men were quiet as they felt their way along the wall, around the pitch dark corner. The trick was to avoid the deep, narrow ditch that ran in front of the house. Sam found the gate with his hand, crossed the little bridge and tapped on the metal sign that warned of a vicious dog inside. In daylight, Chantao's looked like any other middle-class Cambodian house. No signs advertised her enterprise.

"*Oui?*" Rabbit checked to see who wanted in.

"M'sieu Moustache . . ." Sam whispered back.

"*Oui, oui . . .*"

The men followed her down the narrow path alongside the main house and carefully made their way up the narrow steps that led to the den in the back. They could hear whispers and giggles inside the big room.

Stoneman was nervous. He was dressed in his work jeans and a green fatigue shirt, the best and cleanest garments in his wardrobe. Rider argued that Ty should wear the new white korta shirt with the fancy needlework on the front that he'd brought along. Choe looked at it and smiled, touching the threads with her fingers. Stoneman frowned, but put it on.

Claudine hovered over Choe. She had hustled around and found the bride a beautiful red blouse and a snow white sarong. Night flowers were tucked into her black hair, the red blossoms highlighting her sparkling eyes. Sam dumped the rice bag in the corner, next to the case of French champagne liberated from the Malaysian Embassy.

Chantao slipped quietly through the group, looking like the stern mother-in-law, but Sam could tell she was enjoying the occasion. A year ago, she would have never permitted so public an event in her den, but now it didn't matter. Like everyone else here, she felt the end approaching. The old rules no longer applied. She still bribed the police, but their moral vigor was drained like the country. The loss of her business didn't bother her as much as losing her friends. This was her way of showing them she cared.

Sam grabbed a sarong off the peg and slipped into one of the small rooms. Bishop was there, struggling with his sarong, obviously ill at ease. Sam said nothing as he stripped.

"I always wondered how you tied these things," Bishop said, trying to watch how Sam dressed.

"Well, you run the risk of going native, slanty eyes and all that." Sam forced a grin, trying to cover his feelings.

"I run the risk of being shot at sunrise."

"True. What makes this worth the hassles? Not just curiosity." He couldn't resist a dig. "Gathering more fodder for your next cable to Washington?"

"You lost me there."

"Well, it's amazing to me how quickly one's rope can get jerked from ten thousand miles away. I'm trying to go straight down the middle, but someone is obviously trying to convince my bosses otherwise. Somehow, I don't think it's the tooth fairy."

"You think that I'm responsible for that?" Bishop looked surprised.

"Yeah, you, or your boss or someone in that bunker. Just stands to reason."

"I wish you didn't feel that way. We're just doing our job, trying to help these people."

"Yeah, and the Nazis were just following orders. Same logic, isn't it?" Sam's voice was low, but he spoke slowly and intensely.

"Sam, that's not fair. It all depends on your perspective. We know things that you don't . . ."

"A hell of a lot of things . . ."

". . . and if you knew them, you might change your mind." Bishop was holding firm, not giving in.

"Bishop, you people deal in the already known. You pull together all the shit, all the rumors and call it intelligence. The people here tonight know a hell of a lot more about what's happening out there than you think. Since when is a Cambodian general going to tell you something you don't want to hear? They know where the tit is, and they ain't about to bite it. You taught them the rules of the game, and what happened to the gun and in the market is a logical extension of the rules."

"It's obvious you stand by your position."

"Look, we'll never change one another's minds, so we might as well enjoy the party. I just have a couple of things I want to get off my chest. I'm just like you, just trying to do my job. But I don't claim to know everything. To you and Reilly and the embassy, I'm an irritant, something to be gotten rid of and replaced by someone who'll toe the line. But I hate to tell you that Tom Rider can smell bullshit a mile away, and you can bet your ass that his feelers are all stuck out. If it makes you feel any better, I'm in deep shit in New York over this." Sam had finished his speech, and felt strangely relieved.

"Sam, no one is after your job. We've had few problems with your work. Sure, you did that story on the convoy and the gun, and we don't think you can back it up. You're right about one thing. A lot of people hide behind the embassy walls and jerk each other off, claiming they know what's going on. I don't like that either. I'm a military man, and this diplomatic bullshit is starting to turn my head around." Bishop looked Sam straight in the eye. "What else?"

"Sophan. I'll go to my grave knowing you and Reilly were out there, and I'd bet my mother's honor that one of you ordered the attack, or at least didn't discourage it. I got you guys on film, you know." Sam wasn't sure of that, but how was Bishop to know. Let him sweat.

"Sam, part of our job is checking out such incidents.

If it will make you feel any better, we're sorry your man was hurt.''

"Yeah, I bet you lit some candles." Sam couldn't believe that he couldn't think of anything better to say, not after his anger of the past day.

"You're not going to like what I'm about to say, but I think I owe you one. Reilly thinks he's got the goods on you, and he's just waiting for the chance to hammer you. I'll deny ever saying that.''

"What goods?''

"Has to do with the company you keep, Sam, and the funny things that wind up in Saigon. That's all I'll say.'' Bishop tried to end the comment by struggling with the sarong.

"Amazing how quickly the rumors fly, isn't it?'' Sam wasn't about to get into a pissing match over this. Bishop knew.

"Yeah. And how quickly you can wind up on a plane to the States, if you're lucky.''

"Let's leave it, Bishop. There's a wedding here tonight, you know.'' Sam headed out the door toward the big room. Bishop stood still, holding the sarong. "Good luck tying that thing.''

"You two fuckers been in there playing with each other?'' Byers lay on the floor, a bottle of Mekong whiskey in his hand.

"Just a little discussion of current events. Why did you bring him, anyhow?''

"Ease up, Sam. He's here to witness the wedding and to help Choe get her papers. He's doing us a favor.''

"Twenty good deeds and he goes straight to heaven, right?'' Sam decided he needed another pipe.

Byers looked past Sam and grinned. "You sure know how to leave a man looking stupid.'' He nodded to Rabbit, who slipped into the room and tied Bishop's sarong. Sam worked his way through the crowded den, ducked as a

champagne cork exploded and bounced off the walls and
ceiling nets.

Chantao raised her eyebrows at Sam, her way of asking
if he wanted a few pipes. He nodded yes.

The Howdy lamp flickered as she trimmed the wick
with scissors. Sam was the only one in the smoking room,
and he was relieved to have a few moments alone with his
thoughts. Things were coming unglued. Somewhere back
there he had crossed the line, gone through the wall, and
didn't even know it. He was pissed, the network was
pissed, and now Tom Rider was here, breaking his rice
bowl.

Chantao nudged him with the stem of the pipe. He took
it to his lips, determined to swing his mood, even if that
meant doing all the dope in Cambodia. What chewed at
his gut was knowing that he was getting stuck by someone
else. He had lifted a lid someone wanted to stay shut. In
a strange way, Sam understood the Cambodians better than
he did the Americans. The Cambodians knew the rug was
coming out from under them, that the war America had
started would be left for them to end. You could see it in
their eyes, feel it in the air. He could understand why they
would cut their own deals. They felt betrayed, and Sam,
as an American, was an obvious target. He slowly ex-
haled, feeling relieved. Claudine, well that was another
matter. He suspected that he was thinking with his dick.

"My God, the preacher's got to steady his nerves."
Byers stood at the door with Rosen, a scene fit for a comic
book, both of them wrapped in sarongs.

"He always said that he'd found Jesus in that pipe, isn't
that right, redneck?" Rosen pushed by Byers and lay down
across the smoking mat from Sam.

"Nah, I figured all that out long ago. When I was a kid
in Baptist Sunday School, the good teacher would tell us
that looking at a woman in lust was as bad as doing it. It
took me no time at all to decide that if I was going to hell

for looking, I might as well be doing. Besides, they wouldn't let me drink.''

"You really did grow up like that, didn't you?" Rosen was interested.

"Not the worst way to grow up. This place is a lot like a small town. Everybody knows everybody's business." Sam watched as Rosen swiped what was supposed to be his pipe. He didn't care. Byers stayed by the door, alternately listening to them and watching the party.

"How did you wind up with a preacher's license?" Rosen spoke without exhaling.

"Friend Richard sent it to me in 1968. Some people managed to get conscientious objector status from the mail order churches on the West Coast. This one cost twenty bucks. For fifty, I could have received a doctorate in theology. But we already have one theologian in the family, so I stuck to roadrunning.''

"Dr. Michaels. Now that would have been the shits." Byers took the final hit from the whiskey, then eyed the pipe. "The license is legal, right?"

"Bet your sweet ass it's legal. I married off some friends in India with it. The embassy didn't blink an eye." From the front room drifted the strains of a dirty song. He wished his brother were here right now, or that he could get a few days in Singapore with his family. Nothing like a little coddling and warmth from his brother's wife and his two favorite nieces. Sam decided to save the other pipes for later. As he entered the room, a big cheer went up for Kew Son, who pushed through the door with a cake. Behind him was the Swedish nurse, looking brave but a little lost.

"This nice lady, she got out of bed to bake the cake for Stoneman." It was a cake, all right, complete with birthday candles.

"Looks like you went back to bed while it was baking," Moss said, pointing to the sunken middle. The lady blushed.

"Hey, man, this thing is getting out of hand." Stoneman grinned as he spoke, trying to push a garland of flowers off his head. Bishop had found a corner and was contentedly munching some of Stoneman's magic brownies. Sam wondered if he knew they were loaded with nefarious weed. Chan and Marty chatted nearby, both making a show of snubbing Bishop. Sam worked his way through the tangle of bodies and legs to where they sat. "Look who drifted in from the boonies," Chan said, nodding at Satterfield. "Been talking about him doing a little sound work."

"I'll need a visa," Marty said, liking the idea.

"Fine by me. You'll get what Sophan gets. Seventy-five a day and expenses when we sell something."

"That's seventy-five more than I'm making now." Marty stuck out his hand to seal the bargain.

"And no heat. With us you're a pacifist, like it or not."

"No problem. I'll use my Okie charm."

"Sam, I've been thinking about the gun."

"I'm all ears. . . ."

"Satterfield says Pha Doh is pissed about Sophan. He's checked around at where the Chinaman's lab was located. Good part of it was hauled off, and it's probably in the boonies with the gun."

"I think that's pretty solid," Satterfield added. "Pha Doh was hearing rumors about something happening in that village. Now we know, don't we?"

"I take it he's back in the field." Sam played along, letting Chan convince himself that he wanted to go for the gun. They'd talked very little over the past days, and Sam wasn't sure what he knew. Satterfield was slick, that's for sure.

"Yeah, right out in the middle of it. He'll take us in if we want to go. He's listening to the tom-toms, but they've got it pretty well hidden. But if that gun uncorks again, we'll have a pretty good idea, won't we? You want to go?"

"You bet your ass we want to go," Sam exclaimed, checking Chan's reaction out of the corner of his eye. "If I'm going down the tubes over this thing, at least I want to see it for myself."

"We're all going down the tubes. . . ." Chan grinned, but Sam wasn't sure he was joking.

"You willing to go?"

"Check. As long as Satterfield is willing to play point man."

"My original calling in life, remember?" Marty betrayed nothing of their earlier conversation.

"This all sounds great," Sam said, the pipes settling in his brain, "but I'm not sure it will help."

"Tiger," Chan said, nodding toward Rider across the room, "there's only one way to get work when he's around. You've got to hit home runs."

XXV.

Night Life

"I NEVER KNEW she could do that with a beer bottle," Dr. Jake shouted above the din of loud music and yelling at the long bar.

"Yeah, she's got quite a bag of tricks." Kip threw back the dregs of the San Miguel beer, enjoying the opportunity of showing a stranger the seedier side of Patpong Road. The two-block long private street in the heart of Bangkok offered more sin and diversion per square foot than any other street in the world. The bar was his hangout, operated by a couple of Americans who'd found their calling on the Oriental backside.

"Twenty bucks, and she'll do it for you," DeRosa urged, his eyes hooded from constant drink.

"You know, mate," Dr. Jake said, his slow speech indicating a deep thought, "ya give something away when you go into medicine. The graphic stuff just isn't a turn-on. Unfortunately for that lady's pocketbook, I'd rather *think* about what she'd do with a bottle than watch."

"Your cock will thank you for it, too," Kip said, agree-

ing with the doctor. They'd been cruising the street since
sundown, from the time Dr. Jake showed up at the Montien Hotel, satisfied that Sophan was in good hands. At
some point in the morning they'd have to shake off the
cobwebs and fly back to Phnom Penh, but that was tomorrow. The dancer twisted her way toward the far end
of the bar, kneeling from time to time so the patrons could
squeeze a few more bat under the band of her bikini pants.

"Tell you what I would like, my friends." Jake looked
at both men hopefully. "Take me to that place, the one
everybody talks about." He rubbed his forehead, trying
to conjure up the name. "You know the one . . ."

"Caesar's Palace," DeRosa added quickly, the same
idea on his mind.

"The home of the humble 'B Course.' " Kip liked the
suggestion. If he had to fly, a few hot baths and a massage
would go a long way toward getting the poison out of his
system.

"I think the real trick is getting there," Dr. Jake slurred,
trying to stand alongside his stool.

"We'll get you there," Kip said, the rush of blood to
his head from standing up making him doubt his own
words. "All you're required to do at the Palace is make it
to the door. They do the rest."

"Off we go," Jake said, pushing his way through the
patrons. Outside, the road seemed an extension of the bar,
without house rules. Looking for a cab, the three men
turned back propositions from girls, boys, and folks of
questionable persuasion. The hot night pulsed with the
same beat as the muffled music inside the bar. A gaudy
Toyota forced its way to the curb, the driver negotiating
the fare before they got in. The blue tinsel strung across
the top of the windshield served as a canopy for the mixed
bag of idols and symbols glued to the dash.

"Sukumvit, Soy 42," Kip yelled. "You go straight, I
know the way."

"Forty bat," said the driver, smiling.

"Twenty. And drive slow."

"Thirty," the driver sang out as he ripped through the gears, horn blaring, melding into the mix of traffic that makes Bangkok unique in the world of driving. After passing a bus on the curb side, Kip beat on the back of the seat and the driver slowed a little.

"At least he's started out in the right direction," De-Rosa said, pulling a joint from the pocket of his bush jacket.

"I'm at your mercy, mates. If I go during this night, let me go the good way." The doctor studied the joint before taking a small puff. "Is this stuff as bad as they say?"

"It's the best, man. Thai Buddha stick," DeRosa blurted out, proud of his score.

"That's not what he's asking, asshole," Kip said, taking the joint from his hand. "Look at it this way. I've seen a lot of people die from booze and skag, but not from this. Seems to touch a soft spot in the psyche or something."

Horns blared as the taxi ground to a halt in the middle of a major intersection. Cars and trucks seemed to all be pointed at them, their driver yelling curses in singsong Thai out the window, a bicycle rider pounding on the hood, trying to work his way around the jam. On the sidewalk were young people all looking cool, the men in white shirts open to the belly, dark belled pants over Italian loafers. The girls wore silk blouses and tight white slacks, makeup forcing their delicate Oriental features into a parody of western beauty.

"What we going to do about those two guys in the jungle?" Jake asked, the inevitable question coming up.

"What guys? Did you see any guys?" Kip leaned over and stared at DeRosa. He just grinned.

"Yeah, but there were other people on the plane. They saw what happened." Jake was nervous.

"Look, they saw it all right, and they want no part of it. If anyone wanted to yell, they'd of done it at the airport.

Those two weren't friends of anyone else on the plane."
Kip had thought this one through.

"You know what?" DeRosa said, resting his head
against the front seat of the taxi, trying not to get sick.
"I've seen that Chinese guy before. He's the scared one
we picked up that day outside Battambang."

"I don't know. Too many bandages. But if it was the
same guy, he sure knows how to find trouble." Kip felt
like telling DeRosa he was full of shit, but there was enough
logic in what he said to be right.

"Well, whoever he is, he has a lot of friends." Dr. Jake
slumped lower in the middle of the seat.

"What do you mean?" Kip took his eyes off the traffic
and looked at the doctor. "You know this guy?"

"Never seen him before yesterday."

"Then what do you mean?"

"I mean someone showed up at the Bangkok Nursing
Home looking for him, checking on his injuries." Jake let
go a long, deep belch.

"How can that be? He got on the flight at the last minute."

"I don't know, Kip," Jake said, drunkenly waving his
arm in the cramped car, bumping it into both men. "Just
that the nurse came and asked where the patient had gone.
Said some French guy was looking for him."

"Did you see the French guy?" Kip and DeRosa shot
one another a look.

"No. I was busy with Sophan." He belched again.

"Where is the Chinese guy? Isn't he in the hospital?"

"Nope. Last time I saw him he was telling the nurses
to leave him alone. He was on the street, looking for a
taxi."

"He could barely walk."

"Far enough to get a taxi." Somehow Jake thought that
was funny.

"DeRosa, I think our friend did make it to Bangkok."

Kip made the driver go straight through an intersection, saving a five-minute detour.

"Sounds that way. Seems like that Chinese guy is popular." DeRosa sensed they were nearing Caesar's Palace and sat upright. "See there, Jake," he said, holding forth with drunken logic. "The only person we had to worry about is gone, poof. . . ."

"Yeah, if you guys say so." Dr. Jake shook his head, fighting off sleep. "How much farther?"

"Nearly there. Check out the ladies in the glass cage as we walk by. They're for the downstairs clientele. The good stuff is upstairs." They pulled into the drive of the gaudy establishment, paid the driver, and Kip led the threesome through the door. He was recognized by the hostess, and they were led to an elevator. Upstairs, they split up and headed for their private rooms.

Kip had asked for his special girl, and they chatted in pigeon English as she ran a hot bath in the sunken tub. He dug through her cassettes, finding "Dark Side of the Moon," and put it on the small stereo.

She was working on the callouses on the bottom of his feet as he thought through the day. Sophan was in good hands, if in lousy shape. The Chinese guy was in Bangkok, but God only knew where. Maurice had been here, he would bet on that. It didn't take a genius to figure out that the Chinese guy was hot, knew too much about something. There were two stiffs in a clearing near the border, two more victims of the long war. No, they could go on back in the morning, play dumb, and put this down as another day for the Pig Pilots.

Just as he started to think more about the hospital visitor, the girl drained the water, and started rinsing him with the flexible shower hose. She worked from his outer limbs toward the center, and before the water was drained, he'd forgotten all about Maurice.

⊕   ⊕   ⊕

The Chinaman was tired. He was tired of people, tired of war, tired of the lies. He sipped the hot bowl of coffee, broke off another piece of bread and carefully spread it with butter. His stomach was finished, the good food he so loved now a painful part of his existence. He had known this day would arrive, when it was time to let it all go, to disappear, to live as a free man away from war and the chaos that had made him rich.

What set his stomach off this time was the note. This man Chandaran, he was not so smart, but he wasn't dumb. Even President Prek, that shadow of a man who couldn't rule his own bed, was irritated enough to give up the ample rewards of his relationship with the Chinaman, and tell him to end this madness.

Oh, it had been worth the pain. The profits from the upland heroin lab rested safely in deposit boxes from Macao to London. Somewhere along the way, his function had shifted from enterprise to the only dependable method of operation in the country. What had been his goal had now become a curse. Yes, it was time.

He reread the note on the table before him. Chandaran threatened to attack again, this time against the army. The General did know the pressure points. What he didn't know was that the game was up. All that remained were the loose ends, a few scores to be settled. Money, heroin, power, these things were finished. Yes, the only thing he couldn't let go were the insults, the people who thought they were smarter than the Chinaman.

Some were hungry, like Chandaran. He wanted to be the Chinaman. They could have worked together but the General was too greedy. That he understood. Some were frightened and weak, like Prek, but for now he had enough power to resist. And the American, Reilly, he was nothing more than a fool.

But the real reason for his decision lay elsewhere. To be the Chinaman, he needed to remain obscure, his power perceived, not truly known. What tipped the balance was

the newsmen. They kept touching on the edges of his em-
pire, shining just enough light to keep the pressure on
him, to cut back his options. The day would come when
the people he manipulated would turn on him, trying to
save their fortunes and their lives. None could take him
on alone, but the publicity was pulling them together, and
Chandaran understood this.

He had taken care of the master chemist. He no longer
cared what happened to Cambodia. He knew that soon he
could leave the city, fly to Hong Kong and disappear, his
work finished. But that wasn't the mentality that had made
him the Chinaman. He would go, but not until all these
people understood his real power.

He looked again at Chandaran's note. He wanted another meeting. That could never be. Chandaran underestimated the Chinaman, because on this very day he had
the break he'd been waiting for. One of Chandaran's men
wanted to play both sides, and that suited him fine. He
now knew the location of the gun and the trucks, what
they planned to do, and where they planned to go.

His plan was simple. He'd share this information with
everyone: Prek, the Americans, the journalists. Let them
work it out. He wanted to play one more hand, the hand
that held the ace of power.

XXVI.

Stoneman's Wedding

"REVEREND MICHAELS, I think it is time for the service to begin." Rosen called Sam as Chantao entered the room carrying a blazing candelabrum, seven candles stuck in the fine old silver menorah. Sam worked his way to the middle of the room, sat down across from Stoneman and Choe.

"What's this? A wedding or Hanukkah?" Rosen couldn't resist the jibe. Chantao placed it carefully to the side, then leaned over and spoke to Ty and Choe in Chinese. They were ready to begin. The room settled down, everyone watching the three of them. Rosen sat next to Stoneman, Claudine by Choe's side. Sam had thought about being flip, to throw in a little humor, but now he realized that the mood had shifted. In the quiet they could hear the thump of the government artillery, the harassment and interdiction fire that punctuated the stillness of any night in Phnom Penh.

"In this room," Sam started, his voice low and serious, "are gathered people representing every major religious faith." He nodded at Rosen, Chantao and Ali Rahman, the Malaysian chargé. "The marriage of Ty and Choe holds special meaning for us, their friends. It is more than just a coming together of two people, it is the melding of two worlds, two cultures." Rosen nodded approval at Sam's words.

"In a sense, this wedding is symbolic of how we all feel tonight. How we wish we could marry this country, take it away from the misery of the war, put it back together again." Sam paused while Claudine translated into French for Choe. "These two have not chosen an easy way out. They are showing us by the courage of their commitment that they're willing to face the future together, no matter what happens. I just want them to know that a part of us goes with them, that we'll all remember this moment as one of joy and happiness."

Sam tried to remember the wedding vows, then decided to ad lib. "Do you, Choe, take this man, to be your husband?" Claudine translated, and Choe gave a big smile as she turned to Ty and said *oui*.

"And do you, Ty, take this woman to be your wife?"

"Yeah . . ." Ty caught himself, then said, "I do." A soft laugh swept the room.

"Then by the powers vested in me by the card in my pocket, and in the sight of the gods, and the people here, I pronounce you husband and wife."

Stoneman turned to Choe and looked in her face for a full minute. He took both of his hands, pulled her face toward him and gave her a gentle kiss.

Claudine then kissed Ty, Rosen kissed Choe and soon everybody seemed to be kissing everybody else. Sam felt relieved, his chores done. In the corner of the room he saw Chantao wipe a tear from her eye. Ty pulled a Chinese document from his pocket. He read it to her. She squeezed both of their hands, and moved to the back of the room.

"I didn't know you read Chinese." Ty always surprised Sam.

"Learned it from newspapers on opium den walls."

"You're kidding?"

"Nope. True." Ty looked at the document a moment, then handed it to Sam. "It wouldn't hurt if you signed this. We've had a Buddhist ceremony, gotten the blessings of the Chinaman, and now this. I don't want anybody to say it isn't legal."

Someone threw Sam a pen, and he signed on a clear spot. "You sure I didn't adopt you or something?" Stoneman translated for Choe, who laughed. Looking at the unlikely pair, Sam realized what had been bothering him. Stoneman. That he was finally marrying Choe wasn't a surprise. But when someone like Ty decided to settle accounts and plan for the future, the vibes had to be bad. He lived close to the streets, felt the pulse of the country as few foreigners could. He was thinking of the day when he would have to leave. Somehow, this wedding was an acknowledgment that the end was in sight.

"The cake!" Kew Son handed the cake over the crowd to Sam, who placed it in front of the bride and groom. "Damn, I forgot the knife." Son looked flustered.

"I don't need a knife. . . ." Stoneman broke off a corner of the cake and fed it to Choe. Soon hands were reaching for the plate, everyone eating with their hands, champagne corks flying about the room. Rabbit placed a bottle of bubbly in each of the small rooms, making ready for the all-night party. No one intended to leave this one.

Sam kissed the bride, gave Stoneman a hug and ducked back into the smoking room. Someone had thought to bring a tape deck, and Cat Stevens' "Foreigners" played softly under the loud whispers. Sam watched Chantao break out the Number One dope, the stuff Maurice smoked. By the time he'd had two more pipes, the smoking room was packed. Son wanted the nurse to give it a try, Byers needed something to offset the booze, and Moss just wanted more of the good stuff. Claudine appeared at the door, signaling him with her head to follow.

"This is something special," she said, leading him to her favorite room. Marty and Chan were there, hunched over a small mirror. Carefully, Chan cut lines of white powder.

"My wedding present. Been saving it for something very special." Marty rolled a hundred dollar bill into a tube, and they each took two lines. Within seconds Sam thought he was going to be blown out through the walls. He rolled his eyes, then looked at Chan. "Good speed." Chan grinned, bent his head and did a couple of lines.

"Guess again, Sam. Cocaine."

"Oh, lordy . . ." Sam shut his eyes and felt the skag go for his brain. Claudine looked away, a little ashamed, but Sam touched her leg and smiled.

"Hope you appreciate this. Rare stuff in this part of the world." Chan cut some more on the mirror. Stoneman slipped through the door and took a couple of hits.

"No. Just surprised." Sam pulled his nose with his fingers, thought ten whole seconds before sticking the bill back up his nostril. He flopped back on the cushions, the tape deck a foot from his ears. The songs came to life, he found himself in touch with the lyrics, moving from level to level. They were careful to keep the mirror hidden, not wanting the others to find out, like Boy Scouts sneaking a cigarette. Claudine sat at his feet, watching the men. Marty cut her a couple of lines, and handed her the mirror. She paused, looking at Sam. Why not, he thought, shaking his head yes. God knows a little more won't hurt her, not with the amount of the shit already flowing through her veins. As she snorted, Sam glanced around and confirmed that the others didn't think it amiss. Well, maybe they didn't know everything.

When the coke was gone, the others drifted from the room, floating from party to party in the other rooms. Maurice quietly slipped in. He looked tired and preoccupied, not tuned into the wedding. Sam thought about getting his bowels in an uproar, but let it pass. As Maurice and Claudine chatted in French, Sam continued his thoughts. Here I sit with the answer man, and I'm playing right into his lap. God knows this ain't no treatment center.

Claudine stood, signaled to Sam to follow her to another room, quietly shut the door, flipped the knot on her sarong and let it drop to the floor. For several minutes she stood over Sam, running her hands over her body, turning up the heat.

Sam felt his sex drive rising, but held back. There was something missing here. He reached for her hand and pulled her down in front of him.

"You don't want me?" She seemed taken aback by the rejection.

"That's a dumb question. Sure. But right now, we need to talk." He leaned over and kissed her on the tip of her nose.

"You are mad about the coke tonight, yes?" She sighed, reached over and pulled the sarong over her lap.

"No, not what happened tonight. I did it too, remember?" He rubbed his face with both of his hands. "Look. I'm catching it from all sides, and I need some answers. Rider has been pretty laid back about all this, but any day now, someone's going to play twenty questions with me, and I don't know shit."

"What is it you want to know?" She fussed with a string in the mat as she talked, not looking in his eyes.

"Everything. Nothing. Ah, shit, Claudine, I don't know." He paused for a moment, gathering his thoughts. "I guess what I want to know is if there are more surprises."

"Surprises?"

"Yeah, is there anything else going on that's going to jump up and bite me on the ass. Like the heroin in the film bag, that sort of stuff."

"No." She paused, then looked up. "Not like that, no."

"What else?"

"Sammi, there are many things we keep deep in our heart, but that is not your question. I am very sorry that I have gotten you in trouble. You know that was not what I wanted. Now, the others, they know about the drugs, don't they?"

"Only Rider and Moss. It's not something I care to brag about."

"I understand."

"I'm not sure you do, Claudine. On the other hand, I compliment myself thinking that you wouldn't use me."

"Sammi," she said, looking hurt. "I am an addict. I am trying to break the habit, and I will."

"That doesn't solve our problem, Claudine. What I can't understand is that you make good money, and dope is cheap here. I mean, is your habit so heavy that you have to do things like that to keep it up?"

"No. That is not the reason. I did it for someone else."

"Who?"

"Sam, I cannot tell you that. You must believe me when I tell you that it is done, over."

"I have no claims on you as a lover, Claudine. If that's what you're getting at."

"No, that is not it either. Sam, there are things I cannot tell you. That is all. I care for you. More than the drugs. More than this." She sat back against the matted wall, gathering herself. "All right. There is something you should know."

"Yeah?" Sam sat up, dreading what was to come.

"The Chinese man. He is dead."

"You're shitting me. He died in Bangkok?"

"He did not say. Maurice says Kip will tell you all about it. Maurice, he just find out himself."

"The good times just keep on rolling around here, don't they?" Sam looked at her angrily for a long moment. "I'll worry about that tomorrow."

"Sammi?" She called after him as he started to leave.

"What?"

"The gun."

"The gun?"

"Reilly's gun."

"What about it?"

"I can find it." She stood, put on her sarong and walked past him, letting it all sink in. He smoked a cigarette, letting his anger pass. He didn't know why he was mad, or at whom, but something told him that Maurice was the key. Still, if they could get to the gun . . .

"And around and around went the big fuckin' wheel, in and out went the big prick of steel. . . ." Byers was leading a bawdy sing-along in the main room. Sam wandered out and looked around the room. Bishop still sat on a stool in the corner, looking very stoned as he tried to sort out a stack of documents.

"Sam, if you don't mind . . ." Bishop signaled him over. "Sign these where I've *exed* them." He handed Sam a black, GI-issue ballpoint pen.

Sam chuckled when he filled in the blanks. "Universal Life Church," he wrote for denomination. His hands were shaky, his signature not much more than a scribble.

"You did the ceremony very well," Bishop said, sounding sincere.

"Just following my real calling. Think I'll start a church based on Chantao's. 'Temple of the Bamboo Pipe,' we'll call it. Care to join?" Sam found it hard to carry on a light conversation with Bishop, especially now. He had the strangest urge to tell him about the gun. Nah, he thought, let it be a surprise.

"From what I've seen tonight, you'd have a good following." Bishop folded the documents and took them back to the changing room. Rabbit sat in the middle of the room, next to the cake, reading Choe's fortune. Sam spied the sack of rice in the corner, opened it, and started throwing it around the room. Soon, it looked like a snowstorm in the tropics. Chan took a big handful, slipped over to the room where Son was balling the nurse, and chucked a big handful over the top of the wall. Curses and laughs came from the other side.

"Sam, Rabbit wants to read your fortune." Claudine pulled him toward the clutch of people near the cake, now all covered with rice. Rabbit grabbed Sam's hand and started to read his fortune. Claudine translated. "You have a long lifeline . . . for a roadrunner . . ."

"No editorial comments, please. . . ." Sam laughed, but could tell that Rabbit was serious.

"She say that in matters of love, you have many problems. It is hard for you to sustain, keep, but that you love many people."

"Not far off base." Sam noted that Claudine had no reaction.

"Every three, four years, your life, it changes. You have beaucoup highs and lows. You are sensitive, but try to hide it. Your fortune is very broken." Stoneman shrugged when Rabbit gave Sam's hand a squeeze and let it go.

"Hey, this is getting good. . . ." Rosen and Byers had pulled stools next to the wall, peeking over the top into Son's room. Soon, people were climbing on anything to get a peek. Sam shook his head and smiled. Choe looked a little embarrassed, but Stoneman put his arm around her and gave her a hug, the fun of the night overcoming the antics of his friends. They smoked a joint, huddled together there, not wanting to let the good feelings go.

"Man, you should retire to one of the rooms. It seems to be the in thing to do." Sam smiled at Stoneman.

"And let the world watch? You're out of your fuckin' gourd." Ty took a big hit of champagne. "No. Just going to sit right here."

Rabbit turned to Claudine, reached for her hand to read her palm. She stared at it for a long time, her face serious. She looked at Claudine, who shook her head from side to side, as though she were pleading with Rabbit not to say what she saw.

An explosion rocked the den, nearly turning over the menorah. It was followed by a hundred secondary explosions, then another mighty blast.

"Ammo dump . . ." Rider yelled as they tried to get to their clothes. They were all bumping into one another, suddenly shifting gears. Claudine told Stoneman to stay, that she would take pictures for him. Sam fought with the fly on his jeans, which was caught in his shirttail. Nobody paid attention to Son and the nurse, whose intimacy had been finally destroyed by the rush for clothes hung in their room.

Sam was halfway down the sidewalk when he realized he'd forgotten his shoes. He pushed against the wave of bodies on the dark, narrow path. A bright glow from the exploding ammunition dump lit up the night sky. All over the city, soldiers fired rifles into the air to scare off the ghost. He found his shoes and cut through the big room, heading for the door.

Stoneman and Choe sat alone on the floor, surrounded by rice and the scattered remains of the party. A boot had smashed the confection bride and groom into the middle of the remainder of the cake.

XXVII.

After the Gun

CLAUDINE'S BREATHING SLOWED, but the ragged edge of
ecstasy still remained. Sam could feel the shift through
her body, that wonderful time after sex when the mind
creeps back to reality. He hardly noticed the sticks and
little rocks pricking his back through the poncho liner,
only vaguely registered the movements in the camp a hundred feet away. Their passion was what mattered on this
humid, soft night in the jungle. They stayed together, trying to hold on to the moment for as long as they could,
until nature slipped them apart.

The deep jungle that ran beside the small river near Pha
Doh's camp belonged to no one during the dark hours
before morning. They'd slipped away from the camp for
an hour together before the trek at sunrise in search of the
gun. Maybe it was the tension of the coming trip, or that
before they would have never considered leaving the city
at night, much less making love in the jungle. But once
they'd decided to sneak off, the sense of abandon seemed
to spill over to everything, especially sex. Sam and Clau-

dine did all the things they liked the most, wadding the camouflage poncho liner on the riverbank as they groped around, twisted, found each other. Sam's tongue searched Claudine's body. He wanted to absorb every taste, every smell, as though to file them away for a lifetime.

Brilliant stars filtered through the wisp of her hair that tickled his face. Sam breathed through the sweetness. His mind drifted back to the past days.

To Sam, it was all simple enough. They would go with the best Montagnard soldiers, catch the gun in enemy hands and film it being captured. Marty and Pha Doh had worked out the technical part; how to get there, how to get out. Even Rider finally agreed it was a sound plan, if not an unsound idea. No one asked where he got the information. It was obvious that each of them had their own reasons for wanting the gun, that there were questions best left unasked.

Plans had been made over dinner at the Café de la Poste, amidst the chatter and bitching of the retired French prostitutes who lived out their days in the seedy hotel, waiting for their checks from Paris. Claudine told him the location as he was writing the script for the ammo dump attack. From there, the wheels started to spin.

At the restaurant, the conversation had been straightforward, just like a planning session for a mission.

Just when he thought everyone had finished, Claudine launched into Sam, went at him with a vengeance in front of his friends. It was the first time she'd ever questioned his reasoning. He reacted in anger, defensively, afraid that someone would waver and pull out of the trip. Then he'd gathered his cool and realized she was going on the offensive, not letting the situation that had brought on the tensions and contradictions block them from their goal.

Now Claudine shifted on top of him on the blanket, but made no move to roll off. He let his fingers play in the soft nape of hair at the base of her spine. Her breathing was steady, just on the fringe of sleep. What had she been testing in him? Even now, he wasn't sure.

He'd told her in no uncertain terms that she was free to pull out. He needed only Chan and Marty. She shook her head, as if to say that wasn't her point. He was not a soldier, and this was a trip for soldiers. That he could carry his own weight was "bullshit," a term she'd picked up from him.

"You, Sam, are not being honest with yourself. Your mind has slipped into dangerous places. Your *moi*, how do you say, your ego, is on the line. You want to drag all of your friends off into the jungle so that you can embarrass Reilly, lead the evening news, impress New York. It would be better for you to go to Bangkok, Hong Kong, somewhere to rest. You are trying to get it all back at one time." She had seen this before in her friends, she said, the ones who never came back.

"Hey, I'm not forcing anyone to come. And I'm not the only one who will benefit from the trip, either," he answered. "Pha Doh will, if he gets the gun. Chan and Marty make money when I make money. When I gain status in New York, so does Chan."

Sam's temper rose from his gut. He wanted to hit her, to shut her up, a desire he rarely felt toward anyone, let alone a woman.

The argument with Claudine soon spread. Everyone made clear their willingness to go.

Marty needed the pump of the long patrols that he'd relived in his mind a thousand times in the past few years. This is why he'd come back to Cambodia, to go out with Pha Doh just one more time.

Stoneman wanted a big hit, a big score. His stringer status had always suited him, but now he wanted something more, money to get Choe out when the time came. Besides, when he moved his new bride out of the whore-house into their little apartment, he found eight of her relatives and a monkey already settled in. Choe sat next

to him, listening to the strange tongues, but she didn't
need to know the words to understand the tension. For the
first time in his life, Ty told Claudine, he had something
to lose. It was worth the risk.

Rider didn't say much. They'd hashed it out in the room
before dinner, all the obvious questions covered. He was
giving Sam the pucker test, making certain that the decision was based on facts, not emotion or reaction.

Finally, it was Chan who put the argument into perspective. "Each person has a choice," he insisted. "No
one has to go anywhere unless they want to." The plan
was as solid as something like this could be.

"You're really talking about something else," Sam told
Claudine, "not finding the One-Oh-Five."

Claudine got up from her chair and walked around. Sam
followed her. Gingerly, he slipped his arms around her and
for long minutes they stood silent. He could feel her body
jerk from sobs beneath her loose Indian blouse. She turned
and buried her head in his shoulder, crying like a child.
He understood now why she would come along.

After the dinner, the group headed for Chantao's. Chan
and Sam smoked into the morning while Claudine slept in
another room. Even after ten pipes, Chan managed to cut
through to the guts of the problem.

"You can't win, Tiger. The people she loves are all
roadrunners like you, a crazy redneck who hangs it out
day after day." Chan was honest in his opinion that she
was more attracted to the persona than the person, that he
still didn't feel that photography was her main goal. But
he also said that he thought she was in love with Sam.
"Now, because she loves you, she wants to change you,
protect you from harm. Yet she knows that if you change,
she won't love you anymore."

Sam took another pipe from the Poppy Mother, drew
the opium deep into his lungs. He wondered to himself
whether she would have shipped the drugs if she'd felt that
way, then realized that it was the events since then that

had made Chan see their relationship in this light. He thought about coming clean, telling Chan the whole story, but realized that he loved her, too, and that he would protect her as well.

Sam heard someone stirring in the bushes, back toward the camp. A low sigh, the splatter of a stream of water on the ground told Sam he wasn't in danger. He didn't need to move.

"Sam, hey, Sam . . ." Marty called softly through the bushes, snapping him away from his thoughts. "Party's over, man. Better get back into the camp." Sam slowly rolled Claudine over in the blanket, found her clothes. He slipped on his jeans and gently woke her enough to walk, wrapped in the camouflage nylon poncho liner, to the beds that Pha Doh had made for them around the low fire.

A Montagnard sentry stood frozen ten yards away. He couldn't stop looking at Claudine's long, white leg uncovered to the hip. Sam pulled the blanket over her, winked at the young soldier, who shot him a knowing grin, and rolled on his back. The first tiny traces of light pushed at the dark sky to the east. He lay there with his thoughts until the overwhelming need to piss drove him into action.

As he stood relieving himself into the jungle, he detected a movement on the rail of the bridge. Satterfield sat with his feet dangling, looking down the river. Sam's sleep, for this night, was finished. Twice he stubbed his toe trying to get up the bank to the road, but he muffled his curses. The two men sat on the bridge in silence for a few minutes.

"It's the oldest adage of war, you know . . . the most dangerous time is just before dawn." Marty spoke in a low whisper, his voice sounding like it came from another time. "I guess that's why I got in the habit of waking long before sunrise, to keep my private watch." Marty leaned over and spit tobacco juice into the river. "But now it's become my own time, when I sort out my thoughts, decide what to do with the day ahead. Tell you what, though . . . ," he said, turning to Sam. Even through the darkness he could detect a grin on Satterfield's face. "I've never been attacked at dawn."

"You spent a lot of time in the boonies in Nam, didn't you?" Sam fingered the tobacco pouch, but couldn't bring himself to take a chew even though it was still too dark to smoke.

"We were always in the hills. Pleiku was a big city for us. I bet I didn't spend a week in Saigon in three years. Just let the paychecks pile up until I got around to picking them up. Nah, our unit dealt strictly with the 'Yards. I had very little to do with the Vietnamese."

"I guess things are pretty different now, aren't they?" In the camp they heard someone rustling around, poking the fire.

"Yeah, yeah they are. . . ." Marty ran his fingers through his beard, looking at the gray streak of light building in the sky. Sam could tell he was trying to decide if he wanted to talk this out. "Look, ten years ago, when I first met Pha Doh and his merry troopers, the Berets who came to Nam had volunteered to go there. We understood what we had to do, even spoke a bit of the language. Our unit was damn well trained and the 'Yards taught us more. All they wanted to do was kill Vietnamese and get their mountain lands back, which fit right into our program. We just had to make sure their guns were pointed at the right bunch of Vietnamese." Marty chuckled and spit. "Anyhow, I had a lot to give them. Bullets, guns, food, a helicopter for medevacs. You name it, and ol' Satterfield could come up with it."

"And here in Cambodia you're just another civilian. . . ." Sam understood Marty's dilemma better now. Despite the long hair and the beard, he could see the soldier underneath, his posture always erect, his eyes constantly searching the jungle. Sam wondered if the day would come when he would look back on this time in

Cambodia in the same way Marty saw Nam, as the peak of his life.

"Who was the guy who wrote 'You can't go home again'? Well, he was right. The 'Yards have been good to me. Let me stay in their camp, even set up this little trip today . . . mainly because they're bored and want a little action, too. But I'm a liability to them now. I can't compensate for my whiteness anymore with choppers and radios. This trip is my swan song as a soldier, Sam."

"This might be all of our swan songs," Sam replied, half joking. "But when you took over Sophan's job, you stepped over the line. You won't be a soldier today." Sam had wondered how he would handle this. "Marty, I'm going to ask you not to carry a weapon. I'm cutting it close enough coming out on this little trip. If the word got out that one of the crew was armed. . . ."

"I was armed the day of the massacre. . . ." Marty looked him straight in the eye, making a statement more than an argument.

"Right, but you weren't working for the network then. A few months ago, the embassy found out that a photo stringer was carrying a piece out on the highways. They picked the bastard up in the field and put him on a C-130 to Thailand. No explanation, no nothin'. His shit is still in storage at the hotel. He can't get back in." Sam decided it was light enough to smoke. Marty watched him light a Salem. "Look, if you want to be a soldier, I'll carry the sound gear. If it means a lot to you. . . ."

"No, forget it. I told you I'd work for you, and that's what I'm going to do." Marty looked past Sam into the camp, where Pha Doh was picking up a coffee pot and three tin cups. "Just remember this. If the shit comes down out there today, we all may damn well have to cross that line of yours. You understand that?"

"I understand." Sam got the feeling that Marty hoped it would.

"Café?" Pha Doh placed the tin cups on the concrete

rail of the bridge and started pouring hot brew before they could answer. Sam took a sip and nearly choked on the raw, herbal coffee which was bitter like nothing he'd tasted before.

Pha Doh said something to Marty in dialect, and they both laughed. "He says it'll put lead in your pencil."

Sam took a friendly swing at Pha Doh as Marty jumped off the rail and stretched. "The rate you've been going for the past couple of days, you need it."

Sam toasted Pha Doh with the cup and forced down another sip. Like bad whiskey, it numbed the taste buds on the first hit, which made the remainder drinkable. "Ain't life weird? When things are shit with the job, this lady decides to twist the hook. Try that, and you're spoiled for life. She's the only woman I've ever lusted after that was better than I'd fantasized." Sam could still detect her smell on his body.

"Not really. The way she figures it is that when you're on a roll, you don't need her. Chick's a mother at heart, man. A real Earth Mother. Now you're vulnerable and need those strokes. You've gotten more than you deserve. But just wait until you get your confidence back." They mulled over Marty's philosophical statement as they watched the camp come to life.

"Pha Doh, do we really have a chance of finding the gun?" Sam wanted to check one more time before they hit the road. He'd been on short patrols before, but he'd always had the option to pull out when the heat was on. This time it was his party and he couldn't leave.

"We find gun. No sweat. Pha Doh men, they watch." The Major pointed with his eyes.

"What'ya mean, they watch?" Sam was puzzled.

"They've checked out your information." Marty explained.

"Why didn't they take it out?"

"Because a television team from the United States of America wants to take pictures of them doing it. These guys haven't been on television in years." Marty grinned at Sam, knowing he was making him uncomfortable.

"He's not staging this little mission, is he?" That was the last thing Sam needed right now, a staged story.

"Nah. It would take more than two people to wipe it out. Pha Doh keeps an eye on everything around here. Until now, the gun wasn't one of his problems. Maybe he needs the exercise, to keep the boys on their toes." Marty picked up his empty cup and started back to camp. "Any other questions?" Marty grinned slightly, but Sam could tell that he didn't care for his doubts about Pha Doh's tactics and motives.

"Fine, fine . . . just checking." As they walked back, Sam found himself suddenly realizing just what they would be doing today. In a few minutes, they'd be walking away from the security of this camp into no man's land, fair game for anyone. He now questioned every aspect of what they were doing; whether he'd let his desire to score big overwhelm his better judgment, whether Claudine was right accusing him of trying to get it back all at once. Too late now. It was going to be a long day.

XXVIII.

The Gun

THE MONTAGNARDS SELECTED for the mission stood in loose formation, each man checking the pack of the one in front, making certain they had everything they'd need. Sam, Chan and Marty did the same, dividing up the gear, giving the camera a quick run, taking a few pictures of the soldiers, getting rid of extra weight. Sam repacked the ditty bag, putting spare batteries on the bottom, the film magazines and spare film rolls next, with the Bell and Howell windup Filmo on top, as a backup for Chan. He stuck as many C ration cans into the outside pockets as would fit.

Claudine wandered around the camp, taking shots of the Montagnards cooking, getting ready for the day. Stoneman was the most relaxed, cameras around his neck, ready to go. They all wore jungle fatigues, at Pha Doh's request. Where they were headed, civilian clothes would just draw attention. Sam felt for his Buddha, checked for chewing tobacco and cigarettes, a ritual he'd performed three times in the past ten minutes.

They stayed on the road for a couple of miles. The 'Yards seemed confident and loose. The point men were a hundred feet in front, followed by two more soldiers and Pha Doh, his radioman, then Chan, Marty, Sam, Claudine and Stoneman. The remaining soldiers brought up the rear. They were leaving the road and heading for the jungle. Sam's gut rolled in fear.

The jungle trail was narrow, but much traveled. Ahead, the point man was almost out of sight, checking each turn in the trail, his eyes scanning the jungle canopy, the tree trunks for booby trap wires, the ground for any signs of recent footprints or digging. Sam jumped every time the patrol flushed birds in the trees, his nerves sizzled at every sound he couldn't place. He thought of the "Bouncing Betty," a mine on trip wires that would pop up about groin high, de-balling the person behind. Or 105 shells buried in the ground nose up, a solid strike with a boot all that was needed to blow up half the patrol. In Vietnam, booby traps became an art. They took out more soldiers than battles. Luckily, Cambodia hadn't reached that stage.

Sweat soaked Sam's fatigues, even though the sun hadn't really yet warmed the air. He dug out a handful of salt tablets from the pocket on his thigh, and washed them down with brackish water from his canteen. He looked at the people in front and realized that Pha Doh had two weapons slung on his back, including Marty's Swedish K. That irritated Sam for a moment, but he let it pass.

He had just managed to get his nerves and stomach under control when suddenly the 'Yards stopped. The point man had his arm straight in the air, his fist clenched. Everyone dropped into a crouch. Sam didn't breathe. He heard Claudine suck air between her teeth, he could feel the tension from her body. Slowly, he turned his head and tried to give her a smile. The fatigue shirt was too big for her, the neck of her red tee shirt showed through. She pursed her lips, licked the sweat with her tongue.

Then Sam heard the voices. He recognized the singsong

Cambodian, short snatches of conversation followed by laughter. Whoever was ahead of them made no attempt to hide their presence. The chatter seemed to be coming from the bank below them. Marty turned and made a walking motion with his fingers, then signaled the number four, and pointed toward the river, where the trail paralleled the one they traveled.

Sam's legs shook from the tension, sweat poured down his face as the voices came closer. He heard what sounded like a stick slapping against the tree trunks along the riverbank. Marty pointed again. Through the dense foliage, Sam caught a glimpse of the young men, dressed only in black shorts, casually walking by the bushes where the patrol hid, AK-47s slung over their backs, a small towel tucked into the waistbands of their shorts.

Soon the point men pumped his fist up and down in the air and they moved out again. Sam thought he'd been careful earlier, but now he tried to avoid every twig on the trail, anything that made noise. The Montagnards still seemed loose, but more alert. Pha Doh turned his head and shot the crew a big smile and wink.

They rounded a bend another mile down the trail, coming upon a small clearing. The soldiers fanned out, checked the brush, then relaxed, talking quietly among themselves. Through the trees, Sam could see where the jungle cut back from the river, making a floodplain that was covered with paddy dikes, trails zigzagging in all directions. He dropped his pack, welcoming the chance to rest, to settle his nerves. He'd never knowingly been that close to the enemy, and he was still shaken. He took a long drink from the canteen.

"Go easy on that stuff," Marty said, watching Sam take another hit. "It's got to last all day."

"Right," Sam said, screwing the lid back on the plastic bottle. His throat was still dry. He wrung sweat from the red bandanna he wore around his neck. "That certainly was an interesting little get-together back there," he said, trying to hide his fear behind nonchalance. "Guess I'd overlooked the fact that we'd have to get past the Rouge to get to the Renegades."

Marty washed his mouth out with water, broke off a fresh chew of tobacco and watched one of the Montagnards as he honed the edge of a long fighting knife on the leather of his boot. "Well, look at it this way, we saved those fellows' lives." Marty spit between his boots. "If we hadn't been along, that would have been their last bath in any river."

"Sammi . . . ," Claudine called in a low voice from behind him. "You are very funny in the trousers that go plufff. . . ." She spread her hands and grinned. She looked like a ragamuffin herself, completely gobbled up by the borrowed uniform. Her waistline was belted just below her breast, the shirt hung halfway to her knees.

"You're one to talk. . . ." Sam heard the rattling of paper, turned and watched as Pha Doh double-checked the map, discussed the trails with the point man. He turned back to Claudine and took one of the Nikons from around her neck. He took five pictures, two in serious poses, the other three of her cutting up, posing like a fashion model. The rear guard soldiers giggled and looked at the ground in embarrassment.

"We're getting close to the object of our affection," Marty said. "About a klick beyond that far treeline." Marty pried the lid off a can of C ration fruit cocktail with his knife. "The 'Yards had it located before, near here. There's a road over there," he said, pointing along the treeline that paralleled the floodplain, "and they're sure that the gun has been moved that way overnight. Now all we have to do is avoid the spotter planes. We are what the Air Force lovingly calls 'targets of opportunity.' "

"In other words," Sam said, waving his hand at the floodplain, "that is a free-fire zone?" Until this moment, those words contained no meaning. He'd heard them used by pilots on the radio during their attacks.

"You learn quick for a country boy. And we can't talk to them on that thing," he said, nodding toward the radio, "because you just know those guys are listening, too." Marty stuck out the green can. "Wanna sip?" He handed the can to an eager Sam. "If Pha Doh is right, we'll only be a klick from where this river dumps into the Bassac River. Highway 30 parallels the Bassac right back into town. That's where the jeeps will be waiting for us, right at the last government lines."

"We seem to be taking the scenic route. It's what, five, ten miles from Pha Doh's camp down here?" To Sam it seemed like fifty. The sun was high, midway in its track. His watch said twelve-thirty.

"Coming through the back door was one of our old Vietnam tactics, and there is no way we could slip through the government lines on Highway 30. Anyway, we had to leave from his sector." Marty leaned back on the rice paddy dike, revealing a fighting knife in his belt.

"Another hour, huh?" The prospect of finding the gun outweighed Sam's dread of walking in the sun. He heard low laughter from behind, smiled when he saw the Montagnard soldiers dutifully forming a shield around Claudine, who squatted at the edge of the clearing.

"She's going to drive the boys nuts," Marty said. "She's the prettiest white woman they've ever seen."

"Saddle up," Pha Doh called out in a low voice, the Old West phrase sounding far out of place in the jungle.

"That little bastard learned every cliché in the book when he trained in the States." Marty flipped the soundbox on his back, gave Sam a hand and pulled him up.

"One of these days I'm going to bring the son-of-a-bitch who designed this camera along on one of these little hikes," Chan complained. "Let him find out what it's like to carry this sucker. And let's get the asshole in New York who won't give me something lighter to walk point." He stretched his right arm, picked up the camera again and rested it on his shoulder. When Sam first arrived in Cambodia, he'd offered once to carry Chan's camera. Steve had shot him a horrified look, as though he'd suggested molesting Chan's little daughter.

The knowledge that they were closing in on the gun overcame Sam's exhaustion. He kept a wary eye on the sky, praying that a spotter plane wouldn't pop up and decide that they were fair fodder for the day's body count. They finally reached the treeline, paused a few minutes while Pha Doh gave instructions to two of the soldiers, who went ahead as scouts. The pace slowed, as the Major kept the same pace as the scouts. Finally, they hit a road. There were fresh tire tracks impressed deep in the mud.

Marty gave Sam a thumbs up sign and mouthed the word "fresh." The patrol remained in the jungle, skirting the road by a few yards, staying out of the open. Again, the point man's fist went into the air. They stopped, squatted down in position and waited. Scouts seemed to appear out of nowhere, popping onto the trail and huddling with Pha Doh. Their motions were animated, smiles on their faces. The Major signaled for the others to gather round him.

"Beaucoup luck," he whispered, clearing a patch of ground with the flat of his hand. "They stop, hide truck and gun under trees, wait for night. Five, maybe six men with gun. Couple more asleep under trucks. Everything there together."

"Where are they?" Sam could barely whisper the question through his dry throat.

"Half klick." Pha Doh turned to his soldiers. In dialect he explained the instructions as he drew them in the dirt, telling them how he wanted the ambush carried out. Marty watched with an experienced eye. "He's got to finish them off. Otherwise one of them might get on the radio . . . he's telling them not to damage the trucks if they can help it. . . ."

The soldiers nodded, unsnapped the protective loops of their knives, gave their rifles one final check. Pha Doh unslung the Swedish K and looked at Marty. Sam could tell what Marty was thinking, his lips pressed together under the beard. After a long moment, he shook his head no. Sam was grateful . . . and relieved.

Chan reached for the umbilical cord, hooked up the camera and took a light-meter reading. He signaled Marty to hold the shotgun mike near Pha Doh and got a tight shot of the Major's finger drawing in the dirt, then waddled back a few steps to get a wide shot. Claudine and Stoneman were right behind Sam, quietly pulling the film through their Nikons, getting their setup. Sam made a mental note to get some of these pictures from them.

"When we make contact," Chan whispered, "I'll be rolling all the way through. You just stay with me." Marty gave him an affirmative nod. Sam found the record button on the Sony by feel, turned it on and gripped the mike in his hand.

Four soldiers slipped into the jungle, fanning out on both sides of the trail. The point man watched their progress, then gave the signal to move out. Sam's breath was shallow and fast, his heartbeat seemed to be going off the top of the scale. He signaled Claudine to move in front of him, somehow feeling that if he could see her, she would be safer. They moved in starts and stops, the point man keeping them apace with the ambush team. Sam lost all sense of distance, how far they'd moved, where they were going. Birds continued to squawk in the trees, unconcerned by their presence.

Finally, at the edge of a slight rise, Pha Doh signaled for them to move forward, pointing to a grassy spot on the edge. They moved on their knees, holding their equipment tight to their bodies, totally aware of every sound they made. Chan rolled on his back and pushed his body up the rise with his feet. He placed the camera on the ground in position. Sam stayed back, waiting for the cameras to get into place. He crawled on his belly into a space between Marty and Claudine, lifting the brim of his jungle hat and peering over the rise.

In a small clearing, hidden by double canopy jungle, sat Reilly's gun. The long barrel was parallel to the ground, the hitch that extended beyond the breech attached to the back of a deuce-and-a-half army truck. Jerry cans of gasoline were wedged between wooden crates of ammunition in the truck bed. Sam could see the bare feet of one sleeping soldier sticking out from under the truck. Two soldiers squatted in the dirt next to the open cab door, playing a game with sticks and rocks. A short distance away, two more trucks were tucked into the woods, a flash of the green bottles visible under the covers. The chatter of the two soldiers floated the fifty yards to where Sam lay. The sentry walked around the clearing, stopping from time to time to watch the stick game. His rifle was casually draped over his back. Sam raised his eyebrows when Chan turned on the camera. The low hum of the motor sounded louder than he'd ever noticed before.

The guard made a comment, his buddies laughed and he walked to Sam's left, right into the hands of the two Montagnards hidden on the edge of the clearing. Chan hissed a low ''shit'' when he moved out of view.

Without warning, there was a crack, then a roar, as the Montagnards opened fire from three points. The soldiers sprang for cover. One man sprinted for the safety of the jungle. The nearest stick game player lunged for his rifle next to the truck. A burst of Swedish K fire slammed him into the fender, broken in half. He slowly slid into the dirt.

The firefight took no more than thirty seconds. The Montagnards chased the survivors into the jungle. A distant burst of M-16 fire marked the dispatch of the last Renegades into the afterlife.

Camera still running, Chan zoomed in on the dead man next to the gun. Sam talked into the radio mike in a low voice, describing the scene, the burst of fire in the jungle adding to the tension of the recording. Marty was grinning from ear to ear, obviously pleased with the precision of the ambush.

"Renegades . . . *fini bibi* . . ." Pha Doh turned to them, slapped another clip into the Swedish K, and started scampering down the shallow bank to the gun. Sam took a deep breath and relaxed, his body pasted to the ground, feeling like a ton weight. His legs didn't want to move; the adrenaline surge gone, he was drained of all energy. He didn't know whether to laugh or cry. They'd done it, they'd found the gun. Like all prizes, be they guns or Cracker Jacks, the gun looked small and insignificant in the clearing.

Sam struggled to his knees, stumbled down the hill to where Pha Doh stood looking at the dead sentry. The man's shorts were pulled down over his knees. His gun lay in front of him. "Dumb fucker," Marty muttered, pointing to the surgically fine cut that ran across his throat from ear to ear like a meaty red smile. "You always face into the jungle when you shit."

Sam felt his ass clinch when he saw the dead man. He didn't look more than fifteen, a soft layer of fuzz on his face the closest he'd ever come to growing a beard.

The Montagnards were cutting up now, crawling down the barrel of the gun, posing for pictures. Stoneman cursed them in a friendly voice, wanting to get a couple of shots of the gun sitting alone in the clearing.

Pha Doh peered into the cab of the truck and pulled out a map case. He spread a map on the ground near the dead soldier, the cheap paper tearing at the folds. It told the whole story of the attacks on Phnom Penh. Xs marked the spots from which they had fired, the number of rounds dutifully listed alongside each site. At the center of the map, a red line showed where the insurgents had repositioned the gun a couple of miles north. Fifty rounds had been fired.

"That was the market," Chan said, pulling the focus tight on the map. Sam traced the red line to the west, measured off the mileage with his finger, and found where they'd fired twenty rounds. The gun was less than five miles from the ammo dump.

"Fuckers were good, you have to say that for them." Marty shuffled through the papers scattered on the ground. In a small leather wallet was a picture of the man lying next to the wheel. Inside, a government ID card listed him as a major in the Ninth Brigade. A small notebook listed names and addresses in Thailand and the United States, two marked with stars.

"Well, Fort Sill can be proud of this man. Unfortunately, he wound up betting on the wrong players." His ID indicated he'd trained at the huge Oklahoma artillery school. All of the dead men wore the same beret Sam had seen on the day of the sniper attack.

Marty ripped away at a tightly sealed envelope, cutting through the layers of tape to reach the contents, then let out a low whistle. "Oh boy, look at this." He handed Sam a packet of photographs and negatives.

"I'll be goddamned." There was Reilly, swinging from the rafters with a young boy. "I wonder if he knows about these?" Sam asked Marty in a low whisper.

"You can bet on that. I think you should hang on to them, just in case. . . ."

"Right." Sam stuffed them inside his shirt, both delighted with his luck and bothered by the contents. He literally had Reilly by the balls now, but he wasn't sure he quite wanted it this way.

"One thing bugs me," Chan said, resting the camera on the ground after wandering the clearing. "How did they zero their targets. They had a forward observer somewhere." Marty smiled, and headed for the truck cab. He located the rubber ducky antenna of a portable radio that stuck out from under the seat. He pulled the PRC-6 field radio out and flipped it on. Cambodian voices poured out of the speaker. "They use the Army repeater, that's how. . . ."

"First class all the way, it would seem. . . ." Sam took the radio, looked at it and handed it to Pha Doh. Claudine called out to Sam, laughing. Montagnards hung off the barrel, swinging back and forth, acting like children.

"Come . . . I take your picture with gun." Sam moved under the barrel, Montagnards on both sides, his arms around their shoulders. Then the whole crew drifted over, posing like a football team for the yearbook snapshot. They all smiled, kidded, and all the tension of the day drained away. Now Sam knew firsthand the satisfaction of victory. This time he really didn't even notice the bodies sprawled around.

"Let's do a close, then didi. . . ." Chan had loosened up for a couple of minutes, but he didn't take to the idea of hanging around. Sam did at least a half-dozen closes, muffing a couple by laughing, another spoiled by a Montagnard jumping into the frame and giving a peace sign. Finally Marty cursed them, and they moved out of the way, like scolded kids.

"Pha Doh have good idea. . . ." He signaled for Sam and Marty to come back to the map. His men dragged the bodies into the brush, collected weapons and cleaned away any trace of their presence. "We half klick from Highway 30 . . . ," he said, tracing the route on the map. "Then only couple more klicks to bridge, the government lines. We take gun to Colonel Reilly!" The smile on his face would have lit up a room.

"Whaddya you think? . . ." Sam looked at Chan, who shrugged, then at Marty.

"Well, we have two options," Marty said. "I'm all for getting out of here the fastest way possible. That's the trucks. The problem is crossing government lines, but we've got the radios and can tell them we're coming. If we walk out, we'll have the same problem. . . ." Marty rubbed his beard, paused for a moment then said, "I vote for the trucks."

Sam felt Claudine kneel down next to him, listening to

the discussion. As the others rose, she spoke to him in a quiet, soft voice. "You are very brave man, Sammi . . ." He started to argue with her on that point. She gently put her hand over his mouth. "No, you listen. I love you before we come here, and finding the gun would not make a difference. I love you because you worry, because you try to take care of Claudine and everybody. You have a good story, to make New York happy. That what you want. You need rest now, Sammi. My friend has beautiful house in Bali. I take you there. You come with Claudine?" She kissed him lightly on the cheek.

"Yeah, I'll go, but not for a few days yet. Got to wait for the bombing halt. I have to see that through. But, hell yes, I'll go. . . ."

"Hey, redneck, guess who's driving?" Marty leaned around the bed of the ruck. "I can't handle a jeep well, let alone one of these big fuckers."

"If you can't drive a jeep, or sharpen a knife, or build a fire, how in hell did you become a Green Beret?"

"Be an officer, baby, be an officer. Get the enlisted swine to do it." Marty took off his jungle hat and scratched his head shyly. "Now you know why my nickname in training was Jungle Jim."

Sam laughed, helped Claudine into the cab, then got into the driver's seat. His daddy had owned a Ford dealership. He'd been able to drive anything with wheels since he was twelve. The shift was straightforward, five-speed dual axle. His only problem was towing the gun and all the people down the dirt road. Pha Doh sent two soldiers ahead to secure the road, then jumped on the truck bed. Chan and one of the Montagnards cranked up the other trucks.

The motor stalled on the first try, to the hoots and yells from the back, but Sam soon had it underway, leaving the axle in low gear. They bounced and ground over the road, made of little more than two ruts through the jungle floor. Branches brushed over the cab, slapping the people in the back, who cursed and laughed trying to dodge them. Twice he stopped and waited for a soldier to wave him on. He rounded a bend and saw Highway 30 just ahead, the soldiers jumping on the back as he turned onto the paved road. Two more kilometers and they'd be in Fat City.

He brought the truck up to speed, mud from the tires thumping under the wheel wells as the pavement cleaned them off. Marty gave a big "yahoo," and through the rearview mirror, Sam saw Pha Doh work his way toward the cab with the radio. He leaned in the window of the door and shook the radio. Sam took it from him and checked the switches with quick glances. He keyed it twice, but he couldn't hit the repeater. Shit, he thought, we're almost there, and he dropped it on the floorboard. Ditching her hat, Claudine pulled her hair back alongside her head and laughed, someone who'd survived it all and could still laugh.

He ground the gears going into fourth, but was surprised at how well the truck ran. They cleared a slight curve, and through the jungle on both sides of the road he could see the bridge in the distance, with a clump of cars and jeeps parked beyond it. Someone had gotten word about the trip, but he didn't care. He glanced at Claudine and started to laugh. They fed on one another, laughing harder and harder. His eyes blurred, hiding for a moment the sight of the American jet rolling out, its cannons digging a trail of bullets straight down the pavement toward the trucks.

XXIX.

Fini Bibi

RED TAKES OVER. The red of fire, burning marketplaces, exploding trucks, funeral biers. Sam is running in circles, between huts. He needs to find air and be safe. Cambodians babbling in a language he doesn't know point at him, push him toward the flames. They are smiling. But why? Why are they smiling?

The dream recurs over and over. Like a movie flashing before his eyes again and again. There is always the fire, the same taunts, the same faces. Claudine appears, in a red wrapping sheet, the thin cloth swirling in red.

"Come, Sammi . . . you come with me. I have been through the fire already. I can save you. I know the way out." The smoke lifts slightly. Chantao appears, dressed in robes, then Rabbit. "M'sieur Moustache," she calls. Sophan gestures for Sam to follow them. The flames never touch them. The crowd pulls back with fear. Sam doesn't hesitate. He is a survivor. He will follow her into the flames, ask the price later.

"Stay here with me, Sammi . . . hold on to me. You

stay with me," she says, her rigid arms clutching his body
in the cab of the truck. The red of her tee shirt becomes
the red of her blood, then fire. The bullet holes in her
chest, her broken neck, in the dream they don't exist, don't
matter anymore. He holds her against the door of the overturned truck, tight. That's what matters, that they are waiting for the fire to come. "I know the way out, Sammi, I
know the way out. Red is what you want, Sammi . . . stay
with Claudine."

He is running again, through the blazing huts, leaping
across the burning biers. He pushes toward the flames,
following the chorus; Rabbit, Chantao, Sophan chanting
to him, telling him to stay. Hold on to Claudine, deeper,
deeper, deeper. He sees himself, the fear in his face.

Claudine laughs, throws back her head and laughs. The
sound fills the truck cab, the marketplace, Sam's mind.
The fire is everywhere. Claudine breaks away, disappears
into the flames. Fire, red fire, the laughter. He chases her
laughter deeper and deeper into the flames.

Sam jerked awake, the pain in his head only dulled by
the opium. The pipes had been his salvation for the past
five days. But there was a price. He could not escape the
red, the fire dream. The stitches in his scalp and on his
face were only annoying reminders, but deep down he
knew the discomfort triggered the dream. No matter how
he lay, the pain was there. Every part of his body ached.

Lying there on the mat, his eyes closed, he took inventory. A dozen stitches in his scalp, his skull dully throb-
bing from having landed hard on the edge of Claudine's
door. Sticking plaster flecked his face, as though he'd
shaved his entire face with a straight razor while drunk.
Slivers of windshield glass were still lodged in his skin.
The imprint of the steering wheel was etched on his chest,
the gearshift lever on his knee.

Nothing really added up in his mind anymore. What had
driven him so far before was irrelevant now. In the morning he would be on a plane. He would not be headed for

a little house on Bali, but for Paris, with her ashes. Rider had taken care of everything, the tickets, the arrangements. Chantao had let him come to the den well before curfew when the regulars would drift in, and he would stay after they left, unable to return to the hotel, the studio. In the morning, she would give him little balls of cooked opium to fight the stiffness and the pain. He drifted off again, but this time his mind pulled back when he saw the red. Years later, he would hear the song "Dream Weaver" on the stereo and be suddenly overwhelmed by the red. Who would help him make it through the night? But now, his conscious mind told him, this story was done. It was all over. *Fini.*

He heard voices. Tonight they were all here, his friends. They would say goodbye for a while, put to rest this chapter of their lives. Sam knew he would be a roadrunner again, even return to these mats. But he would never belong here again. That was the difference. The next time would be on borrowed time, the Poppy Mother's time. This Cambodia would be no more than a vivid memory. Sam thought a lot about that during those nights sprawled across Chantao's mats. He knew that anything would be better for the Cambodians than this war. Yet it was the war that had brought the roadrunners, the Rosens, the Martys here, shown them this way of life. Yes, all his friends smoking in the next room would agree that anything was better than war for this country. But as Rosen would later write, "Little did we know we were horribly wrong."

Sam slowly opened his eyes and saw Chantao in the blue light of the Howdy lamp. She was sitting in front of a little altar. Joss sticks burned in a wooden bowl, candles bracketed a photograph of a woman in jungle fatigues. Claudine was looking into her own camera, only a few hours before her death. It was the only picture Stoneman had been able to salvage from the roll in the bullet-shattered Nikon. The round had carved a corner from the negative. That camera was packed in Sam's case now. He would keep it.

Sam fought back the memory of that moment, the bullets marching up the hood, windshield glass flying, the steering wheel jerking in his hand, the blown tire whipping the gun like a lash. How the Montagnards screamed when the gun broke loose, crushing some beneath the wheels. Only the angle of the machine gun fire saved the rest of them, the bullets carving off the passenger side of the cab. Claudine's side. The Montagnard's truck behind him had exploded in a flash, Chan barely able to slip through the chaos.

He looked again at Chantao, who gently rocked back and forth, staring at the picture. She hid her grief. Claudine's life had become her own, the lines blurring between sister and daughter. Yet she still cooked pipe after pipe for Sam, never letting him shoulder the guilt alone. She fought his mind with the one weapon she knew well, the pipe.

Marty limped into his room still favoring his sprained knee. "The night has just begun, my man. You going to spend it all lying around in here?"

Sam pushed himself into a sitting position, knowing that he had to leave the dream behind, join his friends. Only he and Chantao knew how he'd made it through the past few days. As far as the others were concerned, Sam had continued working as before, seen the story through. Just the day before, Sam, Marty and Chan stood and watched as the jets dropped their last bombs at the tick of eleven. They monitored the radio as the pilots did climbing rolls in the cloudless sky and chatted among themselves, making the final trip back to Thailand. One of them played a harmonica. "Turkey in the Straw" wafted over the radio frequency. The bombing was over.

The sky hadn't fallen, the capital wasn't invaded. It would be nearly two years before the American ambassador would carry the folded American flag under his arm,

push through the crowd of confused Cambodians, and
climb aboard the last helicopter to a ship sitting offshore.

For now, the newspeg left with those jets. Cambodia
moved to the back burner, so Sam was free to take a break.
He'd won the prize he sought. The network was moving
him to Saigon; he was headed to New York to sign a con-
tract. Some prize. The box was empty, the price far too
high.

Sam was surprised when Rabbit showed Bishop into his
room. Was it all right for him to stay? she asked with her
eyes. Sam nodded yes. The Major sat awkwardly on the
mats, in his civilian clothes, waiting for Sam to speak.
Sam asked Rabbit to bring the pipe into the room. More
silence. Finally, Bishop spoke.

"That's a good picture of Claudine," he said, nodding
at the makeshift altar.

"I took it. May be the only decent picture I'll ever take
in my life."

Rabbit brought the pipe into the room, then left to get
them some tea. Sam reached over and threw Bishop a sarong from the peg. "House rules, gotta wear one." Sam
watched him change, and when he got to the point of
tying, he gave him a hand.

"I was going to use my belt," Bishop said, a small
smile crossing his face, remembering the last time.

"That doesn't mean we're in love, you know." They
watched in silence as Rabbit made the pipes. Sam wondered if Chantao wasn't avoiding Bishop, switching the
blame to him.

"I'm going to Saigon. Staff." Sam squeezed a sore spot
on his arm and picked out a tiny shard of glass.

"I know." Bishop grinned. "I read your cables."

"Not very interesting, are they?"

"Only when you use shorthand. I assume 'five pounds
of cheese' refers to money?"

"Yeah, a pound is a thousand, an ounce a hundred.
They send it over with the next pigeon."

"What's the stuff about a 'drought' in Saigon?" Bishop asked knowingly. "It rained every day I was there."

"Weed, there's a shortage of weed." Sam smiled, strangely feeling at ease with this man.

"I have something for you," Bishop said, digging a telex copy out of his shirt pocket. It was from the fighter pilot.

MOST DISTRESSED CIRCUMSTANCES OF TRUCK TARGET DESTROYED DURING RECENT MISSION SOUTH PHNOM PENH STOP TRUCKS FIT PRIORITY TARGET PROFILE STOP MY LAST INTENTION WAS TO KILL AND INJURE FRIENDLY CIVILIAN AND PERSONNEL STOP PLEASE ONPASS TO RESPONSI-BLE PARTY MY CONDOLENCES STOP CARTER, AARON, CAPT USAF

Sam read it twice, then handed it back to Bishop. "Did he get in trouble?"

"No. As he said, you fit the mission profile, you were in the target area. . . ."

"The free-fire zone, right?"

"You could call it that, yeah. We were after the trucks, you know. That was his mission."

"You knew, too?" Sam wasn't surprised.

"Yeah, but we didn't know you would be in it."

"The Chinaman tell you?"

"Well, our intelligence . . ."

"Bullshit."

"OK, bullshit. Yeah, we were tipped."

"Maurice?"

"You said it, I didn't." Bishop knew that he was talking out of turn, but he didn't seem to care.

"I can't wait to find that bastard. You know where he is?" Sam wanted some answers.

"No, he's gone. That's all I know." Bishop ran his finger through the flame of the Howdy lamp, testing the heat. "There's something else . . ."

"What?"

"Shit, Michaels, I'm talking too much. Let's just leave it lie, OK?"

"No, it's not OK." Sam felt a surge of hurt and anger. "Look, there are a half-dozen good troops dead because of this fuckup, not to mention Claudine. All I want to know is who did what to whom."

"All right." Bishop shifted uncomfortably on the mat. "Maurice was Claudine's brother."

Sam stared at the Major, unable to speak. It made sense; but then it didn't. Why would he let his own sister die for a lousy gun. "Was he the Chinaman?"

"I honestly don't know that, Sam. When the heat turned up on Reilly, he had a check run on Maurice. That little tidbit wound up in the report. Really, that's all I know."

"OK, then, while we're playing get honest, why are you here? To tell me these wonderful things? To tell me good-bye?"

"Yeah, and to ask you a question." Bishop shifted into his best hard-ass officer voice. "What do you know about some pictures?"

"Of Reilly?"

"Of Reilly."

"I have them, if that's what you want to know." Sam stared right back. "Why? Did he send you over here to do his dirty work?"

"No, no he didn't. He's gone, you know."

"When?"

"Last flight, yesterday. He was recalled. He's on his way back to the States, should be retired by this time tomorrow. Goes to the Pentagon for debriefing, picks up a nice set of golf clubs and joins the ranks of retired colonels burned out in this war."

"And he wants the pictures."

"No." Bishop shifted, stalling to collect his thoughts. "Funny, but in a way I feel sorry for him. The shit just piled up faster than he, or anyone else, could shovel. I know you won't agree, but he really wasn't that bad of a guy. Just in over his head. He didn't single you out, you know. He felt the same about all journalists.'' Bishop was eager for the next pipe, the first one just starting to clear his head. "But, God, did he hate you guys. . . .''

"We got that impression,'' Sam replied. Rosen started to come into the room, but Sam signaled him away with his eyes. Rosen saw Bishop smoking, nodded that he understood, and disappeared. "I think we were discussing pictures.''

"Yeah. Look, we all have our ghosts. I know about your problems with the heroin in the bag, I know about Claudine . . .''

"Little late to be threatening me . . .''

"Dammit, hear me out. All I'm saying is that those pictures can't do anything but destroy a man who has very little left. He didn't make Claudine a junkie, he didn't run a lab, and he didn't start this war.''

Sam lay slowly on his back, trying to find a comfortable position. They listened to the chatter from the other rooms, to the laughter, to the weird music.

"Do I make sense?''

"Yeah, yeah you do.'' Sam painfully rolled over and crawled to the corner of the room, lifting the mat. He returned with the envelope. "I have an idea.''

The negatives flashed as they hit the heat of the lamp, the 4×5 photographs smoked and curled as the flames consumed them.

"Satisfied?''

"Satisfied.'' Bishop looked at the ashes in the metal tray. "I didn't know what you'd say. There's no way you'd believe that I wasn't blowing smoke up your ass.'' Now he looked Sam straight in the eye. For the first time Sam realized that Bishop really was a warrior, not the martinet he'd created in his own mind. Bishop's eyes told him that. Like Marty's. Like Pha Doh's. The thousand yard stare. There's little these eyes haven't seen, the stare says. Sam had a good look at similar eyes this morning. His own. In the mirror. It's as though a layer has been stripped away, revealing the soul.

"Sam, there were a lot of guns. . . ." Sam felt his stomach jerk, his neck snap tight. "We took out at least five or six over the past couple of days. . . ." Bishop's voice droned on in a matter-of-fact monotone. The facts. The figures. All the stuff that made Sam know he was right. But the papers we found, Sam argued. "You got the renegade leader. But he was only a small player in the whole thing. I won't say any more."

"Fuck." That was all Sam could say. Fuck.

"Look. Four years ago, I had a patrol out in the Highlands. We staked out an operations center for two days. Counted heads. Did the usual field work. Coming back to the pick-up point, we ran into a company on the move. I lost four men out there." Bishop ran his finger idly over the tip of the blue flame coming from the cut-off Howdy bottle, testing the heat, testing the pain.

"When we got back to Division, I reported." He held his finger still for a long moment. "Colonel told me he'd changed his mind. He'd lost interest in that sector. He apologized for not recalling the patrol. I think he forgot we were even out there."

There was a long silence. Bishop finished his report to Sam.

"What got Reilly was that everyone thought he could find that gun, and he knew we had trouble when your story went on the air. Cambodia got Reilly. Not the Chinaman. Not the gun. Not you. Not these pictures. Funny thing about that, though. Reilly gave the Montagnards all the credit, even talked to Prek about using the Montagnards more in that role."

"I bet I know what he had to say about that. . . ."

"Right. Forget it." Bishop took a deep breath, exhaling loudly. "One thing I've discovered about the U.S. Army. There are 435 generals. Some are real ringers. But most are good. They select their own, you know. They didn't send Reilly here to get his star. They sent him here to have a reason not to give him one. Nobody could survive this tour. It's eaten up an ambassador, now Reilly. And it damn near ate up you.''

''Yeah.'' Sam felt deeply exhausted. He was completely drained. Somehow, realizing that the war didn't revolve around the gun, that no corners were turned, no careers destroyed was a release. He should have been angry, but he was past that now. Tonight, Sam was just sad.

''You happy about going to Saigon?''

''I'd rather stay in Cambodia, but they don't see it that way. I'll still have it as my beat. You're not through with me yet, amigo.''

''You think Cambodia was the Land of Long Knives, wait until you start prowling around Saigon. Good luck.''

''You staying in the Army?'' Sam didn't know why the question popped out.

''Right now, I have two choices. Stay in, or go home with the wife and two kids and take over my father's insurance agency in Dayton.''

''You're in for life.''

''You got it.''

Sam lay back on the mats and watched Bishop fiddle with the pipe. ''You certainly have taken to this part of the culture.'' Sam realized he could like Bishop. He still remembered the village, the soldiers following orders, spoken and unspoken. Bishop bought a part of Sophan's balls. He'd bought part of Claudine. They each owned a share of the misery.

''Hey Sam, Sam . . .'' Rosen called from the other room. ''We're moving the party back to the hotel. Get dressed.''

''Come on to the hotel. It could be fun.''

''Thanks. I'd like to.'' Bishop started to dress as Moss, Chan, and Rosen came into the room as Sam painfully pulled his jeans over his swollen knee. Chantao slipped in, holding out an ornate pipe, the one with the gold and

ivory inlay. It was Claudine's. She put it in his hands, her
red eyes showing the pain. He hefted it in his hands, still
amazed at its rugged lightness. Slowly, he handed it back.
Chantao looked hurt.

"Rosen, tell her that I want to leave it here. To be used
by me and my friends. It belongs to all of us." Rosen
translated, and a slow smile crossed her lips. She pulled
Sam to her, held him tightly for a moment.

"Au'voir." It was barely a whisper.

⊕   ⊕   ⊕

"As is zee tradition . . ." Rosen stood on the balcony of
his room overlooking the pool, holding a Nazi stance. "Zo
that he might know how pleased the Führer is wid hiz
vork, ve have zee following gifts from zee Herr Michaels. . . ."

"All right . . ." The crowd gathered around the poolside nearest the balcony. A portable stereo blasted Pink
Floyd, all the rooms of the Hôtel Royale raided for decent booze. Stoneman and Choe were churning out mon-
ster joints at an incredible speed.

"From zee medical Grupenführer, zee following . . ."
Rosen held up a battered condom. "As zo not to spread
zee nasty things he picks up from the gutter, this *lettre
française*, so kindly broken in by all zee colleagues. . . ."
The rubber drifted down from the balcony and landed with
a splat on the drive. Sam laughed, took a hit from one of
the joints, shifting his sore body in the lawn chair.

"For zee lasting effects of zee food and vater . . .
zee cork . . . complete with zee pins to hold it up zee
ass . . ." The wine cork, filled with colored map pins
landed near Sam's feet.

"Jesus, you guys, you really went all out," Sam said,
giving the cork a closer look.

There was a splash in the pool, followed by gurgles and
giggles. Moss was ahead of the program.

"Herr Moss vill be severely reprimanded for his thoughtless actions," Rosen yelled. "Zee court of Cambodian Truth or Consequences will decide his fate . . . nothing less than five laps around the perimeter of the city at midnight will suffice!" Everyone yelled in agreement. The nice Cambodian ladies giggled too.

"And finally . . ." Rosen signaled into his room. "In zee fine tradition of our Phnom Penh Korps, ve have for him zee little orphan . . . zee adoption papers are all in order, signed by the Führer himself. . . ." Sam laughed so hard his chest hurt. The sight of Mekong Annie dressed like a little French schoolgirl capped the evening. She was stoned, and she started to feel Rosen up as the audience egged her on.

"Nein, nein, mein Fräulein . . . you go to Amerika, teach zee boys zee proper vay . . ." Someone turned the music up another notch, inspiring Annie to start a strip, each article of clothing landing on the drive. Only the hat with the ribbon remained.

Sam felt a soft hand on his arm, turned and saw Ming, Sophan's girlfriend. "Hey, Chan," Sam called out, "could you find this lady a chair?" He wanted to set her aside from the other girls, let the crowd know that she wasn't fodder for Midnight Madness. Rosen joined them by the pool, still talking with an accent.

"Tell Ming that I'll see Sophan tomorrow," Sam asked Rosen. "Tell her I'll send him her wishes."

Rosen translated in a soft voice. She shyly pulled a letter from inside her blouse and gave it to Sam. "She wants you to deliver this letter."

"Sure, be glad to . . ." Sam leaned over and gave her a soft kiss on the brow. At that moment, Marty, Chan, Byers and Rider lifted his chair, carried him around like a Pharaoh, then with great fanfare, dumped Sam and the chair into the pool.

Sam bubbled to the bottom. It was quiet now. No more

thirty shakes, no voices calling down to see if he was all right. He lay there spreadeagled, lost in the moment. His mind drifted. What was it the last pilot said yesterday, as he flew out of Cambodia?

"See you in the next war . . ."